They were at eye level.

Had she noticed the piercing blueness of his eyes before? Perhaps not. Perhaps she didn't dare register such things, because he would become a man and not merely an enemy.

His eyes were so sad—that, she had noticed. He was looking at her so gravely.

Such pain.

What happened to you? she thought.

Maria had no sense that he reached for her, nor she for him, but she was in his arms somehow. He held her tightly, both of them caught in whatever this moment was. Their foreheads touched; their breaths mingled. And suddenly his mouth was on hers. She gave a soft moan, completely overwhelmed by the feel and the taste of him. It was as if she suddenly couldn't get close enough, couldn't touch him enough, kiss him enough. She had never felt such need, such hunger....

Acclaim for Cheryl Reavis's
recent historicals

The Captive Heart
"A sensual, emotionally involving romance."
—*Library Journal*

"A compelling tale that will keep you
on the edge of your seat."
—*Rendezvous*

Harrigan's Bride
"…another Reavis title to add to your keeper shelf."
—The Booknook

1992 RITA® Award Winner
The Prisoner
"…a Civil War novel that manages to fill the reader
with warmth and hope."
—*Romantic Times*

THE BRIDE FAIR
CHERYL REAVIS

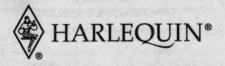

HARLEQUIN®

TORONTO • NEW YORK • LONDON
AMSTERDAM • PARIS • SYDNEY • HAMBURG
STOCKHOLM • ATHENS • TOKYO • MILAN • MADRID
PRAGUE • WARSAW • BUDAPEST • AUCKLAND

ISBN 0-373-29203-1

THE BRIDE FAIR

This edition published by arrangement with Harlequin Books S.A.

® and TM are trademarks of the publisher. Trademarks indicated with
® are registered in the United States Patent and Trademark Office, the
Canadian Trade Marks Office and in other countries.

Visit us at www.eHarlequin.com

Printed in U.S.A.

Please address questions and book requests to:
Harlequin Reader Service
U.S.: 3010 Walden Ave., P.O. Box 1325, Buffalo, NY 14269
Canadian: P.O. Box 609, Fort Erie, Ont. L2A 5X3

"To the red-shod one—with humble thanks."

Chapter One

Salisbury, N.C.
June, 1868

*W*ho *is this woman?*

Colonel Max Woodard watched as the train conductor pointed her in his direction, then stood waiting for her to make her way across the crowded railway platform. The question stayed in his mind as she approached, and it became more and more obvious that she was not happy about having to seek him out. Four years of war and two subsequent years of occupation duty among the vanquished Southerners had made him more than adept at recognizing their barely veiled contempt. Her enmity didn't surprise him in the least. The fact that she was about to speak to him in broad daylight and in clear view of any number of the townspeople did.

"You are Colonel Woodard?" she asked without hesitation. She was wearing black—most of the women in the South seemed to be in a kind of perpetual mourning. Or perhaps it was a matter of economics. Perhaps there was nothing but black cloth available to people who had little money to buy even the necessities.

The woman's voice had a slight tremor in it. Not enough to disarm him, but enough to pique his curiosity as to the cause.

Anger? Fear?

More the former than the latter, he decided. He took the liberty of staring at her. She was too thin and small-breasted for his taste. And she was probably younger than she looked. He had found that to be the case with many of these Rebel women, and he knew from personal experience that near starvation did little to preserve the bloom of youth.

She had ventured out without her bonnet or her shawl, and she was slightly damp from the intermittent rain that had come in fits and starts since his arrival. But she seemed not to notice her missing garb or the weather. *He* was her focus.

"I am," he said, meeting her gaze. She looked away, but not quite quickly enough to keep him from seeing the antipathy she worked so hard to keep hidden.

"If you would come with me, Colonel."

"Why?" he asked, making no effort to do so.

"My father couldn't meet the train. I have come in his place."

"And who might your father be?"

"He owns the house where you will be billeted," she said, clearly determined not to give any more information than she could help.

"I see. And the numerous soldiers who are supposedly under my command. Where would they all be, I wonder?"

Ordinarily, he never objected to spending time in a pleasant and accommodating woman's company—but this one was neither. And there were certain military protocols to be adhered to. He was the new commanding officer in an occupied town, and no one from the garrison had bothered to meet his train. Indeed, but for a few of his fellow travelers, he didn't see any of the military about at all.

The woman took a quiet breath. "Some of the soldiers are maintaining the military headquarters. The rest of them are fighting another fire."

There was a slight emphasis on the word "another."

"What is burning?" he asked, noticing for the first time a plume of smoke off to his left.

"The school."

"The children are safe?"

"There were no children there," she answered, moving away from him. "As you well know."

"Now how would I know that?" he said reasonably, and he still didn't follow after her. "I only just arrived."

She stopped and looked at him. "The United States Congress has seen to it that we here are no longer allowed the luxury of public education—but a fire has *somehow* started in the school building. It is in real danger of spreading. Every able man is required to put it out, lest the whole town go up in flames."

He considered it a just fate for this particular town, but he didn't say so. He glanced skyward. "Perhaps it will rain again," he said instead.

It was clear from the expression on her face that she had no intention of discussing the weather.

"And perhaps the wind will change in time to spare *your* army's storehouses."

Touché, he thought, and he very nearly smiled.

"Do you usually run errands for the military?" he asked to keep her off balance, and she stiffened slightly.

"My father was asked—ordered—by Major Hunt to retrieve you from the station and take you wherever you want to go. But he isn't well enough to do so. I came in his stead. I obey my father's wishes."

"I see," he said again. And he was beginning to. She was going to be a dutiful daughter—if it killed her.

"I've brought you a horse," she said, indicating a nearby animal with a military saddle and brand. "I will show you the way either to the house or to your head-quarters—or to the fire," she added as an afterthought. "As you wish."

She walked on and stepped into a nearby buggy without assistance, then waited for him to untie the horse at the hitching post and mount.

"I am much in your debt, Miss...?"

"Don't be," she said. "It was none of it done freely."

The remark was more matter-of-fact than hostile. He stared at her, impressed by her temerity in spite of himself.

"I prefer the buggy," he said, for no other reason than to inconvenience her. Her remark warranted at least that—inconvenience.

He had already made arrangements for his belongings to be sent to military headquarters, and he climbed into the buggy beside her without waiting for her permission, sitting down on a goodly portion of her black skirts before she could get them out of the way. She sat there for a moment, struggling not to let him see how much his presence disturbed her. Then, she snapped the reins sharply and sent the horse on.

"No," he said, when she would have turned the buggy toward the center of town. "That way."

He pointed in the direction he wanted to go, toward the railroad cut and the outskirts of town. "I insist," he added in case she believed their destination to be a matter for discussion.

She continued in the direction he indicated, her back ramrod-straight. He could just smell the rosewater scent of her clothes and hair. There were only a few people on the street. All of them turned and stared curiously as they rode past.

"I fear I may have compromised your reputation," he said.

She made no reply, reining the horse in sharply when it elected to trot.

"Sir, there is nothing out this way," she said, still struggling with the reins. "If you—"

"I know what is out here," he interrupted. "And I want to see it."

It was the third time in his life he had taken this route. The first time had been in the early summer of 1864. He had disembarked from the train—much as he had today—except that then he had arrived in a boxcar with fifty other men and under an armed guard.

He had made a return trip to the depot in late February of 1865. That excursion he didn't remember at all. He'd been too ill to walk, and several kind souls, who were probably not much better off than he, had carried him. His good friend, John Howe, wasn't among them, of course. He and John had been captured and sent to the Confederate prison here at the same time, but John had made his escape a month earlier—and with a Rebel girl in tow. John Howe had never been one to do things by halves when it came to women.

The horse finally settled down, and Max indicated where exactly he wanted the woman to take him. When she hesitated, he took the reins from her hands and effected the maneuver himself. She made no protest, regardless of how badly she wanted to, and she kept glancing at him as they rode along.

He had no difficulty locating the entrance to the prison—or what was left of it. He drove the buggy directly over the railroad bridge and into the weeds that now covered the grounds. The stockade walls had disappeared, but there was still more of the place left standing than he had expected. Until now, he had liked to think that General Stoneman, who had been a prisoner of war himself, would have celebrated his raid of the town by leveling the prison entirely and sowing the ground with salt.

But the outer walls of the huge three-story factory building used to confine as many prisoners as was inhumanly possible remained. He got some small satisfaction from seeing that the roof and windows were gone and that the hospital and the cookhouses were mostly rubble. Part of a wall stood here, a chimney there—and all of the giant oak trees inside the compound had been cut down. Only the stumps remained. He couldn't tell where the stone wells had been, but he could still see the huge burrows in the red clay earth where men had been forced to live and where so many had died. It was only by the grace of God that he had not been one of them.

He abruptly handed the woman the reins and got out of the buggy, standing for a moment to get his bearings. Then he began to walk. The weeds were taking over, but he could still see the scattered evidence of the men who had been held here. Broken glass, the bowl of a clay pipe, a belt buckle, a brass button. He could smell the jimpson weed, but it was an altogether different stench he kept remembering.

He turned and forced himself to walk in the direction

of what had once been a cornfield and a dead house, but that, too, was gone. He walked up and down, looking for the burial trenches. He wanted—needed—to stand there again—to be reminded why he'd stayed in the army after Lee's surrender, in spite of his precarious health and his family's protests.

It began to rain. A few random drops at first, and then a sudden downpour. He couldn't see any landmarks. Nothing.

He kept walking back and forth in the area he thought the trenches would be, but there were no markers and no sunken earth.

Where are they?

He had friends buried here—good men who deserved better, men who would have never made their own escape and left him behind to die. He could see their faces again, hear their entreaties.

Please, Sir. You tell my mama how to find where I am—

But he couldn't tell anyone's mother where her son had been buried. The lay of the land was different somehow, overgrown and unrecognizable. There was nothing to guide him anymore, not even the foundation of the house where the bodies had been kept until somebody found time for another mass burial.

Where are they!

He felt unsteady on his feet suddenly. He could feel his heart begin a heavy pounding in his chest. It was hard to breathe, and he had to fight down an incredible urge to run. He took a deep breath and abruptly clasped his hands behind his back to keep them from shaking.

It would pass. He knew that. All he had to do was wait.

He glanced back at the woman. She sat in the buggy

where he'd left her, pale and on the verge of becoming alarmed. He turned and walked unsteadily in her direction. He wasn't about to fall on his face and give her any tales to tell about the new colonel.

This time she got her skirts out of the way when he climbed into the buggy. He sat beside her, still fighting down the memories of his captivity.

The rain drummed loudly on the buggy top.

"Do you want to go to military headquarters?" the woman asked after a time.

He looked at her sharply. He'd forgotten all about her.

"Yes," he said finally.

She snapped the reins and sent the horse forward, turning the buggy in a wide circle and heading back in the direction they had come. He paid no attention to the route she took nor the surroundings until she abruptly stopped.

"It's there—the upstairs," she said, indicating a two-story building across from a hotel. Much of the street out front had been taken over by harried-looking civilians—old men, women and children, all of them clearly unmindful of the weather.

"Who are all these people?" he asked, and she kept avoiding his eyes.

"They are...they've come because they're afraid," she said.

"Of what?"

She didn't answer him; she merely shook her head, as if it were too complicated for her to explain—or for him to understand.

He stared at her a long moment. "I expect I shall find out soon enough."

She seemed about to say something, but didn't. He gave her a curt nod and got down from the buggy, then began walking toward the building that housed the North Carolina Western Division military headquarters. He had to literally push his way inside. Women plucked at his sleeve as he tried to pass, some in supplication and others with an obviously more commercial intent. He ignored all of them to put the fear of God into the first soldier he saw—a hapless private who lolled against a wall happily conversing with a painted woman Max had earlier seen prowling the railroad station for customers.

In spite of Max's ire, the private somehow found the presence of mind to lead him upstairs, where Max found an unexpectedly young sergeant major in a crowded and disordered room he assumed was an office.

"This way, Colonel Woodard, Sir," the sergeant major said, as if his new commanding officer hadn't just kicked a private soundly in the backside.

Max stood where he was, ignoring the fact that the sergeant major clearly expected him to take a seat in the chair behind the cluttered desk. He was not yet ready to delve into the stacks of papers his predecessor had left scattered about, nor was he ready to let go of his pique. He knew that Colonel Hatcher's departure had been precipitous—the state of the man's office confirmed that—but he had expected some attempt on Hatcher's part to effect an orderly change of command.

Max walked to the window and looked down at the street below. The crowd was still there in spite of the rain—and growing, he thought. The woman who had brought him here was trying to drive the buggy through, and she was immediately surrounded by bystanders. But whatever questions were being put to her, she didn't answer. She kept shaking her head and finally used the buggy whip to send the horse on, giving the crowd no choice but to let her pass.

"Your name, Sergeant Major?"

"Perkins, Sir."

"What do all those people downstairs want?"

The sergeant major carefully held out a steaming cup of coffee instead of answering.

"I asked you a question, Sergeant Major," Max said sharply.

"Yes, Sir. Petitioners come to talk to the new colonel, Sir."

"How is it they knew I was arriving today? Do you ordinarily keep the civilian population privy to the army's comings and goings?"

"Well, Sir. Sometimes telegraphing gets intercepted up the line—old tricks die hard for some of these so-called *ex*-Rebs. If the message ain't got nothing to do with us, they'll send it on through, like as not. If it does...well—maybe they will and maybe they won't— either way, word gets out as to whatever information happens to be in them." He shrugged. He also offered the tin cup of coffee again. This time Max took it.

"These 'petitioners.' What exactly do they want?"

"Some of them would be wanting the Oath of Allegiance, Sir. People what finally got wore down enough to come in and ask to take it—so's they can get some food on the table."

"It's taken them three years to get here?"

"Well, I expect you know what the Rebs are like, Sir. Especially the women. They hold out as long as they can. I expect the war would have been over a good year or two before it was, if it weren't for them."

Max agreed wholeheartedly—in spite of a noted general's assertion that he could buy any one of them with a pound of coffee—but he didn't say so.

"All of them can't have just decided to take the

Oath," he said. He took a sip of coffee, surprised to find it was quite good. He'd forgotten that some of the best coffee in the world came at the hands of sergeant majors. The skill seemed to come with the rank, regardless of the fact that this particular one didn't appear old enough to have it.

"Well, Sir, one or two of them are here because they *can't* take it," Perkins said. "Them what carried the Reb flag a little too high during the late war—or them what own too much property and ain't about to get rid of it. They couldn't get nowhere with Colonel Hatcher, so they'd be here to ask *you* to pardon them, so they can swear allegiance and get all the benefits thereof. Then there's the usual civilian complaints, Sir."

Max decided to sit down, after all. He was tired. He looked healthy enough these days, but he still suffered from a noticeable lack of stamina. The long train ride from Washington and then the visit to the prison grounds had taken its toll. He took another sip of the coffee, then tried to find a place to put the tin cup among the stacks of papers on the desk. "What kinds of complaints? The men in blue accosting their daughters?"

"No, Sir—not that there ain't plenty of accosting going on, mind you. There's some real pretty girls in this town and don't nothing stir up a soldier's juices more than running into one of them and knowing she'd just as soon gut you as look at you. The boys take it right personal, Sir, if you know what I mean. And they get to feeling all honor-bound to do something about it. Ain't nothing builds a man up like turning some little old girl's head, especially if she thinks she hates the air you're living on.

"But we don't generally hear about any of that up here. If the accosting's mutual, it's either ship the girl off to her relatives or let 'em get married, which is likely what some of them downstairs have come about—permission for a marriage. Getting married to an army officer is pretty popular here of late—what with the latest batch of local females coming of age. They was about too young to get all worked up about the Cause during the war. All they know is there ain't nobody left much to marry—except one of us. Sometimes you'd think it was a regular bride fair around here and a man could just go out and take his pick.

"But now, if the accosting ain't mutual, sooner or later, the accoster gets hisself waylaid some dark night and he don't come out of it looking as good as when he went in. If you get my meaning. And the boys, well, they do have their pride, Sir. They don't want to say they got the bejesus kicked out of them by some unarmed Reb daddy or big brother. The tales I've heard, Sir, about low-hanging tree limbs and stumbling in the dark on the way to the sinks. It's enough to make you think this here town is the most perilous place in the world for a man to go heeding the call of nature after the sun goes down—begging your pardon, Sir.

"No, Sir, there ain't many complaints about 'accosting' coming our way. I'd say some of them people downstairs are wanting to get paid for the goods the army commandeers and for billeting officers in the private residences. It was Colonel Hatcher's policy not to get in a hurry about that. He wasn't exactly what you would call accommodating to the townsfolk."

Max looked at him, recognizing a prelude when he heard one. "How far behind are we on paying them?"

"Well, Sir, I'd say about as many months as the colonel was here—but that ain't the main thing. The main thing is all these here fires, Sir. Six of them, so far. Folks pretty much hold us—that is, Colonel Hatcher—respon-sible for all the incendiary activity that's been going on.''

''Why?''

''Well, he got to saying how the townsfolk didn't suf-fer enough for having the prison here during the war and whatever bad things happened to them was just what they deserved. It didn't take long for some to take that as an invitation to run wild with a torch.''

''Anybody hurt?''

''Not yet, Sir, but there's been some close calls. One of the men barely got a little child out of a house when the fire spread the other night. I guess it's mostly that what's got folks gathering out front like they are. They're wanting you to do something about it.''

Max drew a quiet breath. If he had dared hoped for some quietude here, it didn't appear likely that he was going to find it. He could feel the sergeant major waiting for him to do his job and take command of the situation. He moved a pile of papers instead and uncovered a bat-tered red-velvet box. It contained a pair of garnet-and-pearl earrings of significant quality and value.

''What's this?''

''Those, Sir? I'm thinking Colonel Hatcher meant those for his…ah…''

''His what?''

''Well, his woman, Sir.''

''What woman? His wife?''

''Whore, Sir.''

''His—''

Max abruptly closed the box and tossed it on the desk-top. He was no prude, but it was one thing for an officer to have his entertainments—and something else again to have his staff so privy to them. And Colonel Hatcher's departure must have been even more precipitous than he'd thought.

"Sir, I reckon they might be a problem, too," the sergeant major said after a moment.

"For whom?" Max asked pointedly, and he had to wait for the sergeant major to make up his mind about how much he wanted to tell his new commanding officer.

"For you, I reckon, Sir. This here whor— I mean, woman— I seen her downstairs just now, and I reckon she'll be wanting them."

"Then give them to her."

"Well, they ain't exactly hers, Sir, even if the colonel did promise them to her. Colonel Hatcher, he called them contraband, because of who they really belong to— but I'm thinking it's too late in the day for them to be that."

Max stared at the man, trying to follow his convoluted tale.

"'Who they really belong to,'" Max repeated.

"Yes, Sir. Miss Maria Rose Markham. Colonel Hatcher billeted hisself in her daddy's house. Them earbobs belong to her and they went missing. See, the colonel had a bit of interest in the lady, but she wouldn't have it—she had two brothers and a fiancé killed at Gettysburg—her brothers gave her them earbobs before they went off to war—one of them weren't but fifteen. But even if she hadn't lost her brothers and her beau like that, she just weren't the kind to be impressed with the—"

Perkins abruptly stopped, and clearly had no intention of continuing.

"Speak freely, man," Max said, but Perkins still had

to think about it. It was not a sergeant's prerogative to assess a colonel's character, even when asked.

"Well, Sir," he said finally, "Colonel Hatcher, he was fond of telling people that his family came from these parts—he said he had this here relative what was a big Indian fighter and military advisor a hundred years ago. Only these people here keep records of everything, and somebody found a mention of a Hatcher in the court accounts—how he was put in stocks all the time for drunken and lewd behavior—insulting decent women and the like. Didn't take word long to get around."

"No, I don't expect it did."

"People were kind of laughing behind their hands about it, and that got Colonel Hatcher all the more determined about Miss Markham. Some thinks the earbobs was a kind of punishment for her. That it might have amused the colonel to take something what was dear to her and give it to a whore. Or maybe he thought he could make her trade for them. Sir," the sergeant major added as an afterthought.

Max sat there. He had enough trouble with the apparently ongoing arson in this town. He had no inclination whatsoever to deal with the epic drama his sergeant major had just revealed.

"Dare I hope arrangements have been made regarding my quarters?" he asked after a moment.

"Ah—yes, Sir. The major was thinking to put you in the same house as was Colonel Hatcher. It could get kind of crowded over there, though, Sir, if Miss Markham happened to move a bunch of kinfolk in now that Colonel Hatcher is gone. It might be you'd be wanting a hotel, Sir," he added hopefully. "Mansion House or Howerton's right across the street—"

Max looked at the sergeant major. So. Miss Markham—apparently the woman who had met him at the station—had a champion in this sergeant major, one who wanted the new colonel to know that his behavior regarding her would be duly noted.

But Perkins could rest easy. Max had no designs on Miss Markham's virtue. He did, however, wish to continue to inconvenience her. He wasn't all that different from the men under his command. He had just been on the receiving end of a Rebel woman's disdain, and, like his men, he took it personally.

"No," Max said. "The Markham house will suit me. If there are additions to the household and I find it too noisy, I have the authority to thin them out. My belongings will be sent here from the station. Have them moved to the house—and make sure the Markham pantry is full and there is somebody to cook and to orderly. And find me a decent mount so I can see about this latest fire. Then, I want you to take some men and close this town down. Every store, every saloon, every bar and grog shop. And the whorehouses, too, while you're at it. All church services and public and private gatherings are canceled until further notice. The citizens are to be off the streets and in their homes. Start with that bunch downstairs."

"Yes, Sir! Anything else, Sir!"

"I want all these papers sorted, by date and by urgency—and then I want a burial detail."

"Burial detail, Sir?"

"That's what I said. And find me some small pine blocks—like so," he said, showing him the size with his hands. "Make sure they're finished—no bark—scraps from a lumber mill if there is one—but you can put that at the bottom of the list for now."

"Yes, Sir!" Perkins gave a smart salute and left a

happy man, in spite of Max's choice of residence and his mishmash of orders. Occupation duty was tedious at best, and enacting what amounted to martial law was clearly more to the soldier's liking.

Max sat at the desk, then reached for the red-velvet box again, turning it over in his hands before he opened it. After a moment he abruptly closed the box and put it into his uniform pocket.

Chapter Two

Maria Markham stopped abruptly in the wide center hallway, listening again for the sound of an approaching wagon. The front door was shut, but the downstairs windows were still open to let in the evening breeze until the mosquitoes began to swarm. She stood there, her sense of dread completely taking her attention away from the task of closing up the house for the night and lighting more lamps than they could afford to light.

She had been waiting for the new colonel all afternoon, and she still had no idea what she would do when he finally arrived. She knew what she would like to do, of course. She would like to bar the door and turn him away. She would like to send him and his kind back to whatever hellish place they had come from.

Pennsylvania.

Colonel Woodard came from Pennsylvania. He had served in Rush's Lancers, a supposedly elite cavalry regiment made up of rich young men from Philadelphia society. His having been a Lancer was likely the reason he was in such an elevated position now—or so her father said. Her father made a point of keeping up with what he considered the pertinent details regarding the

occupation army, and he was the one responsible for the
new colonel's being billeted in the house in the first
place—and for the two others before him.

"It is for the money, Maria Rose," he'd explained
patiently when she had protested having yet another
"guest," as if she didn't already know what dire financial straits they were in. The only problem with that
logic was that the Yankees never paid for anything—
least of all their housing. They "appropriated" whatever
they wanted all over town and handed out vouchers the
quartermaster never got around to honoring. The town
was forever sending some kind of delegation to military
headquarters to broach the subject of monies owed, but
far as she knew, her father had received no rent payment
the entire time, Hatcher, the previous commander had
been living here. She had no expectations that this new
one would be any different.

Colonel Woodard.

The man she was having to light the lamps for, because she thought he would come into the house unan-
nounced, barred door or not, and she did *not* want to
encounter him in the dark.

She had been afraid of him today in the buggy. He
had been civil enough, but his civility didn't hide what
she believed to be his true nature. She realized immediately that he didn't suffer fools gladly, but, for whatever reason, he chose to keep a tight rein on his emo-
tions. Even so, she could feel how volatile they were,
how close to the surface, and he had a kind of dangerous
intensity about him she found more than a little disconcerting. She had no idea what people must have thought,
seeing them riding out to the prison like that. It wasn't
proper, and the colonel knew it. He made it very clear

that the delicate sensibilities of the people in this town meant nothing to him.

She was certain she heard a wagon now, and she stepped quickly into the parlor so that she could peep out the front window. If it was Colonel Woodard, she would take herself to another part of the house. The last thing she wanted the Yankee to think was that she'd been dancing in attendance by the front door on his account.

It was nearly dark, but she could see the wagon clearly enough—one of the farmers making a delayed start home, probably because of the fire. Every able-bodied man had been pressed into service. She couldn't see any flames now, or even a glow in the sky, but she could still smell the smoke. The wagon rattled on by, leaving nothing in its wake but the sounds of a warm summer night.

She took a quiet breath and let the resentment she'd been keeping at bay wash over her. She had tried so hard to talk her father out of letting another one of them into the house. It was bad enough having to encounter occupation soldiers all over town. They were always underfoot on the streets and in the shops. Some actually came to church and participated in the services—much to the delight of the young girls, who were more than willing to overlook a Yankee officer's part in the late war for the possibility, however remote, of matrimony.

To that end, some of them had raised simpering to a high art. It had gotten to the point that she could hardly bear to witness it, and she could expect a bevy of eager young females at the front door as soon as word got around that the new—and possibly unmarried—colonel was billeting with the Markhams. If—when—they discovered that he was supposedly from a well-to-do family, too, she would be absolutely inundated with visitors, whether she wanted them or not.

Maria gave a quiet sigh. Perhaps she shouldn't blame the girls—or their mothers, who must surely sanction their behavior. Who else was there to marry? The war had decimated the Confederacy's young men. So many of them were dead or invalid, and it was a bitter thing for those who had survived more or less intact to have to live now in a conquered South. Some of them made no pretense at even trying. They took themselves off to California or to Mexico or to South America, leaving the uncertain resurrection of their homeland to whoever remained.

She resented their departure as much as she resented the new colonel's presence in the house. Having Colonel Woodard here was a classic example of adding insult to injury, and she simply didn't understand why her father couldn't see that. Both his sons—her beloved brothers— had died at Gettysburg. Quiet, scholarly Rob, who had treated her as an intellectual equal simply because she was so eager to learn about matters beyond the kitchen and household. And mischievous, lighthearted Samuel, who could always make her laugh.

She missed them both terribly, and her only comfort was that they had been spared seeing what life here had become. Everything had changed. It wasn't simply the deprivations, the lack of food and money. It was the lack of joy and living day after day in relentless, all-prevailing sorrow.

She caught a glimpse of herself in the gilt-framed mirror on the far wall. The mirror had been cracked three years ago by one of General Stoneman's raiders in an effort to get it out of the house before one of his superiors saw him trying to steal it. She moved to the side so that she could see herself better and immediately wished she hadn't. She was so tired, and she looked it.

What has happened to me?

Her brothers would not have recognized her. She hardly recognized herself anymore. She had never been a beauty, but she had been a cheerful and optimistic person.

Once.

People had enjoyed her company. She had never lacked for invitations to balls and parties. Billy Canfield had wanted to marry her. He had spoken to her father, and they had received the blessings of both sets of parents. It seemed so long ago now, but she had that one small consolation to hang on to, at least. She had once been asked—and only she would ever know that his asking had meant nothing.

But her life was about to change for the worse, whether the new colonel billeted himself here or not. She had no hope of escaping her fate and very little time remaining before she was found out. If only she were devious enough and fetching enough to join the younger girls in their relentless, giggling quests for a husband. A husband would solve everything—even if it were one of them—*if* she could act quickly enough and *if* she could put aside the dishonor of such a venture and somehow dredge up the self-confidence to attempt it. She still smarted at the memory of Colonel Woodard's scrutiny at the train station. His assessment of her had been subtle—not at all like the leering she'd come to expect from Colonel Hatcher and his kind. But it had been no less upsetting. She had seen the new colonel study her face, her breasts—and then totally dismiss her.

Like Billy.

Someone rapped sharply on the front door, making

her jump. She peered out the window again. A carriage had stopped out front, but she didn't recognize it. Apparently the colonel had chosen a conveyance in keeping with his position this time—or perhaps there had been no lone women in buggies handy.

The rapping came again, much louder this time.

"Maria Rose!" her father called from his upstairs sitting room. "Will you answer the door or must I!"

"I'm getting it, Father," she called back, recognizing the threat for what it was. He was looking for an excuse to come downstairs and drink whiskey with a bunch of soldiers—even if they were in the wrong army—instead of coddling his bad heart as the doctor had ordered. She loved her father dearly, but he had to be the most exasperating man in all of Christendom. When his health improved even a little, he never concluded that the doctor's regimen was working. Instead, he promptly decided that it wasn't needed any longer. She ran herself ragged trying to keep him from overdoing, failing and then feeling guilty for his numerous setbacks. It had been the same when her mother was living. Somehow *his* illness was entirely *their* responsibility. If he felt any personal obligation to follow his doctor's advice regarding his own health, she certainly couldn't tell.

"Maria Rose!" her father yelled again.

"I heard you, Father!"

She took a deep breath to brace herself for the coming ordeal, but the door flew open before she could get to it.

"Miss," the soldier standing on the porch said. "I have Colonel Woodard's trunk and belongings."

He didn't wait for her to give him leave to enter. He motioned two other soldiers to hurry along with the baggage and pushed his way into the house, forcing her to step back to give him room.

"Where will the colonel be quartered, miss?" he asked.

"Wherever he likes," she said, because the question was merely a token one, and they both knew it. It wasn't for her to say. She had had enough dealings with these people to understand the fine points. Colonel Woodard wasn't a guest; he was a conqueror. He could pick and choose his accommodations as he pleased—and would, most likely—even if it meant she or her father would have to vacate them.

"Leave that here," the soldier said to the two men carrying the trunk and a number of satchels and leather cases.

Two more soldiers came in through the front door loaded down with wooden boxes, a basket of eggs, a ham and three sacks of flour, tracking red mud on the bare wood floor all the way. The floor was walnut—short pieces done in an intricate chevron pattern that caused much admiration among visitors to the house and cleverly hid the fact that, at the time, the scrap pieces were all her father could afford. It was yet another example of his resourcefulness, but it was she who would have to get down on her hands and knees to brush the mud out of the crevices.

"The colonel's provisions, miss. Light the way to the pantry, if you please."

She didn't please, but she picked up the lamp from the hall table and carried it in the direction of the kitchen. They would have no problem locating which larder had been set aside exclusively for the colonel. It would be the one protected from civilian pilfering by a heavy padlock to which no one in the household had the key.

She looked over her shoulder toward the open front door, still expecting the colonel himself, but she could see no soldiers in the yard or in the carriage.

"You understand that these provisions are for the colonel's use only," the soldier in charge said as his men unpacked the boxes.

She didn't answer him.

"It will save you a lot of trouble and grief in the long run, if you do, miss. The quarters for the colonel's orderly—where are they?" He lit the lamp on the kitchen table.

"Colonel Hatcher's orderly stayed in the room under the stairs."

"See to it," he said to a soldier nearby, handing him the lamp.

"Have you been advised about the new curfew, miss?" he asked as he took a key from his pocket and unlocked the pantry door.

"What new curfew?"

"You—and everybody in this here town—will have to remain in your houses and off the streets. There will be no going anyplace—no public gatherings of any kind—until further notice."

"Surely church services aren't—"

"Church is canceled."

"But why?"

"The colonel means to get to the bottom of all this incendiary activity, miss."

"I doubt very seriously that *we* are the ones responsible for burning our own town," she said.

"Even so—the colonel's got to start somewhere."

"Where is he now?" Maria asked. "I would like to lock up the house after you leave."

"Can't say, miss. He'll be here when he gets here. Somebody will need to stay handy to let him in."

And Maria knew just who that "somebody" would be.

"Maria Rose!" her father yelled from upstairs. "Who is that down there with you?"

The soldier in charge broke into a grin. "Mr. Markham is awake then, is he? I'll just go up and speak to him."

"He needs to be resting," Maria said—to no avail. The soldier went off happily in the direction of her father's voice, leaving her in the kitchen with the rest of the underlings.

She didn't stay. She walked back to the parlor and sat down in a corner by the front windows to wait for them all to leave. From time to time, she could hear her father's laughter upstairs. Her father. What would he say when he found out about her? How could she ever tell him?

But she wouldn't have to tell him, if she stayed here much longer. Sooner or later, he would know. Everyone would know. Her body was already changing. She could no longer rely on it not to betray her at every turn. She was forever on the verge of fainting or weeping or being sick. The smell of frying pork had sent her bolting to the slop bucket more than once this last week. It was a miracle that her father had not noticed.

She tried to tell herself that she wasn't the first woman to be in this situation. She would just have to go someplace until the child could be born—if she could find the money and someone willing to take her in. Perhaps if she said she was a war widow—

But there was no money.

And if there had been, she would have to ask her father for it. She'd have to put his weak heart at risk and tell him why she needed it. And even if she went, people would still find out. They always did. The very fact that a young, unmarried woman left town for a time—no matter what the excuse—was enough to raise suspicions. How could she bear it? For the rest of her life, people would whisper behind their hands, wondering about her prolonged absence and only too eager to share their own opinion about whether Maria Rose Markham had been ruined and who had done it.

If Billy were here—

"He would be no help at all," she whispered.

She abruptly put her face in her hands, trying hard not to cry. Tears were not the answer. She had already cried enough to know that.

"Miss?" the soldier in charge said from the doorway.

She looked up, startled and more than disconcerted that one of them might have witnessed her moment of weakness.

"The colonel said to leave this with you," he said, crossing the room and handing her the padlock key.

She hesitated, then stood and took it.

"Colonel Woodard has the certification that you took the Oath of Allegiance on file in his office. He expects you to honor it—so try not to sell everything off before he gets here."

Maria opened her mouth to say something and couldn't. She was literally speechless. She might *steal* the colonel's provisions if anyone she knew were going hungry and she thought she could get away with it—but she wouldn't *sell* them.

The soldier grinned and touched the bill of his cap.

"Good evening, miss. Oh, and your father is asking for his toddy."

"You didn't give him anything to drink, did you?" she asked, still insulted.

"Ah—no, miss."

She looked at him. He grinned wider.

"I recognize you for the liar you are, Sir," she said.

"Good evening, miss," he said again, chuckling to himself as he led his muddy-footed subordinates out the front door.

Maria waited to make certain they had gone, then walked into the hallway, still holding the padlock key. She stood looking at the colonel's pile of belongings. One leather case was quite large and didn't appear to have a lock of any kind. It took a great deal of effort on her part not to see if she could open it. She liked to think she was an honorable person, regardless of her Pandora-like inclinations. She didn't go around snooping in other people's baggage—even if it did belong to a Yankee— but the temptation was great, nevertheless. She wasn't interested in military secrets, only in knowing what sort of man this Woodard was, and there might be all manner of information about him in the case.

"Maria Rose!" her father yelled from upstairs. "My toddy!"

"I believe you have already had your toddy, Father!" she called back.

It took the better part of an hour to get him finally situated for the night—and even then she had to bribe him with a cigar in lieu of the spirits he wanted *and* listen to him expound on the trials and tribulations of having a "willful girl child" before he would agree to take himself off to bed.

She stayed downstairs and put out the lamps she had

lit, after all. She couldn't—wouldn't—waste the precious oil on the belated colonel. To keep busy, she swept up the muddy footprints as best she could by candlelight, then made sure the doors were locked.

She didn't dare go on up to bed. She sat dozing at the kitchen table instead. Everything was so quiet. Nothing but the ticking of the clock on the kitchen mantel and the creaks and cracks of the house settling. She had left one kitchen window open, and every now and then she could feel the faint stirring of a breeze. If she had been less tired, she might have wondered why the colonel was so late. As it was, she had reached a point beyond caring. She heard the clock strike ten, then dozed again.

She awoke to a whispered curse, and she abruptly lifted her head. The candle was nearly gone, but she could see the colonel clearly. He was standing in the middle of the kitchen, holding a railroad lantern.

"I need your help," he said without prelude. "I had intended not to wake you, but since you're awake—here, take this." He awkwardly thrust the lantern into her hands. "If you'll come outside and hold it so I can see."

He didn't wait for her to either acquiesce or refuse. He walked out the back door. She had little choice but to follow after him—out of curiosity if nothing else. His horse stood tied to the porch post.

"What is it?" she asked, growing more alarmed.

"My horse is lame."

She held the lantern higher—because he took her arm and pushed it upward.

"How did you get into the house?" she asked as he bent down to examine the horse's foreleg and lift its hoof. But there seemed to be more of a problem with his hands than with the horse.

"My new orderly, Perkins. He's very resourceful. I

don't imagine there is a place in this town he can't get into if he's of a mind. If he weren't in the army, he'd probably be in prison. Well, the leg feels all right—no injury that I can see. It think it's a stone bruise. Can you undo the cinch?''

She gave him an incredulous look that was wasted in the dark.

''I am not a stable boy, Colonel Woodard,'' she said evenly.

''I never said you were. I have injured my hands, and I don't think I can do it myself. I was in the cavalry, Miss Markham. Regardless of my current duties, old lessons die hard. I must see to my mount no matter what. I don't want him to stand all night with a saddle on his back. Perkins is off on other business. You are the only other person here at the moment, and you strike me as being reasonably competent. Can we not call a brief truce on behalf of this suffering animal?''

She thrust the lantern back at him so she could undo the cinch. She even pulled the saddle and blanket off while she was at it and dumped them on the back porch.

''Anything else?'' she asked.

''He needs to be fed and watered,'' he said without hesitation.

''Light the way,'' she said, taking the horse by the bridle and coaxing it to limp the distance to the animal shed. She stopped at the trough long enough for it to drink, then urged it into the shed and put it into an empty stall. Her buggy horse, Nell, whinnied softly in the darkness.

''The bridle,'' the colonel said behind her, before she could remove it.

She gave a quiet sigh and struggled to unbuckle the bridle, then handed it to him.

"Shine the lantern there," she said, pointing to a barrel of corn in the corner.

She lifted the lid and reached inside—as much as she hated to when she couldn't really see where she was putting her hands. It was a carry-over from her childhood, when she once lifted out a rat along with an ear of corn.

"Thank you," he said as she dumped as much corn as she could grab in one swipe into the stall crib.

She made no effort to acknowledge his expression of gratitude. She pitched a small clump of hay into the crib instead and turned to go. Her only interest now was in taking her "reasonably competent" self back to the house. It wasn't for *his* sake that she'd assumed livery duties. She had merely appreciated his remark about a truce and determined that none of God's creatures should suffer needlessly—regardless of who the human owner might be.

The colonel followed along after her with the lantern. "I need my trunk opened," he said as they entered the kitchen. He awkwardly set the lantern on the table.

"It's in the front hall—"

"The key is in my left shirt pocket."

She stood looking at him, trying to read the expression on his face. He wasn't ordering her to do anything—and yet he was. And she was certain that he at least suspected that she was afraid of him. He suspected, and for some reason he was determined to push her until he could make her show it.

But she refused to be pushed. She impulsively reached into his unbuttoned tunic to find the shirt pocket with the ring of keys. This close, he smelled of smoke and horse and tobacco. He needed a shave, and he was clearly exhausted.

"Which key is it?" she asked, avoiding his eyes.

"The one in your hand. It opens the big trunk. I need two rolls of muslin and the bottle of brandy—lower left-hand side."

She took the lantern and went into the hall. She had wanted to poke through his belongings, and apparently she was going to get the opportunity.

Except that he came with her.

She unlocked the trunk with some difficulty and located the muslin and the brandy—all the while trying to glimpse his personal possessions. A daguerreotype, a book—anything that would validate her already low opinion of the man. She saw nothing but socks and vests—and drawers. He clearly didn't mind her rummaging through his undergarments in the least. Fortunately, she had had enough brothers not to be alarmed by the sight of normally concealed male clothing.

When she stood up, he was already on his way back to the kitchen. She sighed again and followed, carrying the brandy and the muslin.

"A glass?" he asked. "I'm apt to break things if I look myself."

She got him one from the shelf, amazed that he expected her to pour, too, and even more amazed that she complied. Her one-handed splash was generous; the spirits didn't belong to her.

"That's enough," he said, holding up an injured hand.

But he didn't take up the glass. He shrugged off his tunic and held out his arms for her to roll up his shirtsleeves instead. The shirt was plain but finely sewn and made of a soft, closely woven muslin like the rolls she'd gotten from the trunk. There had been nothing like it available here since before the war.

"If you would be so kind as to bind up my hands,"

he said, still waiting for her to get his sleeves out of the way. "The doctor suggests you soak the bandage in cold water first."

She hesitated, in spite of the fact that she had the skill to do what was needed. The town had had a Wayside Hospital during the war. The trains carrying the wounded had arrived at all hours of the day and night. Even though she was a young, unmarried woman of good family, she had worked around the clock more than once dressing injuries that were so terrible—

She pushed the memory aside. Binding up a soldier's wounds was an expertise she would have preferred never to have acquired.

Colonel Woodard stood waiting. He had asked—more or less—and she couldn't, in good Christian conscience, deny him. Whatever small kindness she would extend to a dumb animal she would also extend to him—except that a good Christian conscience had nothing to do with it. She was going to do this for her own sake, for the chance, however remote, that this Yankee might pay his rent and thereby provide her father with the funds she needed to go away.

She rolled up his shirtsleeves. At first she thought his hands must have been burned, but that was not the case. They were very badly bruised and swollen.

She took down a bowl from the china cupboard and placed the rolls of muslin in it, then carried it to the water bucket and filled it full. She could feel the colonel watching her as she worked to saturate the bandages and squeeze out the water.

"Your hands will have to be wrapped tightly to stop the swelling," she said. "I expect it will hurt," she added, placing the beginning strip of wet muslin across his palm.

"No matter. That's what the brandy is for."

She glanced up at him. He seemed to be expecting her to do just that. She immediately lowered her head and concentrated on the wrapping. She was hurting him, and she knew it. After a moment he half sat on the edge of the table, his hand still extended. She realized suddenly that it was trembling.

"How did you do this?" she asked quietly.

"Someone collected full rain barrels in a wagon and brought them to the fire. The horses shied. My hands were in the way when the load shifted. But your town doctor assures me nothing is broken," he added. His tone suggested that he didn't necessarily believe it. "He also said you would be very capable at wrapping them— if I could get you to do it."

She ignored the remark and tore a split in the last few inches of the muslin, then tied the two pieces in place around the back of his hand. He held out the other one. She wrapped more swiftly now, fully aware that he was inspecting her face while she worked, no doubt verifying his earlier opinion.

"You hate us, don't you?" he asked.

She looked at him. It was a question he hardly need ask.

"As you do us," she said after a moment, tearing another slit in the muslin and tying it securely across the back of his hand.

"Perhaps we both have good reason."

She had nothing to say to that and turned to go.

"Wait," he said. "I think we need to get the rules of the household established. It will save...misunderstandings later."

"I see no reason for our separate living arrangements to interfere with each other—"

"They won't be separate. I expect to be seated at your table for breakfast and—"

"My father is ill. We rarely sit down together in the mornings."

"Then you will act in his stead—as you did today at the station. If I am to execute my duties well—if I am to put aside my prejudices—I must know and understand the people here. I will have questions and you can assist me with answers—assuming that you want to save your people as much grief as possible. I'm not Hatcher. Things will be different in this town from now on. I also expect to be included when you have guests here for dinner or whatever occasion."

"Well, you may have to wait a while for that—since we're all to be kept prisoners in our houses."

"There are worst places to be imprisoned, Miss Markham," he said, and in spite of herself she looked away.

"You need not worry about the added work or expense. You have the key to the larder. You may use those provisions freely whether I'm here or not. And my orderly will help you set a proper table or whatever else—"

"I don't want your charity or your orderly's help," she said. "And I don't want to suffer your presence any more than is absolutely necessary."

"I'm sure you don't—but I don't think I made myself clear. I have the authority to elicit whatever assistance I need from the populace—as I see fit. And at the moment, I require yours. It's not a matter for discussion."

He watched her closely. She could sense how much he wanted her to oppose him, and it was all she could do to keep quiet. Her body trembled with anger.

When she said nothing, he abruptly picked up the glass of brandy she'd poured for him and drained it.

"Now. If you would show me where I am to sleep—so that I don't go stumbling about and wake your father," he said in a deliberate attempt to make it impossible for her to refuse.

She picked up the lantern and walked briskly down the hall and up the stairs, and she didn't stop until she'd opened the door to the bedchamber off the second-story porch. It had once been hers—until Hatcher appropriated it. She now considered it contaminated and fit only for the likes of his replacement.

"This will do," Colonel Woodard said behind her. He pushed past her, immediately lay down on the bed as he was, boots and all. And, without giving her a backward glance, he fell immediately asleep.

Chapter Three

Who is talking?

Max turned his head slightly. At first he thought the lowered voices were coming through the window on the upstairs porch. With some effort, he turned over in the bed, realizing immediately that the conversation originated from the other side of the house.

His hands were still wrapped in spite of his restless sleep and still hurt like hell. He flexed them gingerly and immediately regretted it. Even so, the swelling seemed less, and that was something.

He lay there looking around the room. It was sparsely furnished. A four-poster bed, a dresser, a washstand, a chair and small table, somewhat tattered lace curtains, recently washed. No draperies. No rugs. No framed pictures. The wallpaper had seen better days—some kind of stylized flowers in a vase surrounded by a wreath in a pattern that repeated every few inches. A spotty mirror hung from a braided gold cord over the mantel. It tilted downward enough that he could see a dim reflection of himself lying in bed. It was not his first encounter with a well-placed mirror in a bedchamber. The high-class bordellos he'd frequented before the war were full of them. It was a shame this one would go to waste.

"Perkins!" he yelled suddenly, simply to measure his new orderly's efficiency. He had no idea if the man were anywhere close by or not.

"Sir!" Perkins said immediately on the other side of the closed bedchamber door.

"Coffee," Max said. "Now."

"Yes, Sir!"

Max sat up on the edge of the bed with some difficulty, then unwrapped his hands and flexed his fingers again.

Not too bad, Miss Markham, he thought.

He stood and walked unsteadily to the window that opened on the back side of the house. He had initially been too distracted by the pain in his hands to register that everything else hurt, as well. It had been a long time since he'd participated in the kind of physical exertion necessary to put out a fire. Clearly, the days when he could subject his body to any and every kind of strain and misbehavior and not feel any aftereffects were long gone.

He moved the lace curtain aside and looked down into the backyard. The sun was up. The birds were singing, and there was a fine, cool breeze coming in through the window. Maria Markham stood on the dewy grass below and, unless the man with her lived here, she was exhibiting a flagrant disregard for the new curfew.

Max moved slightly to try to hear what they were saying, but he could only catch certain words. From the look of things, however, the conversation was not going well. Whatever verbal bouquets the man was handing out, Maria Markham was not accepting.

"—how could she be better…they need you. Why can't you see what this is?"

The man reached out to touch her arm, and she stepped away from him.

"You break her heart," she said. Max heard and understood that quite distinctly.

"I can't help the way things are—" the man replied.

"Yes, you can!" Maria said, forgetting to lower her voice in her agitation. "Who can but you?"

But then she suddenly relented. "—I will," she said. "They are always welcome—"

Max looked around at a faint knock on the door.

"In," he said, and Perkins came in with the coffee.

"Who is that with Miss Markham?" Max asked, nodding toward the window. Even from this distance and without much to go on, he didn't like Maria Markham's early morning visitor. It was enough that he was breaking the curfew.

Perkins carefully handed over the tin cup of hot coffee and peered out the window to see.

"You want me to detain him, Sir?"

"No, I want you to tell me who he is."

"That would be…Phelan Canfield, Sir. Ex-Reb artilleryman. Brother to Miss Markham's late fiancé and well on his way to becoming the town drunk. He's married to a friend of Miss Markham's—Suzanne, her name is. I hear that both the Canfield boys admired Miss Markham, though. Some folks here think maybe Phelan would have turned out better if he'd married her instead of letting his brother have her—on account of *she* would have made something out of him. Besides that, *her* brothers—if they had lived—would have half killed him for the kind of misbehavior he's been showing. Good men, her brothers, or so folks say. But you never know about these things that might have been, do you, Sir?

"Anyway, Canfield and this here Suzanne has got two children—little boys. One's five—his daddy got to come home on horse leave one winter and that's where he come from. The other one's about two or so. Suzanne—now, she ain't well enough to look after them or keep up her wifely duties, if you know what I mean, Sir. Most of the time Canfield ain't sober—or he's disappeared someplace and nobody knows where he got to. It's usually jail for being drunk and disorderly or one of the whorehouses down by the railroad tracks. He ain't got enough money to gamble or partake—but I reckon some of the girls take pity on him, him being a Reb war hero and all that."

Max stared at his orderly. "How the hell do you know all this?"

"People talk, Sir. Alls I do is pay attention when they do it. Most of the folks here work so hard at ignoring us, I reckon they really do forget we're around. But I ain't deaf. You can hear all kinds of things at the bakery—it's on the ground floor down at the hotel—Mansion House. And Miss Markham—she's come down to the jail a time or two looking for the son of a bitch and thinking he's been on another one of his binges and got hisself locked up. She takes care of them little boys right much and Suzanne, too. Them boys are a handful—you remember, I did mention, Sir, that this might not be the most restful place for you here."

Max declined to comment. He held the cup precariously with both hands, savoring the warmth against his painful fingers, and sipped his coffee. After a moment he moved to the window and looked out again—at approximately the same instant Maria Markham glanced up and saw him. She immediately sent Phelan Canfield on his way and went into the house.

"Any chance of getting breakfast, Perkins?" Max asked.

"I believe it's in the making, Sir."

"You 'believe'?"

"Well, Sir, I did get myself run out of the kitchen pretty quick—so I can't be exactly sure."

"What the hell did you do?"

"Showed up, Sir," Perkins said. "That's about all it took."

"Perkins, the Markham woman is only this high," Max said, holding up an aching hand in a fair estimation of her tallness.

"Yes, Sir, but she had this here broom and even if she didn't use it, she was about to cry—so I just thought I'd let her win this one. And as long as I was shoved out yonder in the backyard, I got me a campfire going to make the coffee. And I seen to your mount—checked the hooves and got the farrier up here. So that's been done. I got the wash pot filled with water and a good fire under it, while I was at it. It ought to be hot enough about now. Would you be needing it for a shave and the like, Sir?"

"I would," Max said. "Tell Miss Markham I said to hold breakfast until I'm ready."

Perkins made a small sound. Just enough of one to let Max know his orderly wasn't altogether looking forward to another encounter with the daughter of the house.

"Tell her just like that, Sir?" he asked.

"Exactly like that, Perkins."

A "shave and the like" didn't take nearly as long as it might have. Perkins had already set up a place in a small connecting room—in what Max guessed had once been a nursery—Maria Markham's perhaps. The orderly had the tin tub more than half filled. All that remained was carrying the hot water upstairs from the wash pot in the backyard. The biggest delay was caused by finding a wearable tunic. The one he had arrived in had numerous holes burned in it from the sparks at the fire.

Still, the wait would likely not sit well with Maria. It was yet another "inconvenience" he didn't mind perpetrating—or so he thought until he came downstairs. She had gone to a great deal of trouble from the smell of things—fresh bread, cooked apples, fried meat of some kind—bacon or ham—and coffee.

Mr. Markham greeted him in the hall, a stately-looking man in a threadbare frock coat, if somewhat frail. Maria Markham must have taken after her mother. Max could see no family resemblance.

"Good morning, Colonel! And a fine morning it is. This way, if you please," the old man said, leading him into the dining room. "I trust you slept well?"

"Quite well," Max said, the lie coming easily. He had had months of practice when he was still recuperating at home after his imprisonment. Both his mother and his sister, Kate, had asked him that every morning, and every morning he had lied. The truth was that he couldn't remember the last time he'd had a restful sleep. Or even a long one. It seemed to be the way of things. He wasn't the only war veteran to suffer from it—particularly among the ones who had survived a prison. There was no cure, as far as he knew, save laudanum or brandy, not even an accommodating woman helped. He no longer worried about it.

"I see you've sustained an injury," Markham said.

"A minor one. I am much improved this morning—

thanks to your daughter. She very kindly bound my hands last night to keep the swelling to a minimum.''

The old man laughed. "*My* daughter? Ah, well now, that is a surprise.''

Max had the distinct impression that the surprise came not from Maria Markham's handiness at binding wounds but from her willingness to do so for the likes of a Yankee colonel.

The dining room was as sparsely furnished as the rest of the house. The table should have had six chairs, but there were only three and three places set. The china and the silverware were clearly of good quality. The only problem was that hardly anything matched.

"If you would sit here, Colonel,'' the old man said, offering him his place at the head of the table.

"I would prefer the side, Mr. Markham, if you don't mind. I tend to linger to read and work after I eat, and I like room to spread out. I have no wish to usurp your place.''

"As you wish, Sir,'' Markham said. "Maria Rose!''

She came eventually, carrying a tray heavily laden with serving bowls. They were as mismatched as the rest of the dinnerware, and apparently she was foregoing the use of the sideboard and putting everything directly on the table, because there was no one but her to serve.

Max picked up a crisply starched but much-darned napkin and tried not to smile. He understood the not-so-subtle message she was sending him perfectly, as he was meant to do. The Markhams—like the rest of the people here—had suffered for their cause and, vanquished or not, they were proud of it.

He noted, too, that the resolute Miss Markham didn't wear her severe mourning attire at home—or at least, not precisely. She did have on a kind of black skirt, but

she'd put a white blouse with it and then covered over
the entire ensemble with a coarse linen pinafore of a
faded violet color. It made her look young and vulnerable in a way that was not entirely unbecoming.

"Have you seen my orderly, Miss Markham?" he
asked as she set a large compote of a thin, brownish
liquid and a bowl of rice in front of her father.

"He is sitting on the back steps—eating."

"I believe I mentioned that he was to assist you with
the meals."

"And I believe I mentioned that his assistance was
not required," she countered, still unloading bowls.

Her father looked from one of them to the other. "Maria—"

"I must bring the coffee, Father," she said, disappearing through the doorway. She came back almost immediately with the coffeepot and proceeded to pour.

That done, she left the room again, and Max expected
her not to return. She did, however, with a bread basket
full of hot biscuits, which she placed near his elbow.
Then, she sat in the only seat available—across from
him.

"May I take the liberty of saying grace?" he asked
just to see the expression on her face.

"Indeed, Colonel," her father answered quickly, Max
thought to head any remarks his daughter might feel
compelled to make.

Max made his prayer of thanks concise and eloquent,
one that would have done his clergyman great-uncle
proud—if he did say so himself. Rather than bowing his
head, Max kept his eyes on Maria the entire time. She
looked up at him before the prayer ended—as he knew
she would.

He left it to her to begin passing the bowls, and he

managed to serve himself in spite of the pain in his hands.

"Tell me, Colonel Woodard," Mr. Markham said. "Have you learned yet to appreciate our fine Southern cuisine?"

"I'm afraid I haven't often had the occasion to try it," he answered, still watching Maria. His experience with "Southern cuisine" had been the daily ration at the prison—moldy cornbread that was mostly ground-up cobs, and a cup of watery rice soup. On very special occasions, he had fought off other men for the privilege of eating hog entrails that had been dumped over the wall to the men in the stockade in the same way one might feed a pack of animals. And he had been grateful for the opportunity. His ration, pitiful as it was, had been the only thing he had to barter. He'd prolonged his hunger more than one time in order to purchase his desperate notion of what constituted a luxury—once a single, bloodstained page from *David Copperfield*.

He still had it.

But he would have to agree that Maria Markham had set an excellent table, regardless of the hodgepodge of china and utensils. She was a fine cook, but she made little attempt to eat what she had taken onto her plate. She kept halfheartedly pushing her food around with her fork and finally drank a small sip of water from her glass.

Max let Mr. Markham carry the conversation—the weather, street repairs, the impeachment woes of President Andrew Johnson. The most likely topic of conversation—the fire and the subsequent curfew—went conspicuously unremarked upon. After a time he realized that the old man was indeed not well. The effort it took for him to speak left him winded, and clearly worried his daughter. At one point he lost his breath altogether.

"Father—" Maria said in alarm.

"I am...quite...all right, Maria Rose. Don't...fuss over me," he insisted, and he continued with the meal if not the conversation.

Maria Markham had said when Max first arrived that she obeyed her father's wishes. And so she did—but it was all she could do to manage it. They ate for a time in silence.

"May I ask you a question, Miss Markham?" Max said, because he thought she was about to get up and leave.

She looked up at him, her expression startled, as if she had forgotten he was there and, now reminded, had no idea what uncouth subject he might broach, regardless of her father's presence. She also looked very pale.

"I was wondering if you are acquainted with the Howes," he said anyway. "Major John Howe and his wife."

"I...know them by sight," she answered.

"I thought Mrs. Howe was a Salisburian."

"She is—but we did not move in the same circles growing up. And especially not now," she added.

He chose to ignore the remark. "Do the Howes live nearby?"

"The...the Howes—" She abruptly stopped. "You must excuse me, Father. I have things I must see to—"

She got up from her chair and hurriedly left the table, disappearing through the doorway into the kitchen.

Max looked at her father, but the old man clearly felt no need to explain her behavior—possibly because he couldn't. Perkins suddenly appeared in the dining-room doorway, looking as if he didn't quite know how he'd gotten there.

"Did you speak to Miss Markham just now?" Max asked him, because he thought it the only explanation for the man's perplexed look.

"Yes, Sir. Very briefly. I believe the colonel needs coffee?"

The colonel didn't, but Perkins picked up the coffee-pot and poured as much as he could into the already full cup anyway.

"Anything else, Sir?" he asked.

"Stay handy," Max said. "When Mr. Markham is done, you can clear the table. Then you can bring me my leather case. I have reading I need to do."

Mr. Markham cleared his throat. "My daughter is sometimes very…high-strung. The war was hard on the women here."

"The war was hard on the women everywhere," Max said, thinking of the unmarked burial trenches and the women who perhaps still waited to hear what had become of their men.

He took a small breath and tried to let go of the animosity that threatened to overwhelm him. The war was over.

Over.

He had managed to get past the bitterness he harbored after John Howe made his solo escape from the prison. If he could put *that* behind him, surely he could let go of the rancor he felt for the people in this town who had, perhaps unknowingly, tolerated the mistreatment of Union prisoners.

When the old man had taken his leave and Perkins had gone to fetch the leather case, Max kept watching the door that led to the kitchen.

But there was no sign of Maria Markham.

Chapter Four

Maria heard her father slowly climb the stairs and shuffle out onto the second-story porch. He would stay there, reading, until it became too sunny for his comfort. She had a little time before he came inside again.

She heard the front door open and close—twice. The house had gone very quiet. Colonel Woodard and his sergeant major must have left for military headquarters. He would have a great deal to do his first real day in command. Perhaps he would be as late returning as he was last night.

That prospect cheered her considerably. She gave a quiet sigh and wiped her face again with a wet cloth. She was feeling better—less indisposed, at any rate. She wouldn't have to make any kind of explanation to the colonel, but what was she going to tell her father? He couldn't abide rudeness in his children—even if it seemed to be directed at a Yankee invader. And she couldn't explain that she hadn't been rude at all. She couldn't tell him that what he mistook for impoliteness was actually the sudden and overwhelming nausea of pregnancy.

She forced herself to stand up. She couldn't hide for-

ever, and she had a great deal of work to do. She came
quietly down the back stairs into the kitchen. The dishes
had all been washed and dried and placed in neat stacks
on the worktable. Had she been gone that long?

She looked around impatiently for the leftovers—food
she planned to somehow circumvent the curfew and take
to Suzanne Canfield. Phelan had said Suzanne was worse
today; there was no way she could get anything to eat
on her own. And the little boys. Who would feed them?
Phelan intended to get back home through the woods—
if he could keep out of the sight of the army patrols—
but she had no way of knowing if he'd made it. Even if
he had, he wasn't all that reliable when it came to caring
for his wife and children. Suzanne had no family here
to help her, and neither did Phelan.

She kept looking around the kitchen, but she couldn't
find a single cold biscuit. No pieces of ham. No bacon.
Nothing.

She walked into the dining room, thinking that perhaps the bread basket had been left on the table. Colonel
Woodard was still sitting exactly where she'd left him,
only now he was reading a letter. He barely looked up.

"I've been waiting for you," he said when she tried
to back out of the room.

She hesitated, trying to think of a way to escape.
Nothing came to mind.

"What is it, Colonel?" she asked from the doorway,
hoping that he only wanted something fetched or carried
rather than her continued presence.

"Sit," he said.

After a long moment she did so—she still needed the
money. There was a pitcher of water and a small glass
on the table, and a plate with a lemon and a knife on
it—none of which she had provided.

"If you would cut the lemon," he said, "and squeeze some of the juice into a glass of water, please."

Please.

He didn't toss that word around much, and she regarded him warily.

There was nothing to do but oblige. The sooner she did as he wanted, the sooner she could go.

She filled the glass, cut the lemon, picked out the seeds and squeezed in the juice, wondering all the while how much a piece of fruit this fine would cost. When she'd finished, she started to push the glass toward him.

"No," he said. "Drink it. It's for you."

"I don't need—"

"Yes, you do. It will make you feel better if you sip it slowly."

"You practice medicine as well as head the military government?"

"I want you healthy, Miss Markham. Of course, you don't *have* to follow my recommendation. We can have the army surgeon look at you—just to make sure you are not coming down with some illness which might be an…inconvenience."

"Inconvenience to whom?"

"To me," he said easily. "I suspect, though, that you are not ailing. I suspect you are experiencing a mild upset this morning—brought on by a late night and by the worry of having unwelcome strangers in your house—not to mention the concern you must have for your father's health. In which case, fresh lemon juice in water will alleviate it. Please. Drink it."

She looked at him across the table. He was studying her closely—too closely—but not in the lecherous way Hatcher had. She would have to be careful with this man. He meant what he said about understanding the people here, and he would not miss much that went on around him, regardless of his arrogance. She glanced at his injured hands, and he saw her do it.

"Yes," he said. "I'm merely returning the favor."

She waited as long as she dared, then took a small sip of the lemon water. It was…refreshing, and not an affront to her queasy stomach at all. She took another sip, and then another.

"Thank you," she said, her voice low.

"You are welcome, Miss Markham. Tell me about your brothers."

"What?" she said, startled.

"Your brothers," he repeated.

She was so caught off guard that she still didn't say anything.

"They were killed in the war," he said. It wasn't quite a question.

"Yes," she said.

"How old were they?"

"Rob was twenty-eight. Samuel was sixteen."

"Where were they killed?"

"Gettysburg," she said, holding his gaze. She didn't understand why he was asking her this—when it was obvious to her that he already knew.

"I was at Gettysburg," he said.

She looked away, still not understanding. There was no malice in his voice and no apology or sympathy, either. It was merely a quiet statement of fact—and she could make of it whatever she would.

"Your fiancé," he continued after a moment.

"I don't talk about him," she said. "Ever." It was all she could do to remain seated.

"Then you can tell me what I asked you earlier—

before you fled the room. Do Major Howe and his wife live nearby?''

"Major Howe is no longer here. I believe he's returned to Washington."

"Alone?"

She looked at him. "With his wife and mother-in-law, Mrs. Verillia Douglas," she said.

"Ah, yes. Verillia. I would have liked to have been introduced to Verillia. According to Major Howe, she is quite the physician in her own right, is that not so?"

"She has helped my father on many occasions. I wish she were..."

Maria trailed off. She was barely acquainted with the Howes, but she knew Verillia Douglas well. And it wasn't just for her father that she wished Verillia's return, or even Suzanne. Verillia was the one woman in this town to whom she might speak of her current predicament. Verillia wouldn't condemn her—she would help her, even if it were nothing more than to allow her a shoulder to weep on.

She realized suddenly that the colonel had said something.

"I beg your pardon?"

"I asked why Major Howe and his family left."

"I understand there was some concern on his part about the fires—and that he had a disagreement with Colonel Hatcher. My father will know the details. I'm certain he will give them to you if you ask him."

"Perhaps I will. Tell me, how do the people here view Major Howe's marriage to a local girl?"

"I don't know," she said.

"Then how do *you* view it?"

"I have no opinion."

"Because you only know them by sight."

"Because I have no opinion," she said evenly.

"It was a love match," he said.

"So I've heard."

"Major Howe tells me he would be dead twice over but for his wife. Apparently, it was the man that mattered to her and not his politics. All in all, a very romantic story, don't you think?"

Maria made no comment. She was far too busy trying to fathom his intent.

It suddenly came to her. He wanted to point out to her, however subtly, that the people here—the *women* here—had been vanquished in more ways than one. Perhaps Major Howe's marriage to Amanda Douglas had been a love match—but the ones she was witnessing now weren't. They couldn't be more mercenary, and she longed to tell him so.

She glanced at him; he was staring at her across the table.

"Feeling better?" he asked quietly.

"I feel quite fine," she answered.

"And your friend? Your particular friend—Suzanne. How is she?"

"How did you—"

She broke off. Of course. He had been listening at the upstairs window. The question now was how much he had heard and what he would do about it.

"I assume she is not well," he continued. "If her husband would chance being arrested to come here—on her behalf. Is that not so?"

Maria ignored the question and asked one of her own.

"How long will the curfew be in effect?"

"The curfew doesn't apply to you—if you need to see about your friend. I will write you a pass."

"Why?" Maria asked pointedly.

He held up his bruised hands. "I owe you a favor."

"I believe that was canceled out with the lemon."

"Perhaps. But you see, I want you in *my* debt, Miss Markham, rather than the other way around. I believe our association will go more smoothly if you are. I think you honor your debts. I think such things matter to you."

She didn't know whether to be insulted or flattered.

Yes, she did. Without a word, she abruptly stood and walked out of the room, all the while expecting him to object to her leaving.

But he didn't say anything, and she didn't stop until she reached the kitchen. She kept pacing around the room, trying to collect her thoughts. Then, she sat down at the worktable, only to get up again. She did *not* understand this man. Why would he extend to her what anyone would call a kindness—and then go out of his way to make sure she didn't mistake it for that? Were they both to keep some kind of running tally of favors paid and favors owed?

She gave an exasperated sigh. He had offered to help her. The offer itself—and the reason for it—had been plainly stated. But it was what he did *not* say that she found so vexing. He could and would help her—and the only impediment would be that her animosity for him and his kind was more important to her than her "particular friend," Suzanne.

She could hear a commotion at the front of the house: men—soldiers—coming in from the outside.

Officers.

She could tell by the banter. It was the same game of Who's The Better Man? that the enlisted men engaged in everywhere one went, except that theirs, while no less biting, was more sophisticated and subtle.

She looked anxiously toward the doorway at a sudden

burst of laughter, wondering where she could go to escape. Hatcher hadn't held any meetings with his staff here in the house, but clearly that was not Colonel Woodard's plan. She could hear a number of them clumping up the stairs—to see her father on the upstairs porch from the sound of it. It would please him to have visitors, the only visitors possible thanks to the curfew.

And her kitchen was about to be invaded, as well. She looked around in alarm as one of them came in through the back door.

"Well, well, well, what have we here?" he said loudly. She moved toward the back stairs, but he stepped into her path.

"I don't believe you answered me," he said with an all too familiar smile.

She didn't return it. She stood there, not quite sure what to do.

"Pardon me, Major De Graff, Sir," the orderly, Perkins, said in the doorway. "The colonel has remarked particularly upon your absence."

"Yes. Quite right. Thank you, Sergeant Major."

"My pleasure, Sir," Perkins assured him. He waited until the major was on his way to the dining room. "Miss Markham, the colonel needs more chairs. He asks—"

"Tell the colonel there are no more chairs for the dining room—General Stoneman's raiders used them for firewood," she said.

"I'll do that, miss," he said. "Please don't run off anyplace. I'll be right back."

Maria was feeling queasy again, too queasy to run anywhere other than the back door. She stepped outside, hoping some fresh air would help. If it didn't, at least there would be no floor to mop.

The yard seemed to be filling up with Yankees, as well. Several tents had been pitched on the grass since she'd last looked out, and four men were working diligently to make a much larger fenced-in place for their horses than she had for her buggy horse, Nell. And it was much too close to the vegetable garden for her liking. She moved to where they couldn't see her, and she could hear Perkins calling her.

She didn't answer.

"There you are, miss," he said, coming outside.

"What is it now?" she asked.

"The colonel says to tell you he has changed his mind about writing out that pass—no, now, don't go thinking he's breaking his word or it's got anything to do with the chair situation," he added quickly, apparently because of the look on her face.

"The colonel—he's only just got here, see, and some of these men—well, they didn't get a lot of discipline under Hatcher's command—like that there Major De Graff. Colonel Woodard is thinking the patrols might not accept the pass as being official. He says to tell you he will see you about it later."

Maria didn't recall asking for an audience. It was bad enough that he had the power to dictate her comings and goings, and even worse to have to remain in a house full of Yankee soldiers.

She gave a quiet sigh. She had to see about Suzanne, and she had no easy way to get there. She had no food to take her if she could manage to make the trip, unless she pilfered Colonel Woodard's pantry, which she couldn't do—key or no key—with Perkins so close at hand.

She was essentially trapped with nowhere to go. If she tried to work in the garden, she would have an unwanted audience, and inside, she might encounter De Graff again—or the colonel.

"Maybe you should join your father," Perkins suggested, as if she'd spoken out loud.

"No," she said. There was too much work to be done. If she didn't get to the hoeing, the morning glories would run rampant in the corn and beans, thanks to yesterday's rain. The kitchen and the hall—and now the dining-room floors had to be scrubbed free of muddy boot prints. The ironing she should have done yesterday instead of going to the railroad station still sat in the basket in the corner. She had two more meals to prepare. She needed to start a fire in the stove in the summer kitchen to cook the dried butter beans she had soaking. If she didn't, they'd never be done in time. Her father hated butter beans, but it was either that or accept the colonel's bounty, and she didn't want to touch his food, if she could help it.

And she was *tired.*

"They won't bother you, miss," Perkins said.

"What?" she asked, because she had been too busy feeling sorry for herself to remember that Perkins was still close by.

"The men. The colonel has given them all strict orders not to accost you on any account—regardless of their rank."

She looked at him, not at all certain that she believed him.

"I think I will go see my father," she said. She went quickly up the back stairs and just as quickly changed her mind again. Her father was still on the upstairs porch—but he was deep in conversation with Colonel Woodard.

Her alternate plan was to take herself to the summer kitchen. She would be essentially out of sight of the soldiers in the yard and not apt to run into any of the ones who still wandered over the house. She took the basket of ironing with her, giving thanks as she went that the Markhams had once been well off enough to have this alternate place to cook and work in hot weather. There were a number of windows she could raise to catch whatever breeze might at hand. The important thing was that she would be alone there. She could work and she could think—or not think, as she chose.

It took her only a short while to get the cast-iron stove going and the dampers adjusted and the butter beans rinsed and in the cook pot. She put two sets of irons on the stove to heat, and then dampened the clothes with water and rolled them tightly and put them into a pillowslip.

She had to go back into the house once because she'd forgotten the old sheet she used to pad the table when she ironed. Her stomach had finally settled, and she went down into the cellar to get herself an apple. She could hear that the colonel's staff meeting was in session—and from the sound of it, things were not going well.

All the more reason for her not to tarry, she thought. Her only wish was to stay out of his way. She returned to the summer kitchen and ate the apple—and actually enjoyed it. Perhaps there was something to the lemon juice "cure."

When the irons were hot enough, she began pressing her damp petticoats and chemises. From now on, when she did the wash, she'd have to find somewhere inside to hang them to dry. She did *not* want her underpinnings blowing in the breeze for Union soldiers to see.

She kept ironing, kept worrying about how she could get to Suzanne and how she could thwart Colonel

Woodard. She could hear the buzz of insects at the open windows and the murmur of the soldiers still working on their pen. She hummed softly to herself to keep her thoughts from going in a direction she wouldn't be able to endure.

It was so hot. If *they* hadn't been in the yard, she would have done the ironing in the shaded walkway between the house and the summer kitchen. After a time she shed her pinafore and rolled up her sleeves. Then she took off her shoes and stockings, savoring the feel of her bare feet against the cool stone floor. Even so, she still had to wet her face and neck with cold water from time to time in order to stand the heat.

At one point, she looked up at a different sound. Colonel Woodard stood in the doorway.

"I've spoken to your father," he said without prelude—something he did often, she was beginning to realize, as if it didn't matter how he came to a particular point, only that his ultimate demand was met and with total compliance.

She didn't say anything, partially because she had no idea what direction the conversation was taking and mostly because she was mortified that he would see her bare feet. She bent her knees slightly to make sure her skirts touched the ground.

"Your father agrees that it might not be expedient to allow you to go see about your friend under a pass. You will be escorted at his request."

"I will speak to my father about it myself," she said. She wasn't about to take his word for anything.

"I believe he is resting now—"

"I will speak to him, anyway."

"Fine," he said, turning to go. "But put your shoes on."

She could feel her face grow even hotter, and she stood there, her mortification giving way to absolute indignation. If the iron in her hand hadn't been so heavy, she would have thrown it at him.

"Hurry it along, Miss Markham," he said as he walked away. "The Army of the Republic waits for no one."

She slammed the iron down—only to pick it up again because an arrogant Yankee colonel wasn't worth a scorched sheet. She slung the iron onto the stovetop with a loud clang. Then she set about getting her shoes and socks and her pinafore back on, muttering under her breath all the while. When she straightened up, two soldiers were looking in the window, both of them grinning from ear to ear.

"Would you be needing anything, miss?" one of them asked innocently.

She needed a loaded pistol, but she didn't say so. She ignored both of them and walked swiftly back into the house, her head held high.

Colonel Woodard and Perkins stood in the kitchen.

"Sergeant Major Perkins, tell Miss Markham where her father is," Colonel Woodard said when he saw her.

"Mr. Markham is asleep on the daybed in his sitting room, miss," Perkins replied dutifully. "He has had a bit to eat, and he has no complaints—except that he is tired and would like to rest now."

Maria looked from one man to the other. She had every intention of speaking to her father herself.

"I'm leaving now, Miss Markham. You *are* still concerned about your friend?" the colonel asked when she headed for the back stairs.

She stopped, realizing that he was once again deliberately trying to provoke her. She closed her eyes for a moment in a monumental effort to keep her temper in check. She would *not* let him win.

"Yes," she said, turning to look at him. "I am still concerned. I want to go see about her—if you please," she added, though it nearly killed her to do it.

"Excellent—Perkins, you know what to do."

"Yes, Sir!" Perkins said, hurrying away.

Maria moved to get her straw hat down from the peg by the back door, then she stood and waited for her instructions from the colonel and tried not to shred the brim.

"This way, Miss Markham," Colonel Woodard said.

He went ahead of her into the center hallway. A number of Yankee officers stood around, and all of them stared as she passed. The colonel opened the front door for her—in what had to be purely a token gesture of courtesy on his part. No matter how it might appear on the surface, there was nothing civil about the man. But she had no doubt that her father had been fooled or that he had sanctioned her going.

A carriage sat in front of the house—the same one that had brought his belongings yesterday—and the colonel was going to win after all. She was suddenly overcome with consternation at the sight of it. She simply could not bear to be seen in public with this man two days in a row.

He was halfway to the street when he realized she was no longer trailing after him.

"What is it?" he asked, waiting for her to catch up.

She made no attempt to do so.

"I can't," she said, trying not to sound as hysterical as she felt. "My father would not want me to be seen about town with you like this."

"He didn't seem to mind yesterday when he sent you

to the train station," the colonel said. "That aside, I told you I had spoken with him. He feels that my escorting you personally to see about Mrs. Canfield is an excellent plan. I must go to my office, anyway. You can remain with Mrs. Canfield until I—or Perkins—can fetch you home again. Unless you prefer to stay here in the company of a bunch of…I'm ashamed to say, very poorly disciplined officers, who may or may not adhere to the letter of my direct orders and remember that they are gentlemen by military decree, if nothing else. Your choice, of course."

"My choice? It is *not* my choice! You have me in a corner and you know it!"

"Yes," he said agreeably. "Are you coming along or not?"

She was, and he knew that, too. She picked up her skirts and walked purposefully by him and climbed into the carriage, ignoring Perkins's outstretched hand. She had already learned from yesterday's buggy ride that Colonel Woodard would do whatever he pleased, and she moved into the far corner of the seat to keep him from parking himself on her pinafore and skirts.

But he made no attempt to sit beside her. He took the opposite seat instead and watched her closely—which was worse. Maria turned her head to keep him from looking directly into her eyes.

They rode down the shady street in silence. A pack of dogs, unmindful of the curfew, came bounding out from under a house to nip at the horses' heels for a short distance.

"Your father tells me you and Mrs. Canfield have been friends since you were children," Colonel Woodard said. "He said you used to name your pets after each other. I was particularly interested to hear that there was once a little red hen named 'Maria Rose.'"

Maria glanced at him, fully aware that he was trying to annoy her again, but she didn't say anything.

"I believe he mentioned 'The Three Musketeers,'" the colonel continued. "But he didn't say who the third one was."

Maria made no reply to that, either. She was looking at the houses they rode past. There was someone sitting on nearly every porch, all of them watching, waiting to see what indignity would be inflicted upon them next, and all of them trying to decipher the meaning of Maria Markham's letting herself be seen in the company of the new Yankee colonel.

Again.

"Have courage, Miss Markham," he said.

"*I* have no reason to fear," she said pointedly, and she might have meant it if they were not nearing the Kinnard house. Acacia Kinnard ran this town—at least when it came to social matters. Her husband was a man of property and influence—money—even in these hard times. And whenever she snubbed another woman, that woman's social invitations ended.

"Maria!" Mrs. Kinnard called from her second-story porch. "Is the curfew lifted?"

"No, Mrs. Kinnard. I have permission to see about Suzanne Canfield."

"Indeed," Mrs. Kinnard said, obviously pleased. "Well done, Maria!"

"Would you like to visit with this lady a bit?" Colonel Woodard asked under his breath.

"Good heaven's no," Maria said in alarm. "I must see about Suzanne," she added. Knowing Acacia Kinnard, she would want Maria to expand on her success and arrange for all the Kinnard family and friends to escape the curfew, as well.

"I do hope the Ladies' Literary Society will be able to meet soon," Mrs. Kinnard called as if on cue. "I so miss our readings. I was truly looking forward to hearing about the Scottish chiefs. Do you know when the curfew will be lifted, Maria?"

"No," Maria answered, in spite of the fact that the question was by no means directed to her.

"Friday, ma'am," Colonel Woodard said, taking the hint.

"Friday! Are you certain?"

"I am, ma'am. That is, if there are no further... incidents. We will return to the previous rules and curfew—10:00 p.m."

"Excellent, Maria!" she called, as if Maria had been the one who made the announcement. "I believe the next meeting—Saturday—will be at your house."

"No, I don't think—" Maria began.

"Your house, Maria," Mrs. Kinnard said firmly. "At the usual time. And I trust your father will want to join us. *Gentlemen* are *always* welcome."

Maria tried to hide her exasperation and waved goodbye instead of answering. A Ladies' Literary Society gathering was the absolute last thing she needed.

"I hope you are satisfied," she said to the colonel.

"Being helpful always gives one a certain...satisfaction," he said.

"You were *not* helpful, sir," Maria assured him.

"I don't believe it would be appropriate to continue the stricter curfew so that you don't have to entertain the literary society."

"You haven't met the literary society," Maria said,

glancing in his direction. To her great surprise the man very nearly smiled.

The carriage turned onto Innes Street. There were still people on the porches, but none of them had Mrs. Kinnard's audacity. Maria wondered idly how the Kinnards' only daughter, Valentina, was doing in her quest for a Yankee officer husband—and if she knew that her mother had heard enough about the new colonel to have apparently switched quarries.

It would serve Woodard right. Let his new residence be overrun with Acacia Kinnard and her kind.

As they neared the Canfield house, Maria grew more and more anxious, so much so that she barely waited for the carriage to stop before she got out. The front door of the house stood open. She didn't see the boys or Phelan.

Surely he hasn't taken them somewhere, she thought. The last thing she wanted was for Colonel Woodard to find that Phelan was still ignoring the curfew.

"Wait, Miss Markham," Colonel Woodard said. "You forgot this."

She looked around. Perkins held out a basket. She made no attempt to take it.

"It's only food, Miss Markham," the colonel said.

"Phelan Canfield will not accept anything from you."

"It isn't from me. It's from your father."

"My father can't afford to hand out food baskets."

"Perhaps he's come into some money."

Maria nearly laughed. She didn't believe him for an instant, but she came and got the basket—for Suzanne and the boys' sakes.

"Thank you so much," she said with as much sarcasm as she dared.

"It's from your father," he reminded her.

"For the escort then," Maria said.

"I believe you mean for having put you into a corner."

"That is precisely what I mean."

"In that case, you are most welcome, Miss Markham. I will see you later. Perkins!"

The carriage moved off, and Maria stood staring after it.

For Suzanne and the boys, she thought.

For the money.

Chapter Five

"Any trouble?"

Perkins took Max's question as permission to enter and stepped inside the office. "The town's pretty quiet, Sir. There's been a development, though."

Max looked up from the papers he'd been shuffling in spite of the pain in his hands. "What kind of development?"

"Phelan Canfield, Sir. Drunk and disorderly and breaking the curfew. He's in jail."

"Good," Max said, going back to his papers. "What?" he asked after a moment because Perkins was still standing there.

"Well, Sir, he had his boys with him. I was wondering what you want done with them?"

Max looked at his orderly. He didn't want anything done with them—but it was clear by the careful expression on Perkins's face that that was neither here nor there.

"We can't leave them at the jail, can we, Sir?" Perkins said to prod him along.

"I don't see an alternative—with their mother not able

to take care of them. Miss Markham's father isn't well. I don't think she plans to stay there.''

''I sent word to Miss Markham, Sir—so Mrs. Canfield would know where her husband and the little boys got to. They was both pretty upset about it—''

''The man broke curfew.''

''No, Sir—it ain't us they was upset with. It's him— drinking again and what-not.''

Max didn't ask what the ''what-not'' entailed. He drew a quiet breath. He had had a long day—but things were in better order now than they had been yesterday. His first act this morning had been to inaugurate a recognizable chain of command, and by doing so, he'd established once and for all that the perpetual party they had all enjoyed under Hatcher's rule had come to an end.

Max had learned his military lessons from Richard Rush, who had commanded the Pennsylvania Sixth. Rush had been a West Pointer and did not abide military sloppiness of any kind in his subordinates. And neither would Max. He'd given all his officers jobs to do and not enough time to do them in. The results would be…interesting, more telling of the kind of staff he had than a month of observation.

At first impression, they seemed a mixed bunch. Some old veterans who didn't quite know what to do with themselves in peacetime. Some too young to have participated in the actual war, but still looking for a lark. And some like Major De Graff, who wanted to chase Secessionist women around the furniture—and worse.

His mind went immediately to Maria Markham, the sight of her standing barefoot in the summer kitchen, all hot and sweaty, her sleeves rolled up above her elbows and her dark hair coming undone. She should have been anything but appealing, yet he had waited much longer

than he should have before making his presence known.
Everything about her at that instant had affected him—
even the tune she was humming.

Bushes and Briars.

He recognized it easily. One of the Lancer corporals
used to sing it all the time in camp and on the cam-
paigns—Hazeltine had been his name. Benneville Hazeltine, dead now, killed in some skirmish the particulars
of which Max could no longer remember. The song was
a young girl's lament about her lover's long absence and
her longing for him—and her fear that her "boldness"
might offend him when they finally met again. Corporal
Hazeltine had been able to wrap his voice around it in
such a way that left the entire regiment unsettled.

Max wondered what Maria Markham knew about
that—about *boldness*. Nothing, he imagined. And it was
not his business to teach her. Or even his inclination. He
was still incredulous that he had let himself find someone like her fetching. She was pleasing enough, he supposed, or would be, if she were properly turned out—
his mother and sister, Kate, would know what to do with
her. But she was hardly a beauty, and not to his taste at
all. He'd always preferred rosy-cheeked "maids of
golden hair." John Howe used to insist that the popular
song, "Aura Lee," had been written just for him. Whenever he looked at Maria Markham, he didn't see a de-
sirable woman. He saw something else entirely. It was
as if he recognized her—as someone who had suffered
deprivations, just as he had. And every time he looked
into her eyes, he had the annoying sense that she understood things about their mutual trials and tribulations
that he himself did not.

It was suddenly clear to him that he had been too
serious for too long. He needed some kind of diver-

sion—the kind he might have enjoyed with John Howe and the rest of the Lancer officers in the old days. A *man's* diversion. An all-night game of high-stakes poker, free-flowing, aged whiskey and fine cigars.

And women. Accommodating women who knew their art and were nothing like...

Maria Markham.

She had been afraid of him today. Why? he wondered. True, he was in command of this town—and he'd gone out of his way to annoy her. But he'd done nothing to inspire the look she'd given him when she realized he was standing there in the doorway.

"Sir," Perkins said, still prompting. "I'm thinking maybe them young'uns ought to be took over to the Markham house when we go. Maybe Miss Markham can just bring them on home with her—if you think you can stand it, that is, Sir."

Max frowned. Could he stand it? He didn't actually know. He'd never been in a household with children— at least not since he was one himself. Interrupted sleep wasn't likely to be a problem. He never slept anyway. He was beginning to understand what Maria Markham meant by being put into a corner. Jail was indeed no place for the little boys, regardless of their father's past allegiances or his current behavior, and the truth of the matter was that the children would disrupt the Markham household by their presence—or by their absence. He knew Maria Markham well enough to foresee that she wouldn't rest a moment if she thought they were suffering—and subsequently, neither would he.

"Well, go get them, Perkins," he said in aggravation.

"Yes, Sir!"

Perkins was gone far too short a time to have made a trip to the jail and return. The boys must have been downstairs someplace. Perkins brought them both up to the office and herded them inside. It was entirely unnecessary in Max's opinion, but he let it go, because they didn't seem to be living up to their boisterous reputations at the moment. Both children were obviously tired. And dirty. The smaller of the two had wet himself. Even so, he took one look at Max and toddled forward, raising both little arms in a silent entreaty to be picked up.

"Who is this?" Max asked, painfully lifting him off the floor in spite of his soggy state.

The little boy immediately hid his face in Max's shoulder, and Max patted him awkwardly on the back with one aching hand.

"He don't talk to Yankees," the older one said.

"That would be—" Perkins broke off midsentence to grab the boy by the seat of his britches as he tried to make a run for it out the door.

"Jake," Perkins concluded when he had the runaway dangling under his arm. "I'm not sure if this one's got a name," he said, setting the boy on his feet again. The child stood there, clearly worried. He couldn't get out, and he didn't know what to do about Max holding his trusting little brother.

"So which one of the Canfields are you?" Max asked him.

"Phelan Josiah Canfield," the boy said.

"How old are you?"

The boy held up five fingers, then bent down briefly to look under the desk.

"What do they call you—Phelan, like your father?" Max asked when he straightened up again.

"No. Mama and Maria said I had too many names. They just say 'Joe' when they want me. You can say

'Joe,' I guess—but you can't say 'Billy' if you want Jake. Nobody can say 'Billy.'''

"Why not?"

"Because it's Uncle Billy's name. Jake's got all of Uncle Billy's names, but you have to say 'Jake' so everybody don't cry. Mama cries and Grandmother Canfield cries—and Maria, too. I don't cry. I'm too big to cry. I get called 'Joe' and Jake gets called 'Jake'—'cept sometimes Maria calls us 'The Js.'''

"Why is that, do you think?" Max said, still trying to make conversation.

"'Cause she loves us," he said easily, as if he'd already dealt with that question, made the proper inquiries and now had the answer. "Have you got some lots of names?"

"I do—most of them don't bear repeating."

"What *is* your name?" the boy asked, reaching and holding his little brother by the shoe.

"Colonel Maxwell Prieson Woodard," he said.

"Maria doesn't love you."

"No. She doesn't."

"She wouldn't love a Yankee—but I can ask her for a name for you anyway."

"I think I'll just make do with the ones I've got. Right now it's time to go."

"Where?"

"To see your mother."

"Can I go see Maria?"

"Maria is at your house," Max said. He stood up with Jake still over his shoulder. The child had gone very heavy suddenly.

"Is this one asleep?" he asked Perkins, turning so the orderly could see.

"Yes, Sir—and then some. I reckon he's all wore out. Sir, I left the carriage over by the Canfield house—"

"Well, we'll just have to make do," Max said. The house was just down the street and around the corner— not at all too far to walk—unless one happened to be very small and as exhausted as his sleeping brother. "Can you ride a horse, Joe?"

"Yes," Joe said solemnly. "And a elephant."

"Elephants, too—very good. Get my hat, Perkins."

"Yes, Sir. You want to trade the hat for that boy, Sir?"

"Yes," Max said, handing the sleeping Jake over. "Come on, Joe," he said. The boy immediately latched onto his most painful hand, and he had to switch him to the other one.

"Where are we going?" Joe asked, looking up at him.

"Your house, remember?"

The boy shook his head. "Mama's sick."

"I know…but she's worried about where you are."

"I hope we get supper," Joe said.

"Don't worry—"

Maria's there, Max almost said.

The thought popped into his mind unbidden. He didn't take time to examine it or the reason for it. He led the boy down the stairs to the street, letting him clump as much as he liked, which was considerable. A private scrambled to attention at the sight of them—a much better response to Max's appearance than yesterday's. Of course, the real test would have been if the private had been trying to amuse a town trollop at the time.

The private had a horse ready and waiting—also an improvement.

"Take his head," Max said to him, because his hands hurt too badly to try to manage the horse and the boy.

He placed Joe on the saddle and mounted behind him. "We're going to go the long way, Perkins," he said to his sergeant major. "Advise Mrs. Canfield that young Master Canfield will be there directly."

"Is that me?" Joe asked, trying to turn around enough to see Max's face.

"It is," Max said. "Now. Which way shall we ride?"

The shadows were long, but the afternoon was still hot and muggy. Typical for the time of year here, Max knew from his imprisonment. There was enough of a breeze to rustle the tops of the trees along Main Street, but it never seemed to reach the ground. He could hear the sparrows under the eaves of the buildings, and, except for a few soldiers here and there, everything was deserted. At Joe's direction, Max took the horse first north and then south before he finally turned toward the Canfield house. Maria was standing on the porch, and she walked out to meet them.

"Look at me, Maria!" Joe cried at the sight of her.

"I see you, Joe," she said, smiling. "What a fine rider you are."

"Am I fine?" he asked, turning around look at Max.

"Very fine," Max said. "Shall we show her how fine we look?"

He urged the horse into a small trot down the street and back again, both of them sitting tall to show off for Maria Markham.

At the end of the demonstration, Max handed him down to her and dismounted.

"Perkins told you about—" he began.

"He told me," she interrupted. "Joe, thank Colonel Woodard for bringing you home," she said to the boy.

"Thank you," Joe said dutifully, but at the last moment he abruptly wrapped his arms around Max's knees in a brief, hard hug.

Max reached down to pat the boy's head. "Perhaps we can ride again sometime, Joe."

"His father won't permit it," Maria said quietly.

"One never knows—"

"*I* know," she said. "If you have a moment, Colonel Woodard, Suzanne would like to speak with you."

Max looked at her, then at Joe's upturned face.

"Run inside now, Joe," he said. He waited until the boy had disappeared into the house before he continued. "If Mrs. Canfield intends to ask for her husband's release—"

"She does not," Maria said. "She would merely like to thank you for bringing her children home—and for allowing me to come see about her. It's the way things are done here," she added in a not too subtle reference to *his* claim to want to understand the people he was supposed to govern.

"Very well," he said. "Lead the way."

The house was two-story, one of the "shotgun" styles with a long center hall front door to back. As an invading cavalryman, he had ridden more than once right up the front steps of a house like this one, down the hall and out the back—as more of a hell-raising lark than a military necessity.

He could smell something cooking—Joe clearly had no need to worry about getting his supper. As he followed Maria inside, a loud crash sounded toward the rear of the house.

"In there," Maria said, pointing out a doorway on his left. "Suzanne, this is Colonel Woodard," she called as she rushed away to investigate.

He stood for a moment, then entered the room. A

young, fair-haired woman lay on a daybed by the windows. She had on a faded but clean calico dress and her hair looked as if it had been freshly braided—Maria's doing, he supposed. She appeared weak and delicate, but pleased to have company, even if it was a Yankee colonel.

"Colonel Woodard," she said, extending her hand. "Will you come sit by me?"

He did so, pulling up a nearby chair so that she could see him without having to turn. She seemed a little breathless, but she didn't look feverish. He wondered precisely what her ailment was. That particular detail regarding Suzanne Canfield, Perkins had left out.

"Mrs. Canfield," he said to acknowledge her, and he placed his hat on his knees, aware that she was looking at him intently.

He waited.

"I never expected to invite a Yankee colonel into my home," she said finally.

He realized by her slightly mischievous expression that he was about to witness what must have once been Southern belle coquetry at its best. It had been made frail by her illness, and perhaps by her marriage, but it was still in evidence. And quite charming, actually, he decided—if a man didn't get taken unawares. He wondered if Maria had been mistaken, and Suzanne Canfield was about to petition for her husband's release, after all.

"I don't think I ever expected to be invited," he said, and she smiled. He thought she must have been very beautiful—once.

"I understand you are from Philadelphia," she said.

"Germantown, actually."

"I've been there—to both. With my father—before I was married. He was a scholar of Revolutionary War history. I recall there were some very interesting houses in Germantown. Perhaps, at the very time I visited, you lived in one of them.''

''Perhaps,'' he said.

She was still looking at him in a way he could not fathom. He was willing to make idle conversation, but he was acutely aware of the things that could not be remarked upon. The late war. Her incarcerated husband.

''You must be nostalgic for your home,'' she said.

''No, actually, I don't believe I am. I've been away a long time.''

''You joined the war early then.''

''Very early.''

''And you were a prisoner here.''

It wasn't a question, and he frowned slightly, wondering how she had come by that information.

''Maria told me you went to see it—the prison—when you arrived. I guessed that you must have had a particular reason to go there.''

He didn't have a reply to that, and she didn't seem to expect one.

''Maria says you have told her you want to learn how to get along with people here. She doesn't believe it. She thinks you only want to show *her* who has the upper hand.''

The remark was so indicative of his true motives that he shifted slightly in his chair.

''We've been friends since we were children, Maria and I,'' Suzanne Canfield said.

''Yes. So her father told me. I believe you were 'musketeers.'''

She smiled. ''There were three of us.'' The smile faded. ''Then two. And soon...'' She closed her eyes for a moment, then suddenly brightened again. "I could advise you how to get along with Maria, if you like."

"Do I need instruction?"

"I would say so—but only if you seek a certain civility in your society with her. There is no reason why you should, of course. You are the conqueror, and she— we all—are the conquered."

He didn't say anything.

"You *are* living in the same house and must tolerate each other," she said after a moment. "There really is a secret, you know. I'm not sure even Maria recognizes it."

"All right, then. Tell me. What is the secret to getting along with Miss Maria Markham?"

"She will never rely on anything you tell her."

"I would expect that—given our opposing politics—"

"It has nothing to do with your politics, Colonel. It has to do with Maria. She will not believe what you say, she will only believe what you do."

"I see."

Suzanne Canfield smiled again. "No, I doubt it. But what I've told you is the truth. It's the deed, not the words, that Maria will value—no matter if the deed is good or bad."

"Why are you telling me this, Mrs. Canfield?"

"Because I can. I haven't shocked you, have I?"

"No, you've piqued my curiosity."

"I think it's because I'm ill that I'm making suggestions," she said. "I see things that need saying and I say them. I can get away with it now, you see. It's very strange—and very…satisfying in a way—not to be bound by convention anymore. Maria is very dear to me and to my sons. I want her to have whatever ease of mind she can. But I'm keeping you, Colonel," she said, completely changing the subject. "I really only intended to say thank you."

"It isn't necessary. I haven't done anything, Mrs. Canfield."

"Of course you have. You are bound to do whatever you see as your duty, but you've still extended a kindness to me and to Maria—when you didn't have to."

He wasn't quite sure if she alluded to the curfew or to Phelan Canfield's being in jail.

"I wanted you to know that I'm grateful, Colonel Woodard," she said. The mischievous smile returned. "And I wanted to get a look at you. It will be all over town that you actually paid me a visit. The members of the literary society are going to be so very envious that I have seen you first."

Maria appeared in the doorway. She had flour all over her skirts.

"Joe was stacking boxes so he could climb on the flour barrel," she said.

"Is he hurt?" Suzanne asked in alarm.

"No, thank heavens. Some of the flour has spilled though."

To Max's alarm, Suzanne Canfield suddenly covered her face with her hands and began to weep. He immediately stood, then left the room to let Maria handle it, waiting in the hallway for her to come out. When she didn't appear after a time, he walked out onto the porch and lit a cigar. He had nearly finished smoking it when she finally appeared.

"I am taking the boys home with me," she said, her tone of voice, her stance, everything about her suggesting that she expected opposition from him and was prepared to do battle if need be.

"How is Mrs. Canfield?" he asked to divert her purpose.

"Suzanne is quiet now—asleep. She's asked if I will look after her boys until Phelan comes home. I have said yes. I am taking them with me."

Max stared into Maria Markham's eyes. She was so determined, and so certain that he would oppose her.

She will not believe what you say. She will only believe what you do.

Now why is that? he thought.

"Have we misplaced Perkins?" he asked.

"He's on the back porch trying to get the flour out of Joe's hair."

"If you would send him to me," he said, throwing the cigar away.

She hesitated. She clearly didn't like running errands any more than she liked playing stable boy. Max also noted that she looked pale—the way she had at the breakfast table this morning.

"Are you—"

She didn't give him time to complete the question. She left, nearly at a run, and she didn't come back. Perkins appeared almost immediately, carrying the still flour-covered Joe.

"Sir!" he said as if he were presenting himself at his martial best.

"Bring Miss Markham and the boys along—whenever she's ready."

"Yes, Sir!"

Max rode the distance to the Markham house alone, but he didn't stop. He gave the horse his head and continued on, as long as there was a street. Then, he rode into the wooded countryside, following any bridle path he could find. The sun was nearly gone when he returned, and whatever good had come of having his hands bound last night was no longer apparent. He was in pain, and he arrived to find the Markham house in chaos—both boys crying and the butter beans burned. He took one look at the situation and left immediately for the hotel across the street from military headquarters—where the proprietor made the mistake of informing him that there were no vacancies. Unfortunately, two of his lieutenants suffered for the man's impertinence. Perkins had them routed from their room and relocated to who knew where before they knew what had hit them.

By the time that had been accomplished, the pain in Max's hands had reached monumental proportions. With Perkins's help, he repeated last night's cold water treatment, but the sergeant major, as handy as he might be, was no match for Maria Markham when it came to wrapping injured hands.

Max finally fell asleep well into the morning hours, and he woke just as aggravated as when his head hit the pillow.

He stayed in the hotel for three days. Long enough for the curfew to be lifted. Long enough for Maria Markham to think she had her father's house back. But Max had no intention of being quartered with a bunch of rowdy soldiers, regardless of the fact that there was a time in his life when he was just like them.

He returned to the Markham house early Saturday evening—to find the little Canfield boys returned home and a chaos of a different kind. The Ladies' Literary Society. The house was full of chattering women—young and old. And women were still arriving, most of whom seemed to be carrying their own chairs. The parlor was full. The overflow spilled into the wide hallway. His arrival caused even more of a stir.

He saw Maria standing at the edge of the crowd, and it was clear to him that she expected him to turn tail and take himself back to the hotel. But he wasn't about to capitulate this time. He waded right into the midst of the society to reach her, feeling a buzz of attention all around him as he approached.

"I think introductions are in order," he said, just to see Maria give him her best exasperated look.

"This way," she said quietly, but her quietness didn't fool him for an instant. Miss Maria Rose Markham was quite ready to box his ears.

"I don't believe I see your father."

"My father is in hiding," she assured him.

She took him to the Kinnard woman first—a good indication of the pecking order, he thought. He already knew that Mrs. Kinnard felt her importance—as must her husband, given the number of petitions from him on Max's desk.

"And this is my daughter, Valentina," Mrs. Kinnard said of the young girl next to her.

"Miss Kinnard," Max said. Valentina was striking; there was no doubt about that. She was the only one in the group wearing a new and decidedly fashionable frock, a pale gray and blue thing with black stripes. It was that as much as anything that made her a rose among the weeds.

"You *will* come to our house for dinner soon, won't you, Colonel?" Mrs. Kinnard asked. "At your convenience? Mr. Kinnard and I would be so honored."

"Yes, please do, Colonel," Valentina said, lowering her eyes so that he could get the full effect of her long lashes. At the right moment, she looked up at him in a way that was so calculated he nearly laughed.

So this is the "bride fair," he thought.

"I'm afraid that wouldn't be possible," he said. "As much as I regret it, I must strike an impartial pose and not seem to have particular favorites."

"Are the Markhams not your fav—"

"Of course," Mrs. Kinnard interrupted, squashing her daughter's impertinence. "I did not think. Appearances are so important, because they are so easily misconstrued. But you will join us this evening then, Colonel Woodard—so that we may enjoy your company here? Perhaps even read for us?"

He had every intention of outmaneuvering the Kinnards on this matter, as well, then abruptly changed his mind. It was obvious to him that Maria was annoyed by the entire business—and that alone was reason enough for him to choose to remain.

He had a brief conference with Perkins—who looked very much like the proverbial fox in the henhouse—then returned to the parlor, allowing Maria to continue to make introductions all around the room and into the hallway again. He recognized a number of the surnames as being on petitions for favors like Kinnard's. And one young woman's name was the same as one of his officers.

"Carscaddon?" he said. "I believe I have a Lieutenant Carscaddon."

"Lieutenant James Carscaddon is my husband," she said, blushing.

"Indeed? Well, I can see I must compliment the lieutenant on his excellent choice of brides when next I see him."

The blush deepened, and Maria moved him along to the next eager presentee. He kept glancing at Maria as they moved from person to person. She avoided his eyes at every opportunity. Clearly, she still considered this distressing gathering all his fault.

"Will you sit here, Colonel?" she asked finally, showing him to a chair by Mrs. Kinnard.

He took it, just in time for Perkins to arrive with a huge platter of neatly quartered oranges and a large bowl of sugar in case any were too sour to be edible—the United States Army's contribution to the evening. Max knew oranges to be a rare delicacy in the town, and he sat there amid the exclamations of delight, feeling every pair of eyes on him—save Maria's. She kept busy, opening or closing windows, according to the desires of the guests nearest to them, finding napkins to accompany the orange platter. He watched her closely as she moved about. She was wearing the black dress again—which must be her only good one.

"Oh, my!" Valentina Kinnard cried next to him. "Forgive me, Colonel Woodard, but have you a handkerchief?"

He glanced at her. She had made a pretty mess with her orange quarter, and she looked at him coyly. He found his handkerchief, one of several his mother had sent him, and gave it to her. But he had no interest in observing her dab her pretty mouth with it. He looked for Maria again. She was no longer in the room.

"Colonel Woodard," Mrs. Kinnard said, determined to keep his attention from straying.

"Yes, Mrs. Kinnard?" he said, still trying to locate Maria.

"I asked if you would read for us?"

She was already pushing a green leather book into his hands.

William Wallace—*The Scottish Chiefs.*

He took the book and opened it where she directed.

There was an immediate hush in the room. He hesitated, then began to read aloud to the wives, the mothers, the sisters of men he had likely wished dead many times over. The irony of the situation did not escape him.

He was well into the jealousy Lady Mar felt for the beautiful Helen when Maria returned. She was carrying a large tray of mismatched glasses and a pitcher of water.

He kept reading.

"'Wallace will behold those charms!' cried her distracted spirit to herself, 'and then where am I?'"

He glanced up at Maria just in time to see her sway. She fell forward, hitting the floor hard amid the shrieks of alarmed women, the clang of the serving tray and the shattering of glass.

Chapter Six

"*U*nlace her!"

"Colonel—"

"Unlace her, damn it!"

"We can hardly do that with *you* present!"

"Get out of the way, Mrs. Kinnard. You! Mrs. Carscaddon! Come with me!"

The voices swirled around her, and Maria felt rough wool against her cheek. Rough wool that smelled of tobacco and leather and the out-of-doors.

"Billy," she whispered, pressing her face into it, savoring the warm feel of him. "Billy—"

He lifted her up, and she leaned into him, giving herself up to the sensation of being held close. She tried to say that she was so glad he was here, but the words wouldn't come.

Then she was in her own room, lying on her bed, and Ceily Walker, now Carscaddon, was removing her stays. Maria took a deep breath to fight down a ridiculous urge to cry. Billy wasn't here. He would never be here again.

She tried to sit up. Her head swam so she couldn't manage it.

"Maria, lie still—"

"What…is it? What's wrong?"

"You've swooned in the middle of *The Scottish Chiefs,* that's all. I think you were laced too tightly."

Maria closed her eyes. "Yes," she said, grateful for an acceptable excuse.

So much better than the real one, she thought. She gave a wavering sigh, then suddenly tried to sit up again.

"The literary society…I must—"

"The literary society is long gone. Colonel Woodard certainly is a forceful man. When he wants the premises vacated, vacated they are. No wonder James is scared of him. The colonel has sent for the regimental surgeon—"

"No!" Maria said in alarm, trying to get up in earnest now. "I'm quite all right."

"Don't worry, Maria. I've met the doctor on several occasions. He really is a nice man—"

"No. I can't. I won't. Ceily, please!" Maria managed to sit on the side of the bed after all.

"Maria—"

"Please!"

Ceily gave a sharp sigh. "I think you'd better tell the colonel, then. In the mood he's in it shouldn't come from me—for James's sake. Are you all right sitting there?"

"Yes. Yes, I'm much better now. Am I decent?" she asked, looking down at her dress.

"Well, almost—" Ceily said, helping her button up. "And I think you'd better just sit there and let Colonel Woodard come to you. I'll fetch him—you practice not falling on your face."

"Ceily," Maria said when she was about to open the door. "Thank you."

Ceily Carscaddon smiled the smile that must have led Lieutenant James Carscaddon directly down the path to matrimony. "You're welcome, Maria. I would have helped you any way I could—but you should have heard the colonel barking orders at me. I think he had me confused with James. Oh, and Mrs. K. is all irked,'' she added, lowering her voice.

Maria all but cringed at the news. "Why?"

"Because the colonel wouldn't let her say what was to be done with you. *He* took charge—and he volunteered me. You certainly stole Valentina's thunder, I can tell you. Valentina thinks you did it on purpose—so that the colonel would make a fuss over you. She was *not* happy—my guess is because she didn't think of it herself.''

"I didn't faint on purpose!"

"Well, of course, you didn't. You toppled like a felled oak tree. It's a wonder you didn't really hurt yourself. You're very lucky, Maria. I'll be right back. Are you sure you're all right sitting there?''

"Yes," Maria said, in spite of the throbbing in her head. But whether she was or not, she couldn't let herself be examined by a doctor.

She took a deep breath and waited. She didn't have to wait very long—just long enough for it to occur to her that perhaps she shouldn't be sitting on her bed when she spoke to Colonel Woodard.

But the realization came too late. He strode into the room without knocking—before she could move—and he had no compunction whatsoever about coming very close and peering into her face.

"Are you all right?" he asked, still staring at her.

"I'm fine," she answered, her voice shaky in spite of everything she could do. "I don't need a doctor."

"I believe what you mean to say is that you don't need *our* doctor.''

She looked at him. "Yes."

"You've got a knot on your head."

She instinctively reached up to touch the place on her forehead that hurt.

"It's nothing."

"It looks like something," he assured her.

"I don't want your help!" she cried. "How difficult can this be for you to understand!"

"I understand," he said quietly. "Even so, the regimental surgeon will be at your disposal...should you require him. If you're feeling up to it, I think you should speak to your father. He is very concerned about you."

"Yes. I will. Thank you," she added as a token afterthought—mostly because she wasn't entirely sure what he'd done, other than alienate Acacia Kinnard. She wasn't worried about Valentina. Valentina hadn't come into her own yet.

When the colonel had gone, Maria gave a heavy sigh of relief and lay back on the bed. If there was anything good about this situation, it was that Suzanne's boys weren't here. She'd never manage looking after them in her present state. Her head pounded so, and she closed her eyes. She would go see her father in a moment.

Or so she thought. She awoke with a start, not knowing what had awakened her. She had no idea what time it was; the room was completely dark. In spite of the warm night, someone had covered her with the velvet quilt that had been folded and placed on the cedar chest at the foot of her bed. Her father, she supposed. He used to do that when she was a little girl and fell asleep in his chair. It was likely the only thing he knew to do for her, and for a brief moment she had to fight back the tears again.

Soon.

She would have to tell him soon.

She pushed the quilt away, and perhaps she drifted off to sleep again—she didn't know. She thought she heard someone call out, and with some effort, she sat up on the side of the bed. The dizziness had gone, but her head still hurt, and she was so thirsty. She got up and tried to find her shoes, finally giving in to the pounding in her head and abandoning the search. Her hair was coming undone, and she took out the remaining pins and raked her fingers through it before she stepped bare-footed into the hall.

The house was very quiet. If it had been even a few years earlier, she would have been able to hear the grandfather clock that had stood for as long as she could remember in the downstairs foyer by the front door. But it was gone now, like so many other things, and so many people. All of them gone, leaving nothing but silence in their stead.

Colonel Woodard's door was firmly closed. Maria had no way of telling if he was there or if the latest disruption in the Markham house had driven him back to a hotel. If it had, then it served him right. She couldn't help but feel a certain satisfaction that he had erred in his assumption that a household consisting of an old man and his spinster daughter would be peaceful and serene.

Maria slipped down the hall to her father's room, opening his door slightly and listening. He was snoring softly, and she stood there for a time to make certain all was well.

She closed the door again and felt her way along the hall to the back stairs. The steps creaked as she went down into the kitchen. Her father was not a heavy sleeper, but she didn't make enough noise to disturb him.

The back door had been left open; she hadn't realized that it was raining. She could hear it pattering on the stepping stones outside. She stood for a moment looking out into the darkness and listening to a lone frog croaking in the meadow beyond. She could hear a rumble of thunder as well. A storm coming, she thought.

She couldn't see any activity in the yard where the soldiers were camped. If they were keeping any kind of watch, she saw no evidence of it. Lightning flashed on the horizon, and the ensuing thunder sounded nearer. She pulled the door closed and latched it, then fumbled around in the dark until she found a small piece of candle to light. As long as she was downstairs and wide-awake, she wanted to see what state the parlor had been left in.

She saw a plate covered with a frayed but crisply starched napkin on the worktable. Oranges left over from the Ladies' Literary Society meeting. She was more thirsty than hungry, but she ate two of the pieces, pushing aside a nagging realization that she was accepting the colonel's charity, after all.

Colonel Woodard.

What an unfathomable man, she thought, reaching up to touch the swelled place on her forehead. It still hurt.

She picked up the candle and walked to the parlor doorway and peered inside. To her surprise the room was in perfect order. No overturned furniture or scattered orange peels. No broken glass. She supposed that her "thank you" to Colonel Woodard earlier had been appropriate, after all. If Acacia Kinnard had indeed been upset by the situation, Maria doubted that any of the literary society would have remained to set things right. It naturally followed that *he* must be responsible. He must have assigned Perkins to cleanup duty. Hopefully, he hadn't conscripted poor Ceily into helping, as well.

When Maria stepped out into the wide hall hallway,

she heard a noise upstairs. She waited, unsure of what it was. It came again—a voice—someone calling out.

It was not her father—it had come from the front of the house. She climbed the stairs quickly and rushed down the hallway, but she stopped short of knocking on Colonel Woodard's door. And she didn't take the liberty of simply opening it. She had no right to enter his bedchamber, regardless of the precedent he had set earlier when he'd barged into hers.

She stood listening, hearing nothing. When she was satisfied that the episode—whatever it might have been—was over, she stepped away, her bare feet making no sound on the cool wood flooring.

Maria walked quickly to her father's room to make certain he had not been disturbed and was halfway to her own door when she heard Colonel Woodard again.

"There! Get him! Get him, damn it! Watch...watch him—bring him down! Somebody bring the son of a bitch down!"

Maria looked in alarm toward her father's bedchamber. Surely he must hear. Something overturned inside the colonel's room, making a loud crash. She threw open the door and stood there, shielding the candle flame from the sudden draft with her hand.

The table at the bedside had fallen over. A tall candlestick and several books lay scattered on the floor. Colonel Woodard sat on the side of the bed, breathing heavily, staring straight ahead. He was dressed—except for his tunic. His shirttail was half out of his trousers. He kept making small gasping sounds—as if he had been running—and it was clear to her that whatever he was seeing was not in the here and now.

She didn't know what to do, and she still had a small hope that whatever he was experiencing would pass.

"Noooooooo!" he suddenly shouted, his body rigid, and she jumped in alarm.

He was standing now, lurching forward, crashing into the dresser.

"Colonel Woodard—" Maria said. She came closer, but she didn't dare try to touch him.

"Colonel Woodard!" she said more forcefully.

He suddenly reeled in her direction and was now between her and the door. He was speaking again, unintelligibly. She tried to edge by him. The last thing she wanted was to be trapped in here with him in his present state.

Where was Perkins? she thought suddenly. Surely he must be somewhere about.

But obviously he was not, or he would have been on the scene by now.

Maria set the candle on the mantelboard. If she was going to have to tussle with Colonel Woodard to get out, she didn't want to be carrying an open flame, and she didn't want to be in the dark. He still didn't see her, of that she was sure. If she was careful, she could get by him.

She began to move toward the door, and he abruptly stopped talking and faced in her direction. When she moved toward the door again, he moved with her.

"Colonel?" she said quietly. "Colonel Woodard?"

He stopped—but whether he actually heard her, she couldn't tell.

"Colonel," she said again. "Wake up. Wake up now."

"The marksmen. Did they get him?" he asked, his voice strained and hoarse.

"Colonel, you were...dreaming."

He stood there, weaving slightly, and just as she decided that the episode was over, he suddenly looked heavenward and gave a loud, anguished cry.

"Colonel Woodard, stop it!" Maria yelled. "Wake up!"

But he didn't stop. He lunged in her direction, grabbing her by her forearms before she could get out of the way. She couldn't get free of him, and she tried to push against his chest.

"Colonel! Stop it! Stop it!"

His grip suddenly relaxed, but he still had hold of her.

"Colonel?" Maria said more quietly. "Colonel Woodard—"

"What is it?" He let go of her arms.

"You were having a bad dream."

"I—" He stepped away from her, but he still seemed dazed and unsure of his surroundings. A clap of thunder rolled overhead, and it seemed to confuse rather than ground him.

He stumbled toward the bed and sat down on the edge again. After a moment he looked at her.

"Are you all right now?" she asked, but she didn't come any closer.

"It's—" He broke off and was silent for a moment. Maria could hear the rain on the roof.

"What...why are you in here?" he asked.

"I told you. You were having a bad dream."

"I see. You...heard me, then."

"Yes."

"What...what did I say?"

"You were reliving a battle, I think," she said much more calmly than she felt. He had frightened her, and perhaps he knew it.

"Did I hurt you?"

Her arms still ached from the strength of his grip, but she said nothing.

"I...apologize. I didn't mean—"

He broke off again, and she turned to go.

"Miss Markham."

"Yes?"

"It would be...helpful if you would sit here...in the room...for a moment. Over there by the window."

The request—if that was what it was—took her by surprise. She wondered if he remembered that he meant for *her* to be indebted to *him.* Her staying like this, now and under these circumstances, would go a long way toward shifting the balance.

"Why?" she asked bluntly. In the dimness of the room, she could barely make out his features.

"Because of...how well you bandage."

"I don't understand."

"Wherever you learned the skill, I think you must have witnessed the many kinds of suffering a soldier might endure. I think perhaps you are accustomed to things other women might find...alarming."

Maria continued to stare at him in the soft darkness. The candle flame wavered in a breeze from the half-open window, making the shadows dance around the room. She thought he still wasn't quite saying what he meant to say.

"Conversation is helpful?" she asked finally.

"Yes."

There was another clap of thunder overhead, and he flinched. He was not a man to fear a thunderstorm; she believed that with certainty. It was the memories the storm brought to life that troubled him, the ones still so strong that he needed her to keep them at bay.

"Where is the brandy bottle?" she asked.

"The same place—in the trunk."

She moved to get it.

"There is a glass on the table—or there was," he said, realizing that the small table by the bed had been toppled.

Maria brought the bottle to him. The glass had rolled near his feet, and she bent down to retrieve it. She handed it to him and righted the table. Then she began to gather up the books lying on the floor, as well.

"Leave those," he said.

"I can't leave a book where it might get trod upon," she said, setting the stack on the bed.

He poured some brandy into the glass. His hands shook visibly. "Are you a book lover then?"

"Yes," she said, keeping her distance now. This situation was far from proper. She knew that—but still she didn't go. It was a matter of checks and balances, she reminded herself. If she stayed—even for a little while— once again he would be in her debt.

He downed the brandy in one swift motion. "I wonder…"

"What?" she asked when he let whatever he was about to say trail away.

"I wonder how long they last—the bad dreams."

"I don't know."

"It's been three years. I think they're worse when there is a storm. The cannons—one can't help but remember the cannons."

"Perhaps if I lit the lamp—"

"No. The candle is enough."

"It will burn out soon."

"I don't want any light!"

"Very well," she said. She sat down carefully in the chair by the window, and she didn't say anything more.

"I haven't asked," he said after what seemed a long while. "If *you* are all right."

"I am quite fine."

"So you invariably say."

"Because it is true."

"You always tell the truth, then?"

"Always," she assured him.

"Even to Yankees?"

"That doesn't count," she said, and in the dimness she thought he might actually have smiled.

"What with your swooning and my nightmares, this has been a...riveting evening, has it not?" he said.

"Perhaps."

"There is one good thing that has come out of it."

"Is there?"

"Indeed."

"And what is that?"

"I don't think you're going to have to worry about hostessing the Ladies' Literary Society for a while."

Incredibly, Maria laughed. She broke off immediately, but the damage to her hard-won self-control had been done. It had been so long since she had laughed like that. She couldn't even remember the last time she had allowed herself any kind of emotional spontaneity. She couldn't afford to be spontaneous. She had far too many secrets.

But somehow she had forgotten—everything.

She had forgotten who she was, and where she was, and with whom.

She abruptly stood. "I must go," she said, her voice barely audible. The candle sputtered and went out. She couldn't see, but she stepped blindly forward anyway, not realizing he had stood up with her. They collided in the darkness, and for a brief moment she felt his warm hands on her, strong hands that steadied her and then let go.

"Miss Markham," he said as she reached the door.

She hesitated, then looked back at him.

"Thank you."

Max lay awake in the dark. He could hear the night sounds—tree frogs and cicada and whatever else had been encouraged by the rain. A solitary dog barked from time to time, and from time to time one of its kind answered. Once, he heard the whistle of the supposedly tri-weekly, Charlotte-to-Greensborough night train.

The storm had faded, and a cool breeze came in through the open window. The nightmare had faded, as well, and he felt peaceful enough now, he supposed, but sleep still eluded him.

Nothing—no one—stirred inside the house, but perhaps he would not have heard her. Maria Markham, whom he kept catching without her shoes. He wondered if she had any idea how erotic it was, seeing a woman fully dressed and her hair tumbling down her back and her feet bare. He doubted it. He doubted if she knew much at all about what happened between a man and a woman.

But then, she had called him "Billy."

Billy.

It had taken a great deal of effort on his part not to ask her about him, in spite of the fact that he already knew. Billy was the Reb artilleryman Perkins had told him about. He was young Joe Canfield's uncle—the one whose name couldn't be said aloud for fear of making the women in the family weep.

Maria Markham was not nearly as buttoned up as she always seemed. Max had heard the longing in her voice when she'd said the dead man's name. Worse, he had felt it and felt it deep. Her soft whisper against his neck as he'd carried her upstairs had affected him more than he would ever have cared to admit. He still wasn't certain what to call the emotion he had experienced.

Yes, he was. It was jealousy. Primitive and absolute and male. He had been jealous of the man—his enemy— who, even dead, could inspire that kind of yearning in the woman who had belonged to him. And, it was because of it that Max had wanted to keep her in the room as long as he could. It went beyond his usual need to inconvenience her. The comfort her presence might have offered him in the aftermath of his nightmare wasn't simply another item on the list of things owed him by the people of this town. It was much more than that, and he knew it.

He had wanted her to stay with him. With *him*.

He had wanted her in his bed.

He took a quiet breath and closed his eyes, remembering. Not the dream and not prison, but Maria Markham's laugh. He wondered if the artilleryman had made her laugh. He must have. He must have heard her laughter bubble up like that many times, just as he must have heard her whisper his name.

Billy…

Chapter Seven

Maria made no attempt to go to Sunday church services, regardless of her usual custom. She was too overcome by morning sickness and too disinclined to face Acacia Kinnard to chance it, no matter how much she herself was in need of a sermon. All that aside, she had no intention of encountering Colonel Woodard if she could help it.

Thus far, she had managed to elude him. She still didn't quite understand what had passed between them in the dark. Nothing, she kept telling herself. Nothing that she could put into words, at any rate. And, there was the distinct possibility that her ability to interpret last night's events could have been somewhat impaired. Fainting in the middle of the Ladies' Literary Society reading alone would have been enough to increase the chance of misinterpretation on her part. Perhaps she had still been dazed or perhaps she hadn't been quite awake. Perhaps both those things *and* the bump on her head had made her misconstrue everything.

She closed her eyes, remembering. The feel of Colonel Woodard's hands on her had nearly been her undoing. She tried to tell herself that it was simply the basic—and in her case—unmet desire for human comfort. She had been worried for such a long time, so much so that she had become exhausted by it. In her weakness and for that one instant, she had needed a warm embrace. In lieu of kindly Verillia Douglas's solace, she had been willing to accept his.

Any port in a storm.

No, she thought immediately. She hadn't wanted comfort from anyone else. She had wanted comfort from him. Colonel Woodard had sought her presence, he said, because she understood. It came as a great revelation to her that that ran both ways, that she had felt the same desire for a kindred spirit. Even now, she wanted his arms around her again, wanted to rest her head on his shoulder.

"What is wrong with you!" she said out loud.

The man was her enemy, just as Hatcher was. Her brothers were dead—and it was possible, however remotely, that *he* could have had a hand in it. And Billy—

She didn't want to think about Billy. She had to get herself together—and right now. She still had the threat of the regimental surgeon hanging over her head. Her eyes burned from the lack of sleep. She had only just managed to get through breakfast before her nausea overwhelmed her. She still marveled that she had managed to escape in time and without running into the colonel. She had no idea what her father and he had done in her absence. Perkins, she supposed, would have been called upon to take over.

And now she had to put some kind of meal on the table that would pass for a Sunday dinner. Her horse hadn't been fed, and there must still be dishes and pans to wash from this morning.

She stayed hidden in the privy until she was certain

her father would have left for church services. She had
made her excuses to him regarding her church attendance early on, and thankfully he didn't feel the need to
hunt her down and have her reiterate.

She took a deep breath. Her stomach still lurched at
the mere thought of food. It was too bad she didn't have
another one of the colonel's lemons.

She went quietly down the stairs to find Perkins sitting
at the kitchen worktable. He got up immediately, as if
he thought she would report his idleness to his colonel.

"Miss," he said, watching her closely.

And Maria couldn't blame him after her behavior yesterday and this morning—or perhaps he had been appointed to send for the army surgeon at the first sign of
her being out of kilter.

"Would you happen to know where Colonel Woodard
is, miss?" he asked

"No," she said. "I haven't seen him."

"Must be at church, then," he said.

Maria looked at him doubtfully.

"I believe the colonel had some particular business
there this morning," Perkins said.

Maria had no reply to that. Colonel Woodard didn't
seem the church-going type—but she firmly believed his
attendance could be a part of his plan to manage the
people here.

"Miss?" Perkins said as she was about to go out the
back door. "I've got the pine blocks the colonel
wanted."

"Pine blocks?"

"Yes, miss. About like so." He held up his hands to
show her. "I put them out there on the porch—he didn't
say where he wanted them. Would you tell him that? In
case you see him first—before I do."

"Yes, all right," Maria said. But she had no intention of seeing the colonel, first or otherwise.

She grabbed her straw hat and went outside, stopping at the summer kitchen first to stoke the fire in the stove and to fill some pots with water and put them on to boil. She opened the warming oven. The bowl of dough she had set aside to rise was still there. She punched it down again and returned it to the warming oven. Then she washed her hands and tied on her hat and went to the shed to feed old Nell, ignoring the interest of the soldiers still camped at the edge of the yard.

The horse whinnied softly at her approach.

"I didn't bring you anything," Maria said, caressing the velvet-soft nose as the animal tried to search her pockets. "And I'm ashamed of myself. You're lonely out here, aren't you. Nothing to keep you company. Not even a cow." There *were* the horses the Yankees had penned in the new fence they'd built nearby. Maria thought they were now working on a stable—yet another uninvited intrusion.

Nell propped her head heavily on Maria's shoulder. She'd had the sorrel mare since she was a little girl; Nell had been her tenth birthday present. What joy Maria had felt that day at having a horse of her own. She smiled slightly at the memory of it.

Poor Nell. She was ready to be let out to pasture, but she still had to serve as the Markham buggy horse—and would for the foreseeable future.

Maria took the animal out of the stall and into the yard, brushing her down a bit before she tethered her to keep her out of the corn stalks. Maria could feel the continued interest of two soldiers near the tents, but they kept their distance and their counsel. At one point she glanced upward at the windows of Colonel Woodard's bedchamber, in case he still happened to be there.

She did *not* want to encounter him today.

She went back into the house, to the cellar to get potatoes and whatever else she could find. The logistics of preparing meals was beginning to wear on her. She didn't want Colonel Woodard's charity—but if he insisted on sitting down at the table with them, then she had to use food from his pantry. And her father wasn't about to keep to the Markham butter beans if there was anything else available, regardless of where it came from.

Nothing was simple anymore.

She found some decent potatoes—and took a dozen ears of corn still in the husks from the brine barrel. Storing unshucked corn in a tightly packed barrel of salt water—as if one were making pickles—had been another of her father's clever solutions—like the pieced flooring. And she would have to admit that the salting process worked well. The corn kept without rotting and when cooked, it was reasonably tasty.

She carried everything out to the summer kitchen and set to work scrubbing the potatoes and cutting the corn off the cob. When she had put each into a pot of boiling water, she took the corn husks and cobs to a most appreciative Nell.

The mare, in the hope of more, followed Maria back to the summer kitchen as far as the tether would allow. She lingered long enough to give Nell one final pat, then turned to find Colonel Woodard standing just behind her. It caught her completely off guard, and she stopped just short of giving a shriek.

"Sorry," he said. He looked quite polished and official and military, in spite of his disturbed sleep. "I didn't mean to startle you."

Maria didn't say anything. She sidestepped him and went into the summer kitchen ostensibly to see about the potatoes and corn.

"I've taken a liberty," Colonel Woodard said, following behind her.

She made no attempt to acknowledge his presence or the remark.

"It's Phelan Canfield. He's in jail."

The word "again" hung unspoken in the air between them. Even so, Maria appreciated his effort at diplomacy, meager though it may have been.

"Perkins is going to check on Mrs. Canfield and bring the boys here if necessary—if that's all right."

Maria glanced at him. He stood waiting for her to answer him, a token gesture at best. The disposition of the Canfield children had clearly already been decided without her.

"I'll go see about her—"

"I don't think that will be necessary. At least not yet. Perkins may already be on his way here with the children. I'm sure he can tell you how Mrs. Canfield fares. You'll know more what needs to be done after you speak to him."

She found his logic perfect—and maddening. And for all its perfection, she still wanted to defy him.

"Very well," she said, attending to her pots as if they required it. She could feel his eyes on her, but she dared not look at him.

"Perkins brought your pine blocks," she said, still avoiding his eyes. "They're on the porch."

"Yes."

Yes, she thought. No "Thank you." No "Very kind of you to mention it, Miss Markham." Just "Yes."

"Will you be here for the noon meal?" she asked, busily stirring the corn.

"No," he said. He waited until she glanced at him again. "I have an invitation for Sunday dinner."

Maria looked away, her curiosity definitely piqued. She moved the pots around as she considered this information carefully, but when she turned with a mind to perhaps glean some additional details from him, he had gone.

She stood for a moment, still considering the possibilities. She had heard him decline Acacia Kinnard's dinner invitation. He couldn't show favoritism—or so he said. Perhaps he'd changed his mind, after all. She certainly hoped that was the case. He had essentially snubbed Acacia at the Ladies' Literary Society meeting—a very new sensation for the formidable woman, to be sure. If he had turned around now and accepted someone else's invitation, Maria's life would be worthless. Entirely innocent or not, she would suffer the consequences by mere association—if indeed she wasn't already on Acacia's list, thanks to his not-so-diplomatic meddling yesterday. She would be ostracized soon enough; she had no wish to hurry it.

Still, it was a relief to know that he wouldn't be underfoot.

Perkins arrived with the boys almost immediately.

"Ah! The Js!" Maria said when she saw them. They both ran to her and hugged her knees. Joe let go almost immediately, but little Jake clung to her until she had to bend down to pick him up.

"Come here, sweet boy," she said. "How is Mrs. Canfield?" she said to Perkins.

"The doctor's been to see her, miss. He's given her something to make her sleep—and there's a lady coming later to sit with her. I'm to tell you that it's a Mrs. Warrie Hansen. The doctor says he will wait until she arrives."

Maria looked at him in surprise. Warrie Hansen had been gone from this town for well over two years. Thanks to the downfall of her only daughter, Warrie had become one of those people Acacia Kinnard had declared unfit for decent society. And thanks to Maria, her own poor father would likely join the group.

But, outcast or not, Suzanne couldn't be in better hands than Warrie's. For the first time in months—years, perhaps—Maria felt a certain element of relief.

She glanced at Perkins, who seemed to be waiting for some reason.

"Are you hungry, little sir?" she abruptly asked Jake, who was holding on to her pinafore with both hands in case she held any notions of putting him down.

He let go with one hand to put his fingers in his mouth and nodded. Maria smiled, and he smiled his own endearing smile in return. He looked so much like Phelan—and Billy. Both boys did.

"Oh, good. Let's go pick out our plates. Come along, Joe."

Joe was already on his way to see what the soldiers camped at the edge of the yard were about, but he turned around and came running.

Picking out a plate had become a great treat for them at the Markham house, because Maria had such a variety of remnant sets to choose from. Some had belonged to her mother's family, and some she had bartered for during the war—more to accommodate a friend who was in need of the dried fruit Maria offered than because she wanted another mismatched piece of earthenware or por-

celain. And she let the children select any one they
wanted, no matter how rare the plate might be. Jake was
very partial to flowers and gold bands. Joe liked the En-
glish ''castle house.'' But it wasn't the varied selection
that pleased them so much as the process—the fact that
they could actually choose.

They decided on a plate for Maria's father, while they
were at it, and set his place carefully in the dining room.
Then they went outside again to pick some wildflowers
for the table—daisies and Queen Anne's Lace—which,
if there happened to be small children around, became
Kiss-Me-And-I'll-Tell-You. The game was a time-
honored tradition in the Markham family, and Joe had
already learned it well.

''What's the name of *this* flower,'' he would ask mischievously.

''Kiss-Me-And-I'll-Tell-You,'' Maria would say dutifully, much to his delight, because the reply was an
open invitation for him to plant one of his wet, little-
boy kisses on her cheek, supposedly to her great aston-
ishment.

Today, they played the game at length as they gathered the flowers from the meadow behind the house.
Each time little Jake saw a kiss coming, he hid his
face—which brought him even more kisses from Joe and
Maria both—which led to a wild chase and more giggling and kissing.

In the midst of it, Maria realized that Colonel
Woodard had come to stand on the back porch, the cue,
apparently, all of his subordinates to snap to attention.
An eager private, at Perkin's hand signal, quickly
brought a magnificent red dun gelding around, and Maria
had to grab Joe by the seat of his pants to keep him from
running and soliciting another ride.

Colonel Woodard gave Maria and the boys a curt nod, mounted the horse and rode away.

He stayed gone a long time—which Maria was certain suited her perfectly. The less she had to worry about running into him, the better. She fed the boys—and her father—washed the pots and the dishes while trying to keep all three of them out of mischief, and she remembered too late that she had never baked the bread she had rising.

She took the boys to the summer kitchen and set about making loaves for supper, standing both children on wooden boxes and giving them each a piece of dough of their own to worry. The project went well, as long as she refused to be overly concerned about flying flour.

While the bread baked, she set the boys on Nell's back and walked them around the yard under her father's supposedly critical eye. The truth was that he was as taken with the Canfield boys as she was, and he praised their horsemanship at length. At one point they let Nell return to her grazing, and all four of them sat under the big shade trees in the yard. The boys hunted for bugs and sticks and acorns while her father dozed.

Or so she thought.

"Maria Rose," he said, his eyes still closed. "You have the makings of a fine parent."

"I had a good example," she said without thinking, meaning her mother more than he. He was a loving father in his way, but his idea of raising a child was to disappear into his sitting room and close the door.

"I had hoped to see you settled by now."

"I know, Father."

"I can't help being concerned, when I can feel it so acutely."

"Feel what, Father?"

"Time. I can feel time going, running fast."

She looked at him, thinking of Rob and Samuel and how much their dying had taken from him. He was so frail now. His family name would not be carried on—and she had ruined whatever chance she might have had to give him legitimate grandchildren.

He reached out to pat her on top of her head, the way he had often done when she was a little girl. The gesture left her throat suddenly aching with unshed tears, because she knew exactly what he meant. Time was running out for her, too.

"My bread!" she said suddenly, and escaped to the kitchen. The bread had not burned, but she shed a few tears as if it had. When she had composed herself, she brought out still-hot samples spread with apple butter, much to the boys' delight.

It was midafternoon when her father went to his sitting room and she finally put the boys down for a nap. She let them lie on quilts on the floor of her room, deliberately placing them near the window that opened onto the upstairs porch, because there was a breeze there and because she planned to sit on the porch to recover, and she wanted to be able to hear them if they woke up. It took a bit of doing to get them settled down. She'd had to sing to them and ultimately resort to issuing them an irresistible challenge to see who could go to sleep first.

She stood watching them for a moment before she left the room. She did love them so much—in spite of the exhaustion they inspired. After a moment she stepped out onto the upstairs porch.

Colonel Woodard sat in a rocking chair on the shady end—in his shirtsleeves and whittling, of all things. She had no idea that he had returned, and once again his presence startled her.

"Wait," he said when she would have left without a word.

She stood there, then turned to face him, but she didn't say anything.

"Would you be so kind as to take a seat?"

"I don't think it would—" she began.

"Please," he interrupted.

She drew a quiet breath and sat down as far away from him as she could.

"You're very high-strung, aren't you?" he said.

"No, I just don't expect to see you at every turn."

"I live here," he said reasonably.

She had no argument for that, and so again she said nothing.

"Your turn, Miss Markham," he said after a stretch of silence. The remark was designed to annoy her—and did. He was coercing her again. Perhaps he had forgotten who now owed whom.

But he would not best her this time. She could hold a conversation with the Devil if need be.

"I see you found the pine blocks Perkins brought," she said.

"Yes," he answered.

But he didn't say anything else. Neither did she. In that one foray into polite dialogue, she had changed her mind. She had made an effort and that was it, as far as she was concerned.

She looked out across the front yard toward the street—and prayed that no one she knew passed by. He kept whittling, and she found herself watching his hands. He had beautiful hands. They were still bruised, but didn't seem to cause him trouble as he worked the wood.

And he was using such a peculiar instrument—not a knife exactly, but obviously sharp enough. It looked as if it had been fashioned by someone who didn't quite understand what he was making.

"My given name is Max," he said, still whittling away.

Disconcerted, she looked at him. "I cannot call you by your given name—"

"I didn't mean to suggest that you should. I only wanted you to know it. It's Max. Maxwell, actually. I already know yours," he added.

She frowned and went back to watching the curls of wood drop onto the porch.

"This is something I never expected to do," he said. "Whittling."

"You seem very…accomplished at it," she said in spite of her decision not to participate.

"An old infantryman taught me. I never had much use for the walkers before then. I learned well because there was nothing else to do." He stopped and looked at her. "In the prison."

She could feel her face flush.

"I'm making a train," he continued. "For Joe and Jake."

"Their father won't allow—"

"Yes, I know. But I'm making the train for them nonetheless."

Maria looked at a robin running across the yard.

"Tell me," he said. "How would you assess my performance as the military commander here so far?"

"Your establishing what amounted to martial law the first day you arrived has stirred up a lot of resentment," she said without hesitation.

"Perhaps. But I think the resentment people feel now

is considerably less than it would be if I had allowed the arsonists to continue as they please.''

Maria stood, intending to go—because she didn't want to sit here and spar with him and because he was right and she didn't want him to be.

"Before you leave, I have something I've been meaning to give you," he said, shaving another curl of wood off and letting it drop to the floor.

"That is not necessary." Maria took a step toward the door.

"It is necessary. It's your property."

She turned to look at him. He reached into the uniform tunic that hung on the back of the rocking chair and held out a red-velvet box.

"Where did you get this?" she said, snatching it out of his hand.

"Hatcher left it behind. I understand it belongs to you. I apologize for the delay, but the truth of the matter is that I forgot I had it."

She looked down at the box, clutching it tightly.

"The earrings are still there," he said.

She was going to cry—if she didn't get away from here, he was going to see her do it. And she was in real danger of fainting again. She could feel her heart pounding in her ears, feel herself sway.

She made her way blindly back into the house. She had but one thought in her mind. To get away from Max Woodard.

Chapter Eight

"They've found them all, Sir," Perkins said.

Max gave no indication that he heard. He continued to stare out the window at the street below, his attention taken by a passerby—the prostitute Perkins had identified as belonging to Hatcher. Max wondered idly if the woman knew the earrings she'd coveted—or perhaps earned—were back in Maria Markham's possession.

He hadn't spoken to Maria since he'd returned them to her—more than a week ago. She had been deliberately avoiding him, all the while making certain that he had no complaint about the timeliness or the quality of the meals he took at the Markham table. She was quite adept at absenting herself. Her father's shirts and dirty linens had to be boiled. The weeds had to be pulled before the sun got too hot. She had to make a shut-in visit to Suzanne Canfield. Once or twice, she was simply "indisposed." And she never presented her excuses herself. They all came via Mr. Markham.

In Maria's diligent absence, Max had had a number of worthwhile conversations with the old man. Mr. Markham had given him more information about all three of his children than Maria herself ever would have. The problem, however, was that he missed the challenge.

And perhaps—incredibly—he missed her.

Apparently his having Sunday dinner with the Kinnards had been the right move. As far as he could tell, Maria hadn't suffered because he had unwittingly aroused the Kinnard woman's wrath. He knew something of how these things worked from his mother and his sister, Kate—but, all in all, the ins and outs of polite society were far too complex for him. He'd entirely missed that he had affronted Mrs. Kinnard at the reading, and even if he hadn't, it would never have occurred to him that Maria would be the likely candidate to bear the brunt of the retaliation for his uncouthness—until Lieutenant Carscaddon's wife enlightened him.

He'd accepted her interpretation of the situation, and made his apology to the Kinnard woman at church— with a considerable audience—and he had gotten stuck with an invitation to dine at the Kinnard house, after all. He'd put himself out well above the call of duty, endured all manner of unsubtle manipulation for what seemed an endless meal, and all for one of those Southern woman who, as Perkins had so delicately put it, would just as soon gut a Yankee soldier as look at him.

Perkins was still fidgeting behind him and pointedly cleared his throat. "Sir?"

"What?" Max said, finally acknowledging the sergeant major.

"The burial trenches, Sir. They've located all of them now, as far as we can tell."

"Have you got the chaplain on hand?"

"Yes, Sir."

"What about the local preachers—is there a priest in this town?"

"I'm not sure, Sir. It's never come up. I ain't run into one."

"Well, find out, and if there is, get him over there. And the rest of the clergy, as well."

"All of them, Sir?"

"Yes, all of them. Get the mayor and his bootlickers, too, while you're at it. They tolerated having that hell-hole of a prison on their doorsteps. The least they can do is be on hand when these men finally get a decent burial."

"Am I to invite them, Sir, or just bring them?" Perkins asked, still working on the fine points.

Max gave him a look.

"Yes, Sir!" Perkins said. "Would you be wanting the entire garrison on hand, Sir?"

"I would. And I mean everybody."

"Yes, Sir!" Perkins said again, saluting and barreling down the stairs to rattle the composure of any number of privates on the street below. The man absolutely lived to exercise military authority.

Max stood looking out the window again, but he was no longer mindful of the street below. He'd sent letters to Washington to get the prison burial ground established and maintained as a military cemetery. That had been the easy part. The hard part was yet to come. For all the effort he had put into it, he wasn't looking forward to this. The news that the quest for his comrades' remains was finally over had made them all real again. He kept seeing their faces in his mind, hearing their voices, little flashes of memory that seemed to come at him from every direction.

He reached into his pocket and pulled out the make-shift knife he still used to whittle. The old soldier who had helped him make it and who had taught him how to carve wood lay somewhere in the trenches. Max had done the best he could for him—for them all. It had been apparent immediately that the bodies couldn't be separated, and so they had been left as they were. The recovery detail had continued to dig ever-widening probes, branching out in all directions to try to locate the unmarked graves.

And now it was finished.

He looked around because Perkins was back again.

"What is it?" Max asked.

"Well, Sir, see, this is what happened. Major De Graff was wanting to marry this here town girl—Miss Russell, her name is—but her family wouldn't have none of that, so they up and hid her from him. And ever since—"

"The short version, Perkins!"

"Yes, Sir. Major De Graff and Phelan Canfield is about to fight over a whore, Sir—and Miss Markham is right smack in the middle of it."

"For God's sake, where?"

"Right down the street, Sir. I figured maybe you'd want to handle it—there's a pretty good crowd gathering."

"Pretty good" was a sizable underestimation. Max couldn't see the ruckus over the heads of the people who had gathered, but he could hear it. He left the task of getting through the throng to Perkins and his men and followed in their wake. Maria was indeed in the middle of things. And Canfield, for once, seemed to be only moderately inebriated. In any case, he was in a better condition than De Graff. It appeared to Max that Canfield was actually exercising some sense—at least he seemed to be listening to whatever Maria was saying to him. She had him by the arm, and as badly as he obviously wanted to push her away, he didn't.

The fourth person in the melee was the woman he'd watched from the window earlier—Hatcher's former strumpet. De Graff clearly had plans for her, which, for whatever reason, she neither welcomed nor found convenient. He kept trying to get to her—and Canfield kept trying to get to De Graff. The woman moved in front of Canfield, digging in her heels and pressing both hands against his chest to keep them apart. De Graff suddenly grabbed her by her hair and hauled her backward. Canfield lunged for him, but the woman was in the way, and Maria was still hanging on to his arm.

"Get Miss Markham out of there, Perkins. De Graff!" Max bellowed when De Graff's side arm came out of the holster. "That is enough, Major!"

The authority in Max's voice deterred him—but not for long. De Graff hesitated then raised his revolver and leveled it at Canfield's chest, just as Perkins bodily removed Maria to the sidelines. The other woman screamed and put herself in between the two men. Canfield shoved her aside.

"Go ahead!" Canfield yelled at De Graff. "What are you going to do—shoot her? Shoot me? She's not armed! Neither am I! What's next, you Yankee bastard!"

But Perkins had his men well trained in the art of maintaining order. One of them put a hard thrust of his rifle butt into the back of De Graff's knee, causing his leg to fold under him. The revolver discharged as De Graff hit the ground, and the women in the crowd screamed. Two more soldiers piled on top of him.

"I will not tolerate this kind of behavior!" Max said as they wrestled De Graff's side arm away from him. "De Graff! Get to you feet, damn you!"

De Graff struggled to get up, and he by no means had

himself under control. He stood weaving for a moment, then, amid a string of epithets, lunged at the woman again.

It took some work to get the two separated again.

"Lock them up, Perkins!" Max said.

"Both, Sir?" he asked, still keeping Maria out of the way. "We ain't got accommodations for the officers—"

"I said lock them up!"

"Yes, Sir!"

"And break up this damn congregation. Now!"

"Wait!" Maria cried, pulling free of Perkins's hold on her. "Colonel Woodard—Phelan wasn't to blame. It's my fault. I interfered when I shouldn't have. Can't you—"

"No," Max said.

"But he didn't start this!"

"He is drunk and disorderly, Miss Markham. I will not excuse behavior in an ex-Confederate that I do not tolerate in my own men. Perkins! Escort this woman home!"

"You have no right—"

"I have every right! For a damn wasted Sunday dinner, if nothing else!"

"Sunday dinner! What are you talking about!"

Max looked at her, but he said nothing. If she didn't understand what participating in a tussle between two drunken idiots on Main Street in broad daylight was apt to do to her standing in Mrs. Kinnard's pecking order, far be it from him to try to explain it. He began to walk away.

"Now, Perkins! Take her home and turn her over to her father!"

"Maria!" Phelan Canfield yelled. "Leave it alone! Woodard, I don't need any of your damn favors! Did you hear me! I don't need your favors! My *boys* don't need your favors!''

Max spun around and walked back to where the man stood. ''Then maybe you should try to stay sober long enough to look after them.''

''I look after them!''

''I see. And where are they now, I wonder? Who's looking after them so you can get yourself—and Maria—into another one of your drunken brawls?''

''You don't tell me how to look after my boys! My boys and Maria are none of your goddamn business!''

Max had had enough—enough of Phelan Canfield, enough of all these damn Rebs. He turned and walked away, knowing the person he was really angry with was Maria Markham—for her flagrant disregard for her reputation, not to mention her life. And all for a man like Phelan Canfield.

''You don't worry about Maria, Woodard!'' Canfield yelled after him. ''Goddamn you, Woodard—''

''Shut up, Phelan! Haven't you done enough!'' the prostitute, who was at the heart this ridiculous uproar, yelled. ''Colonel Woodard! Wait! Please!''

Max didn't stop.

''Colonel Woodard!''

He finally stopped—because it was either that or have her yelling after him all the way to headquarters. ''Yes, what is it!''

She smiled in spite of his displeasure. She was quite pretty up close—dark red hair and blue eyes—and she knew it. She was showing an impressive amount of cleavage, and she knew that, too.

''I just wanted to thank you, Colonel Woodard,'' she said, putting her hand on his arm.

''Who are you?'' he asked bluntly.

"Eleanor. Eleanor Hansen. I wanted to thank you for getting Maria out of that mess and for not letting Major De Graff hurt himself. He's a good boy most of the time. Well, he hasn't been so good lately—since he got jilted by the Russell girl. Just now it was the whiskey talking, but he'll get over it."

"You know Major De Graff well, do you?"

"I have made his acquaintance," she said demurely, refusing to take offense at the insinuation behind the question. "And don't you mind about Phelan, either—"

"I don't mind about Phelan," Max assured her.

"Well, that's good. He was trying to help me—or maybe he was just using me as an excuse to get at one of you Yankees. It doesn't matter, I guess. You know, he's just one of these people you can't ever decide about—whether you want him drunk or sober. Either way, he's still a pain in the ass."

Max laughed in spite of himself. He had all but forgotten about this particular kind of woman, brash and audacious and fun-loving. The kind who expected nothing of a man and who would forgive him anything—as long as he had the fee. Max had wasted many an hour and a great deal of his father's coin on Eleanor Hansen's sort in his reckless, pre-war youth.

"There!" she said, clearly delighted. "I just *knew* you had to let yourself go now and again. You should come see me sometime, Colonel. I expect we could find *something* to laugh about, you and I."

"I'll keep it in mind," he said trying to move on.

"And would you do something else for me?"

"What is it, Miss Hansen?"

"If and when Maria ever speaks to you again, would you tell her I said thank you? Just say, 'Nell says thank you.'"

"I should think you can do that yourself."

"Well, of course, I can't, silly. Maria can't be seen talking to *me*."

"But she can participate in a brawl on your behalf?"

"That is entirely different. Will you tell her, please?"

Max stood looking at her. Perhaps he needed more help understanding these people than he realized.

"If and when she ever speaks to me again, I will tell her," he said, and she smiled her best smile, bent and picked up her skirts so that he would get the full advantage of her plunging neckline, then hurried away—stopping once to blow him a small kiss.

Max returned to his office; the dark mood that had come down upon him earlier came back again. A timid private brought the mail sack that had arrived on the afternoon train. When Max finally opened it, there were a number of personal letters for him in it. Two from his mother. One from his sister, Kate. And one from John Howe.

He picked up John's letter and turned it over in his hands, but he didn't open it—or any of them. He sat at his desk, surrounded again by ghosts from the past, and he waited until Perkins came to tell him that everything and everyone was ready for the official burial at the prison.

"Cancel it," Max said when he did so.

"Cancel it, Sir?"

"That's what I said."

Perkins hesitated, then apparently thought better of pursuing the matter. He went downstairs, and Max continued to sit.

The men lying in those trenches needed more than he had provided for them. No, *he* needed more. He needed every man, woman and child in this town to be in attendance. He needed the soldiers who had survived that place, as he had survived, to be there. As many of them as he could find.

He heard a commotion downstairs.

"Miss—no—you can't go up there!" Perkins said.

Now what? Max thought.

Someone came running up the stairs; Maria burst through the doorway, with Perkins on her heels. Max held up his hand to keep the sergeant major from grabbing her. She didn't stop until she was leaning against his desk.

"I am *not* going to change my mind about Canfield," Max said.

"It's…my father," she said, her mouth trembling. "I can't find…the doctor. I need the…regimental surgeon. Please, Max—please!"

She wiped at her cheeks with the heels of her hands, struggling hard not to let him see her cry.

"Perkins will know where the surgeon is," he said. "I'll have him send a man to get him."

Maria stood for a moment, staring into his eyes, poised on the edge of something she couldn't quite make herself say.

Then she turned and ran down the stairs.

Max stayed late at headquarters. Numerous papers had arrived in the mail bag that had to be read and signed. When that was done, he lingered to open his own letters.

His mother's were filled with news of people he once knew and now hardly remembered. There were some sketchy details of his father's latest business concerns and the fact that he would be leaving for London soon— sketchy because she never really paid any attention to that sort of thing. Her job was to spend her husband's profits wisely and well, not concern herself with how he acquired them. Near the end of her second letter, she mentioned a recent society with the Howes and how much she liked John's "little wife," in spite of her origins and her politics.

Max smiled slightly at his mother's acceptance of John's Rebel bride. John's mother, on the other hand, would have happily seen her Southern daughter-in-law banished to Hell. He wondered if Mrs. Howe realized that there were situations here where the reverse was true, where young women like the Russell girl had been literally hidden away in order to protect her from the attentions of men like her beloved son.

He moved on to the letter from his sister Kate. Hers was just as he expected—filled with her observations about young Harry Howe, John's supposed younger brother.

Poor Kate, he thought, skimming the page. Harry was the only child she would likely ever have—and he had been sacrificed on the altar of moral propriety. She had been fourteen years old when she became pregnant with John Howe's child. Max still remembered that terrible time. Kate, in the throes of early pregnancy, having to jump up and rush from the table and no one even remotely suspecting the actual cause. When the truth had finally come to light, he had been incensed, ready to challenge John to a duel—illegal or not—in spite of the fact that John had been more than willing to offer his sister marriage.

The two families had come to a terrible impasse. Kate was too young to marry—she and John both were—and Mr. Howe had no intention of seeing a grandchild of his lost. So the Howes and the Woodards hatched a plan. Mr. and Mrs. Howe would go abroad for a time and take

Kate with them. She would deliver her child while they were gone, and when the Howes returned, Mr. and Mrs. Howe would pass the baby off as their own. The bleakness Max had seen in Kate's eyes the day she had sailed for Europe had never left her. Even now, whenever he looked at her, he could see the abject sadness of a woman who had lost her only child. And what torture she must endure every time she saw him, knowing, for his sake, she could never tell him the truth.

Max picked up John's letter. When it came right down to it, he had quite a lot to forgive his friend John Howe for. But, he had managed to do it. He had successfully rid himself of the anger and resentment he'd felt, both for Kate and for having been left behind in the prison— most of the time.

He stuck John's unread letter inside his tunic and went downstairs, leaving the soldiers still on duty to maintain the hard-won military presence. The streets were deserted, in spite of the fact that it was not yet ten o'clock. He had every intention of going to the hotel. Even after he mounted his horse and rode down Main Street that had been his plan.

But somewhere in the short distance between military headquarters and Howerton's hotel and then the Mansion House, he changed his mind. Another crisis or no, he was going to the Markhams' instead.

The moon was so bright that the stars were barely visible. He rode through the empty streets, listening to the peaceful sounds of the warm summer evening. Cicada and whippoorwills. Tree frogs. Ordinarily such a night reminded him of the war, of being on the campaign.

But tonight he was thinking about Maria. She had called him by his Christian name. He wondered if she even realized it, and the possibility that she hadn't made it seem perhaps more significant to him, as if her saying his name unawares indicated that in her heart of hearts she didn't think of him as Colonel Woodard, the despised occupation commander—but as Max. He thought, too, that Suzanne Canfield had been wrong. In this once incidence, Maria Markham had taken him at his word. She had looked at him, and she had believed him when he said he would send for the surgeon.

He rode past the Kinnard house. It was dark—but someone was playing the piano. All the houses he passed were dark—until he reached the Markham house. The front parlor windows and Mr. Markham's bedchamber windows were alight. As he approached, a seemingly alert private dashed forward to take his mount and stable it.

Max didn't see Maria when he went inside. There were two women in the central hall, women he had had introduced to him at the literary society meeting. One of them immediately pounced upon him.

Fortunately, he was very good with names.

"Mrs. Russell," he said. "And Mrs. Justice, I believe," he said to the other woman.

He recognized the significance of the Russell woman's name immediately, and he wondered if she were the mother of *that* Russell, the one who, for all intents and appearances, was going to be the ruination of one of his young officers.

"Colonel Woodard," the Russell woman said. "We weren't expecting to see you."

She paused as if she expected him to try to justify his intrusion at a time like this. He said nothing, letting the silence lengthen until she became uncomfortable.

"Have you eaten?" she asked, smiling a smile she did not mean.

"I'm not hungry—"

"Nonsense," she said. "You shall have some coffee and pie, at least." She looked at the other woman, who immediately bustled off, he supposed, to get it.

Max very nearly smiled. Here was someone to usurp Mrs. Kinnard's throne, given half the chance. "How is Mr. Markham?" he asked, certain that the Russell woman would know.

"He is unchanged."

"What has the surgeon said?"

"He believes it to be a case of the dropsy. Maria found him fallen in the kitchen when she returned this evening—your men carried him upstairs. *Your* army physician says it is a matter of waiting. Either he will recover—slowly—or he will not recover at all. Only time will tell."

"Where is...Miss Markham?" he asked.

"She *should* be lying down," Mrs. Russell said pointedly. "She has run herself ragged of late, trying to keep this big house and see that her father is comfortable."

And waiting hand and foot on a sorry Yankee colonel.

The woman didn't actually say it, but the way her eyes flicked over him, she might as well have.

She was indeed De Graff's potential mother-in-law, Max decided. This woman would take that old axiom about hiding one's daughter from the attentions of the regiment literally if anyone would.

"I have never known her to be so puny," the woman went on. "Always swooning and feeling sick and the like. Maria's constitution was always as strong as a horse. Nothing upset her until *now.*"

"I ask you again, Mrs. Russell. Where is Miss Markham?"

"I don't know, Colonel Woodard—but I'm sure you wouldn't want to disturb her."

"Your pie and coffee are in the dining room, Colonel Woodard," Mrs. Justice said, returning. "And Maria is in the kitchen."

"Thank you," Max said. He left both women standing and went straight to find her.

But the kitchen was empty. He thought she must have gone up the back stairs but then decided to see if she might be at the well or the summer kitchen instead.

He caught a glimpse of her as she disappeared into the shed where her horse was stabled.

He didn't follow her. Perhaps she needed a respite from the events of the day—or from the Russell woman. *He* certainly found Mrs. Russell exhausting. He would hate to ever have to endure her and Mrs. Kinnard simultaneously.

He lit a cigar and sat down on the stone steps, once again appreciating the summer night. After a time, he realized that Maria was talking to someone, that she wasn't alone. He could just see the other person at the edge of the shadows—another woman. He recognized her. It was Eleanor Hansen.

The conversation ended, and the Hansen woman slipped away into the shadows. Maria walked quickly toward the house, and she was becoming better at not reacting when she found him where she didn't expect him to be.

She didn't jump this time. She only stopped and stood looking at him. She was tired, exhausted. Even from here he could see it.

"I am beginning to believe it is an exercise in futility

to think for one moment that I can enforce any kind of curfew in this town,'' he said after a moment.

''It isn't ten yet,'' she said, swaying slightly. ''Is it?''

''Perhaps not. Would it be too uncouth on my part if I suggested that perhaps you should sit down?''

He wanted very much to ask her what Eleanor Hansen had been doing here, but he didn't. He supposed that the irrepressible Nell had decided she could deliver her own ''thank yous'' to Maria, after all.

Surprisingly, Maria came and sat down on the stone steps—but not *too* near him. And she stayed quiet for what seemed a long time.

''Nell…and I were childhood playmates,'' she said finally.

''The third Musketeer, perhaps?''

She looked at him in surprise, as if she'd forgotten that her father had told him of the little girl Maria and the playmates he called The Three Musketeers. ''Yes. The earrings you returned to me—Hatcher had them. He took them away from me—as a payment.''

'' 'Payment?' ''

''Reparation. For the prison being here. He…appropriated things when it suited him—especially jewelry and especially…''

Especially if the owner wouldn't cooperate, Max thought.

''Nell had been trying to get them away from Hatcher for me.''

''I see.''

''I didn't want her to have anything to do with the man, but she—''

''I see,'' Max said again when she didn't go on.

''My brothers gave me the earrings. I was to wear

them when I married. They wanted me to have them in case they couldn't...get home.''

She gave a quiet sigh before she continued. ''It's because of my brother Rob that Nell meant to get them back. She loved Rob once.''

''Once?''

''Now she hates him, I think.'' Maria looked at him. ''For dying. I think that's why she lives the way she does now—she's punishing him, even if he's dead and gone. It's the only way she can endure his leaving her.''

She didn't say anything more, and neither did he, for a time. A night breeze stirred the leaves on the trees. Once again, he could hear a whippoorwill.

''I'm sorry about your father,'' he said quietly.

She looked at him, but made no reply to his expression of condolence. ''I have been remiss in not thanking you,'' she said. ''For the earrings and for sending the surgeon. I find it very difficult to express the gratitude I feel—to you.''

''I don't require—''

''Colonel Woodard, Sir?'' Perkins said behind him.

''What is it?''

''Another fire, Sir. Downtown this time.''

Even as Perkins spoke, church bells all over town began to ring the alarm. ''Looks like it was set, Sir.''

Max swore and got to his feet; he could already see the glow in the night sky. A soldier came running with a fresh mount. Max looked back once as he was about to ride away. Maria stood watching from the steps, her face a pale blur in the moonlight, her arms crossed over her breasts as if for comfort.

Maria.

Chapter Nine

Max's mount had been well trained somewhere along the way and had already detected his rider's agitation. The animal was eager for the fray, and Max made no effort to hold him back. He left Perkins to follow as best he could.

In spite of the line of tall shade trees along the street, the glow from the fire was clearly visible. Max could see townspeople who had come out onto their porches, but none of them dared venture any farther or call to him as he rode past. When he reached the town well in the main square and was still several blocks away, he could see the sparks shooting high in the air, and he reigned his horse in. It sidled and pranced in protest.

"Perkins!" he called over his shoulder. "You said the fire was set?"

"Looks like it, Sir," the sergeant major called back. "Big burned spot on the ground—next to an outside wall—"

"What's burning?"

"Sir—it's Phelan Canfield's house—"

"What about Mrs. Canfield?"

"She's dead, Sir."

Max looked at him sharply. "Are you sure?"

"Yes, Sir. The surgeon was there. He says she suffocated from the smoke."

"And the boys?"

"Some of the men were trying to find them when I came to fetch you."

Max gave the horse his head again. He arrived on the scene at a gallop and in the midst of chaos. Soldiers from the garrison and the men from the civilian fire brigade rushed back and forth trying to get water on the flames.

But there was little doubt that the house would be lost.

"Mrs. Canfield is over yonder, Sir," Perkins said.

Suzanne Canfield had been wrapped in a quilt and placed in the back of a wagon left standing in the middle of the street. Max came up beside it and peered in. In the flickering light of the fire, she could have been sleeping.

"The boys—have you found the boys?" Max asked the nearest soldier.

"No, Sir. Sergeant Briggs thought he heard them, but they don't know him and they wouldn't come to him. One of the men—he thinks they'll hide. He says little 'uns will do that—try to hide from a fire."

Max dismounted and ran to the back of the house. The flames were not as bad here, but the smoke was heavy. He leaned into an open window.

"Joe!" he yelled. "Hurry up, son! We've got a ride to take! Joe! Did you hear me? Hurry! Bring Jake! We've got to go!"

He listened hard, straining to hear something, anything, above the sounds of desperate men and crackling flames.

"Joe!" he yelled again. "Answer me, boy!"

This time he heard something.

"Sir," Perkins said as Max was about to go headfirst in through the window. "I'll go, Sir—"

"No. You stay here by the window," Max said. "So I can find my way out. The boys know me a little. I think—hope—they'll come to me."

"Wait, Sir," another soldier said. He tied one end of a rope around Max's waist, then threw a sopping wet blanket around his shoulders.

"You give us the word, Sir, and we'll drag you out. But if the smoke gets to you and you can't, you ain't going to be left in there."

Max gave him a curt nod and worked his way through the open window into the room. When he stood up, the smoke hung in a heavy layer at his face, and he crouched down into better air, moving along the floor toward the center of the house, looking under tables and behind chairs as he went. The farther he went, the more searing the heat became. It hurt to breathe.

"Joe! Jake!" he kept yelling.

He heard something, but not in the direction he was going. He could hardly breathe now. He began crawling in the opposite direction, still yelling their names. As he passed a flour barrel, a little hand reached out and grabbed his sleeve.

"Joe!" Max said, dragging him out. "Where is your brother!"

Little Jake came crawling out from behind the barrel on his hands and knees. Max scooped them both up and wrapped them in the wet blanket. There was a sudden burst of heat and flame behind him, and he began to run. Overhead timbers fell all around him. A burning two-by-four clipped him hard on the forehead.

He kept going, but he was disoriented now, blinded by the smoke and the pain.

"Which way!" he yelled. "Perkins!"

"Here, Colonel!" Perkins yelled. "Here!"

Other men took up the cry, and Max kept going, following the sound of their voices and the pull of the rope, finally locating the window by feel. Hands took the boys from him and dragged him through to the outside. He took several steps and fell on his knees. Two of his men dragged him into the road away from the heat. He couldn't stop coughing, couldn't stop retching. And he was struck by the ridiculous thought that it was a good thing he hadn't eaten the pie or drunk the coffee Mrs. Russell tried to force upon him.

One of the men poured a bucket of water over his smoldering uniform coat. Max looked around to see the surgeon, Major Strauss, kneeling on the ground with the boys, and he made himself get up and walk in that direction, only to collapse again in a fit of coughing.

"Are…they…all right?" he finally managed to ask.

"I think so," Strauss said, coming to his side. "I can't find any obvious damage. They've likely breathed in a lot of smoke, though. Let me look at you—"

"I don't need—"

"I think I phrased that wrong," the major interrupted. "I made it sound as if you had a choice. You don't. Sir," he added. "Bring me a lantern!"

Max suffered the compulsory examination, his eyes on the two little boys lying on the ground.

"Your head's going to hurt," Major Strauss said, poking at the place where the two-by-four had struck Max's forehead with all the disdain of a veteran army doctor who could cut a wounded soldier's entire leg off in a matter of minutes. But Max was way ahead of that prediction. His head pounded with every movement, however slight.

"Are you sure the boys are all right?" he asked.

Both children started to cry suddenly, and Max went and knelt on the ground beside them. Without hesitation, they came to him. He stayed there, with his arms around them. He knew nothing of soothing children, but neither of them seemed to notice.

Perkins came to offer him a swallow of brandy. He took it gratefully in spite of the rawness in his throat. A shower of sparks went up as the house began to fall in upon itself.

"Was anyone else...supposed to be—inside?" Max asked.

"No, Sir."

"I thought there was a woman staying...with Mrs. Canfield."

"She weren't there when the fire started. She'd gone to the apothecary—to get Mrs. Canfield some medicine. Something different the doctor ordered made up for her because she was in so much pain. I reckon her regular medicine wasn't working anymore. She just got here. She's over yonder with—"

He didn't finish the sentence, and Max looked around to see a completely distraught woman kneeling in the back of the wagon with Suzanne Canfield's body, keening loudly, tears streaming down her face.

Max tried to get up, but the boys clung to him for dear life. He looked down at them. Their faces were black from the smoke. They were no longer crying, and it struck Max that neither of them had asked for their mother, he supposed, because they were so used to her being unavailable, so used to being left to the kindness of people even as unlikely as himself, that they no longer expected her to be a source of comfort, no matter what the crisis.

The church bells continued to peal, but, in spite of the fire, he saw no civilians, save the fire brigade, who had dared to break the curfew. He looked toward the wagon.

"Perkins."

"Yes, Sir."

"I want you to send somebody to the Kinnard house. Have them tell Mrs. Kinnard that I need her help and advice. Understand?"

"Yes, Sir. Help and advice."

"Maybe you should go yourself."

"Yes, Sir."

"Tell her I don't know the customs here, and I want her to take charge of the arrangements for Mrs. Canfield. I don't want her left like that."

"Yes, Sir. If she wants to see you?"

"I'm going to take the boys to Miss Markham's. And then I'm going to the jail. I want you to make sure nobody tells Canfield what's happened here. I'll do that myself."

"I reckon you know, Sir, he's going to blame you for it."

Max didn't respond—but he knew. And he wasn't going to hide from it. "All right, Joe—Jake. Come on. Stand up now. We've got a ride to take."

"Where are we going?" Joe murmured.

"To see Maria," Max said. "Stand up."

"Is Jake going to ride, too?"

"I think we can make room for him if he's good, don't you?"

"He's not bigger enough," Joe assured him.

"Well, you and I are going to help him."

The boys reluctantly let go of Max long enough for him to stand, but he had to immediately pick them both up again. He carried them part of the way, then handed them over to Perkins so he could mount.

"Sir?" Perkins said.

Max looked at him, but it took the sergeant major a moment to say what was on his mind.

"Miss Markham—she's got her plate full already. I reckon this is going to break her heart, and that's the god's truth, Sir."

Max had nothing to say to that, and Jake began to cry again. The horse was still skittish from the excitement, and the crying didn't help.

"Take his head," Max said to another soldier.

Joe was a willing enough rider, but it took a show of complete exasperation on Joe's part to convince his little brother that he wanted to participate in this venture, too. Max finally got them both more or less on the saddle in front of him. "Hold on to your little brother," he said to Joe. "Hold him tight. Perkins, give the Kinnard woman any assistance she needs—or will accept." He didn't feel any compunction at all about imposing on Mrs. Kinnard in this way. She needed to learn that even the appearance of favoritism had its price.

He spurred the horse and rode slowly down the street. Miraculously, Jake stopped crying. Max knew that Maria had her hands full with her father—but he didn't know what else to do but bring the boys to her.

The image of her playing with the children amid the wildflowers suddenly came to mind.

What is this flower, Maria? What is this flower!
Kiss me and I'll tell you…

He judged the Markham house to be a little over a half mile away—but it seemed a hundred. At one point Perkins caught up, then left him as they reached the Kinnard house.

The horse walked steadily on, no longer looking for a cavalry charge. "Can we go fast?" Joe turned around and asked him.

"Maybe next time," Max said. It was all he could do to hold on to both of them as it was.

The lamps were still lit at the Markham house. Max rode through the boxwoods right up to the front porch, thinking he could just set the boys off and then dismount with no fear of them getting stepped on.

No such luck. Both of them had clearly decided that he was their anchor in this madness, and they wouldn't get down or turn him loose. He didn't want to chance just sliding off and perhaps dropping one of them or having the horse shy, and he didn't want to yell for someone to come, because of Mr. Markham.

Jake began to cry again. Max swore under his breath—only to have Joe repeat it verbatim. He sighed and managed to free one hand from the death grip the boys had on him to get into his pocket. He pulled out several coins, and tossed one of them against a pane in the front window.

It clattered loudly against the glass. Jake cried harder, and still nobody came. Max decided to ride around to the back of the house, on the slight chance that all the soldiers camped at the edge of the property hadn't been drafted to fight the fire.

He couldn't see anyone at the tents—but he did see Mrs. Russell coming out of the privy. She was carrying a lantern, and she was *not* happy about having him find out that she actually observed the call of nature.

"Where is Maria?" he asked without prelude.

"Miss Markham is not available at this hour," she said with a haughtiness that made the hair on the back of his neck stand up.

"Get her," he said.

"Surely you don't mean to—"

"Now!" Max bellowed in spite of his desire not to disturb the household, making the horse prance and Jake cry even harder.

The woman left at a near run, and Maria appeared almost immediately with the lantern in her hand. Max didn't realize how bad the three of them must look until he saw her lift the lantern so that the light would shine on them.

She gave a small cry and rushed forward, setting the lantern down hard on the ground.

"Take them," Max said. "Jake, don't cry, son. Maria's got you."

"What's happened?" Maria asked, catching his sleeve. "Suzanne?"

"Not now," Max said. "Can you get them to bed? I didn't know where else to take them."

She nodded, handing Jake over to Mrs. Russell, who had dared to return. Max handed Joe down to her.

"I'll be back," he said.

"Wait!" Maria cried. "Where are you going?"

"I have to go to the jail."

"Tell me what's happened—"

"Not now. When I come back."

"Has something happened to—" She broke off, he thought because she realized what the answer would be even as she asked.

"Yes," he said, because he couldn't see any way out of it. She drew in a sharp breath.

"And Mrs. Hansen?" Her voice trembled.

He had to guess who she meant.

"She's all right. She's with Suzanne. I'll be back."

He meant to go, but Maria grabbed the horse's bridle in spite of having Joe over her shoulder.

"Has Phelan been told?"

"No."

"I should do it."

"No," Max said. "You have the boys to see to."

"Don't you understand? He shouldn't hear it from you."

"It has to be me. If I bear any blame in this, I accept it. And he will know I accept it. I will not hide from him."

He spurred the horse and wheeled away from her. And he didn't look back.

"Let him out."

"Yes, Sir," the soldier said, in spite of his obvious surprise.

The key in the lock made a lot of noise. Canfield ignored it. He was sitting on the floor in the corner, his eyes half closed.

"Get up, Reb," the soldier said.

Canfield did as he was told, but he took his own good time about it. Max waited.

"What's this about? Don't tell me Maria finally got to you," Canfield said as he stepped out of the cell. "I shouldn't be surprised. She can be very hard to resist—"

"I have bad news," Max interrupted.

Canfield looked at him and then at the other soldier, still cocky. His eyes were bloodshot, and he swayed slightly on his feet. "What do you mean?"

"There was a fire. The boys are all right—they're with Maria. But Mrs. Canfield—"

"What about Suzanne?" he interrupted.

"I regret to tell you that Mrs. Canfield died as a result of the fire."

"You regret— No! It's not so!"

"There was nothing that could be done for her," Max continued. "I'm having you released so that you can see to your boys and to the funeral arrangements."

"And what am I supposed to do—say thank you very much! Kiss your damn boots!"

Max ignored the outburst. "I've asked Mrs. Kinnard to help. I understand she's already seen the undertaker. If you have no objections, your wife's body will be taken to her house until such time as—"

"By God, you're enjoying this!"

Max had to work hard for control. "I can assure you, I am not. I had occasion to meet with your wife once— after one of your binges. We spoke at length. She was very gracious and kind."

Canfield ran his hand through his hair. "Gracious— and kind. Yes," he said absently. "Did she—" He broke off and exhaled sharply, as if he were having trouble breathing, and he stood there, clearly not knowing what to do.

"Maria has the boys," he said finally.

"Yes," Max said.

"Good. Good, then."

"Mrs. Kinnard's carriage is waiting. She will give you the details and take you where you need to go."

"The fire—what happened?" Canfield suddenly demanded.

Max didn't answer him.

"What happened! Did the boys knock a lamp over— what?"

"The fire was…suspicious."

Canfield stared at him. "Deliberately set, you mean."

"There are...some indications."

"Ah, God! Suzanne—" Canfield took a deep, wavering breath and struggled for control. "If that's so, it was one of *you* that did it! What are you going to do about it, Woodard? Are you going to look for the son of a bitch who did this?"

"I am."

"Liar!" Canfield said, lunging at him.

"You have a lot to do, Canfield," Max said, holding him off. "I suggest you go do it while you still can."

He gave Canfield a shove and braced himself for another round. The man stood there for a moment, then wiped his hand over his eyes. He gave Max one last hostile look before he let himself be escorted out.

Max left the jail immediately, going out the back way to avoid Mrs. Kinnard's carriage. He had done all he would do for Phelan Canfield this night.

Now he wanted to see Maria. He rode back to the house at a gallop, hoping to lose some of the misery he felt along the way.

He didn't go into the house immediately. He dismounted and led the animal to the small stable where the Markhams kept their buggy horse. It rumbled softly in response to the intrusion.

The shed smelled of dust and hay, manure and weathered wood. Max stood for a moment then began the cavalryman's ritual of seeing to his mount, clinging to the familiar chore in the hopes of settling down his rattled nerves. He had seen death many times and many ways, and still his mind was filled with the image of Suzanne Canfield's body wrapped in a quilt and her pale lifeless face.

He put the horse into the closest stall. Perkins had

been absolutely correct in his observation. The news about Suzanne would break Maria Markham's heart.

When he finally entered the house, a lantern burned on the kitchen table, and Maria was sitting there, her head resting on her arms in much the same way she had been the first night he'd come here. He stood for a moment, watching her.

She lifted her head before he could make his presence known.

"Suzanne is dead," she said. It wasn't a question.

"Yes."

"Have you told Phelan then?"

"Yes."

"How is he?"

"I don't think he quite…grasps it yet," Max said instead of saying what he really meant, that the man was too hungover and hostile to realize much of anything.

"Tell me what happened to her," Maria said.

"Are the boys asleep?"

"Yes—"

"How is your father?"

"He wants a toddy and a cigar," she said. "Tell me what happened to Suzanne."

"Are Mrs. Russell and Mrs. Justice about?" he asked, because he wanted to get through this without interruption.

"Mrs. Russell is with the boys. Mrs. Justice is sitting with my father—because she doesn't get on his nerves quite so much. I expect they both have their hands full."

He nodded and sat down at the table. He was so tired, his stamina suddenly leaving him in the way it often did since his imprisonment. He drew a deep breath and looked at her in the dim light from the lantern.

"Most of what happened is just conjecture at this

point. The fire may have been deliberate. The men got
Mrs. Canfield out early on—she wasn't burned, Maria—
but it was too late. The surgeon says she suffocated from
the smoke. Perhaps she had taken laudanum for her pain
and couldn't respond to the danger. Perhaps she didn't
even know. I can't say.''

Tears were rolling down Maria's cheeks, but she said
nothing, made no sound.

''I've asked Mrs. Kinnard to make the funeral arrangements. I trust that is all right. I don't know the
customs here and I thought it best that she oversee everything, so there would be no hard feelings on anyone's
part—in so much as can be helped. And I didn't know
what Canfield's disposition would be, and I didn't want
to just...leave Suzanne—Mrs. Canfield—unattended until somebody would volunteer to do what needed to be
done. She was very kind to me that day we talked—
when she had every reason not to be.''

Maria still wept. Tears streamed down her face, completely unheeded. She was so silent about it, but her grief
was almost a tangible entity in the room. He wanted to
reach out to her, but he knew better than to presume that
she would accept his comfort.

''I don't know how much the boys saw or how much
they understand,'' he said after a moment. ''But I trust
their father will come talk to them.''

Maria wiped at her eyes with her fingertips, then
stood. He could see the effort she was making not to
lose control.

''I am very sorry about Mrs. Canfield,'' he said.

She looked at him, but whether or not she believed
him, he couldn't tell. She walked out of the room, leaving the lantern with him and disappearing into the shad-
owy recesses of the house.

* * *

Maria stood in the dark upstairs hallway a long while. She had to see about the boys—and her father—and all she could do was cry.

For Suzanne. For herself.

She stayed there, just past the second-floor landing, until she thought she heard Max Woodard climbing the stairs. Then she quickly moved on, furtively wiping her eyes as she went and slipping into her father's room, out of sight.

Mrs. Justice dozed in a chair at the edge of the circle of light from the lamp, and Maria's father seemed to be sleeping, as well. She touched Mrs. Justice lightly on the shoulder.

"I'll sit with him now. Would you see if Mrs. Russell and the boys need anything? And then please rest. There is no need for all of us to be awake. I'll call you if I need anything," she whispered.

"Those poor, poor babies," Mrs. Justice whispered back, but she gave her no argument about leaving the room. Maria silently blessed her for it. Mrs. Russell wouldn't have been so amenable. She would have wanted to stay and reiterate her hatred of the army of the occupation, a hatred Maria herself shared.

Or so she had always thought.

She stood at her father's bedside, listening for the door to close behind her as Mrs. Justice went out. When it did, she gave in to the burning in her throat and eyes and began to cry again.

She didn't know what to do. Somehow she had to get through these next few days—for the boys' sakes if nothing else—and she simply didn't know if she could do it.

At one point she cracked the door and peered into the

hallway. She didn't see Max anywhere—it was silly of her to have run from him. She tried to think that she just hadn't wanted him to see her weeping, but that wasn't it at all. She was afraid. Afraid of the memory of what it had felt like being in his warm embrace—regardless of how brief the encounter had been. Tonight she needed someone's warmth and strength—*his* warmth and strength—no matter who they both were or what animosity lay between them, and she was so afraid that her neediness would show.

He had his own worries, and perhaps he didn't even know it. How little he understood of the people here. Yes, he had done the right thing in letting Acacia Kinnard see to Suzanne's funeral arrangements—but people would still blame him for her death and hate him for it.

He was being so *kind*. Why was he being so kind? Now she was forever in his debt—for his having sent the army surgeon to her father and for the regard he'd shown for Suzanne and her boys.

"Suzanne," she whispered, feeling the tears come anew.

Among "The Three Musketeers," Suzanne had been the first to experience all the milestones of a young girl's life. She was the first of them to be courted, to marry, to have children. Maria had seen Suzanne's vitality ebbing away every day, but still she was not prepared for *this*. How could Suzanne be so suddenly gone? Maria wanted desperately to believe what Max had suggested, that perhaps she had been asleep and never knew what was happening to her. It was unbearable to think that she might have been trying to get to her children.

Maria gave a wavering sigh and sat down in the chair Mrs. Justice had vacated. She hadn't wanted Max to be the one to bring Phelan the terrible news of Suzanne's death, because he was the one Phelan would blame.

But if the truth be told, there were a host of people who had precipitated what had happened tonight. Maria's mind reeled from all the "if onlys."

If only Major De Graff hadn't accosted Eleanor on the street.

If only Phelan hadn't taken exception to De Graff's demand—and he wouldn't have if he'd been sober. Eleanor had long since forfeited the right to have her honor defended, even by the likes of Phelan Canfield.

If only Maria herself hadn't tried to intervene and thereby escalated the situation until Max had had no choice but to exercise the law. If only Hatcher hadn't made his reckless statement about the town needing to be punished in the first place. If only Eleanor hadn't fallen so low and Phelan hadn't become a worthless sot and made it his life's work to insult every Yankee within earshot.

Maria had been angry with Max Woodard on the street today. Even understanding his position perfectly, she had been angry. But she truly didn't blame him for Suzanne's death. They were all to blame, each playing his or her own part, however small, in the events that would ultimately cost Suzanne her life.

Maria had no idea what would happen to the boys. No one could guess what Phelan would do. She had heard of drunkards who, because of some great tragedy, had turned their lives around, but she held out no such hope for him.

She sighed again and wiped her eyes on the corner of her apron. When she looked up, her father was awake and watching.

"What...is...wrong?" he asked, the shortness of breath

that was so indicative of the seriousness of his illness very much evident. "Damn silly...woman... wouldn't tell me... a thing."

"How are you feeling, Father?"

"Maria...Rose, do not...put me...off. It...makes me... cross. I see...the shape you...are in...and I have... heard...the bells. Or...would...you prefer I go...and see... for myself?"

She knew her father well enough to know that he just might try it.

"There was a fire," she said after a moment.

"And?"

"Suzanne...is dead."

She glanced at her father.

"Poor...child—" he said, and her eyes filled with tears, because she didn't know if he meant her or Suzanne.

"Go get the...boys..."

"They're here, Father. Colonel Woodard brought them."

Her father closed his eyes, and Maria thought he had dropped off to sleep.

"I want to...see him."

"Who, Father?"

"Colonel...Woodard."

"I'm not sure he's still here."

"Go...look."

"Father, you have to rest—"

"Go...Maria Rose. I have...finished business—with him."

"Unfinished business, you mean?"

"No—*finished*. I must see...him. Now—"

She stood, but she made no attempt to leave. Her father feebly waved her away with his hand, and she had no choice but to do as he asked. Or at least seem to. The last thing her father needed was a visitor, and the last thing *she* needed was for the visitor to be Max Woodard.

She took a small lamp from the mantel and lit it, then finally stepped into the hall. She only had to go a few steps to see that his door was closed. She would make an attempt of sorts, she decided, and then she would return and essentially lie to her father.

She came and stood for a moment outside the door and, just as she turned to leave, it opened.

"What's wrong?" Max said.

"I—I didn't mean to disturb you."

"What's wrong?" he asked more pointedly.

"I—my…father has asked to see you."

"I see. Did he say why?"

"No. I'm not sure he's in his right senses—I can tell him you aren't here."

"I thought you didn't lie."

"This is different. He's very ill."

"If he's asked, perhaps I can give him some peace of mind about something. But I will leave it to you."

Maria looked at him. He was doing it again. Being kind.

"All right, but please don't—"

"I won't stay if he seems the worse for my being there," he interrupted.

He stepped back into the room and picked up his uniform jacket. Maria was glad of that. She wouldn't want to encounter Mrs. Russell in the hallway in the company of a Yankee officer in his shirtsleeves.

"You don't have any cigars in your pockets, do you?" she asked as he put it on.

"I don't think so. Why?"

"Because, if you do, ill or not, my father will try to talk you out of them."

Max Woodard actually smiled. "You know, I think I rather like your father."

He felt an inside pocket and removed a letter. The letter appeared to be wet. He took the time to open the envelope and spread the sheets of paper inside it on the small folding table he apparently used as a desk.

And all the while, Maria watched. The movement of his hands. His profile, limned in the light from the lamp.

"No cigars," he said.

He followed her down the hallway to her father's bedchamber.

"I mean to consult you about Mrs. Russell—at a better time," he said as they reached her father's door.

Maria opened it and went inside, hoping that her father would be asleep now. He wasn't. He opened his eyes immediately.

"Go…away…Maria Rose," he said. "The colonel… will fetch you…when we're done."

"Father—"

"Don't…vex me, girl. Run along. Pull the…chair closer—please…Colonel. You can tell me…why you… have mimicked…my daughter…and are going around… with a knot on your…head—"

Summarily dismissed, there was nothing for Maria to do but to go. And she was as tempted to stand outside the door and eavesdrop as she had been to go through Max Woodard's belongings the night he arrived.

But she had other things to do, not the least of which was to see why Mrs. Justice had suddenly rushed up the stairs and was motioning for her to come there.

Maria had to force herself to walk in that direction.

"It's Phelan Canfield," Mrs. Justice whispered.

Chapter Ten

It was only by the merest chance that Max saw them. The wick in the lamp needed to be turned up, and when he got up to do so, he glanced out the window. There was just enough moonlight for him to catch a glimpse of someone outside in the yard below. He turned the wick down instead of up and moved closer to the window where he could see.

It was Maria, talking to Phelan Canfield. The man had what looked like a cloth sack of some kind, and he held it out to her. She wouldn't take it. At one point, she turned and walked away from him. He caught her arm.

Max could hear them now—or at least some of the conversation, and it struck him that he was making a habit of eavesdropping on these little tête-à-têtes with Phelan Canfield.

"I can't stand any more, Maria!" Canfield said.

Max couldn't hear her response, but he could tell she was trying to get away from him.

He glanced at Mr. Markham. The old man was sleeping now—exhausted by the effort it had taken to say what he wanted done. Max quietly left the room with every intention of going to fetch Maria—as her father had indicated he wanted done when he had finished talking. Fortunately or unfortunately, Max knew exactly where she was.

He went down the back stairs into the kitchen and stepped outside, but he stopped short of interrupting. He waited by the well where he could hear but not see them. For all intents and purposes, he just wanted to be...on hand, in the event that some intervention was needed. Who knew how drunk Phelan Canfield was by now? The man certainly had the justification to be as inebriated as possible.

But it occurred to Max as he stood there how much he didn't like this association between Maria and Canfield, in spite of the fact that they had probably known each other all their lives. He didn't like that Maria had risked her reputation on Canfield's behalf, and he didn't like the man coming to the house to see her now, even if his children were inside.

"Take it, Maria!" Phelan suddenly said. "It's for the boys—don't look at me like that!"

"They don't need this," she said. "They need you."

"Maria—"

"Goodbye, Phelan," she said.

Max could hear her walking in his direction, but he made no attempt to evade her. When she came into view, she was carrying the cloth sack.

"Out keeping the peace again, Colonel?" she said without stopping.

"If need be, yes," he answered truthfully.

"I'm not on a public street now. Whatever happens here is none of your concern—and I don't need your help."

"Perhaps. Perhaps not," Max said. He stepped in front of her. "Are you...all right."

"No. I am not."

She slipped by him into the house. And she didn't stop. When he came into the kitchen, she had already gone up the stairs.

Max stood for a moment, then followed after her, but he didn't see her anywhere. The door to her bedchamber was open when he passed, and he looked in. There was a lamp lit. Except for the two little boys asleep in her bed, the room was empty.

He went inside and looked down at them. Their little faces were clean now. He had no idea how he had managed to establish such rapport with these children in so short a time—but he realized suddenly that he was glad of it.

He left and went down the hall to his own room. He was tired, but not sleepy enough to retire. He sat for a time, smoking a cigar and shuffling papers—and listening for Maria in the event that her business with Canfield wasn't finished.

He heard Perkins come in and go to his place under the stairs. He should have told Maria to send the sergeant major to fetch the doctor if her father required him during the night—and he would have, if she'd given him half the chance.

At one point he picked up John Howe's letter. It was dry now, but the ink had smeared in places. He attempted to read it. The man was still happy. Max could tell that much.

and you must take care while you remain there in the town, John wrote. *...if you are of no mind to take a wife. There is something very compelling about Rebel women—particularly the ones who desperately need your help, but would rather die than say so. When they turn their eyes upon you, eyes filled with a sadness that* *perhaps you and your kind have caused, it is most hard to resist. Believe me, my friend, I know...*

Max skimmed the readable parts of the letter again, then put it aside. He was suddenly overcome with sleepiness, after all. He went and stretched out across the bed, not bothering to turn it down.

He woke to bright sunshine and giggling. Both Joe and Jake sat on the foot of the bed. He had no idea when they'd come in. He still had a soldier's wariness even in sleep—or so he thought. He must have been extremely tired to have let two little boys sneak up on him.

He sat on the side of the bed, wondering where the hell Perkins was. He didn't have to wonder long. The sergeant major appeared with a pot of coffee almost immediately.

"Whoa, Sir!" Perkins said when he saw the boys. "Where did these two come from? How did these rascals get in here?"

"I'm sure I don't know," Max said.

He glanced at the boys. They both grinned. "Any news regarding Mr. Markham?"

"The surgeon's come already this morning, Sir. Him and the town doctor both. I don't think there's much change."

"We like coffee," Joe said as Perkins handed Max a cup.

"You're too young for coffee," Max said.

"We like baby coffee," Joe amended. "Don't we, Jake?"

"Baby coffee," Jake assured him.

"And what would 'baby coffee' be?"

"Mostly milk and sugar, Sir," Perkins said.

Both boys were looking at him hopefully. "Can you find some for these two, Sergeant Major?"

"I can, Sir."

"Good," Max said. "Go with Perkins then."

They clearly liked the sound of that and hopped down immediately. Both boys were wearing—Max didn't know quite what they were wearing. Maria's blouses perhaps.

"Have you seen Miss Markham this morning?" Max asked as Perkins herded the boys out the door.

"Not exactly, Sir. I heard her. I reckon she's sick again. Oh, and I brought you another mail pouch, Sir. It got overlooked when they delivered the first one. I thought you might want to look at it here—get a head start, so to speak."

Max nodded absently, thinking about Maria. He took the mail pouch and sat down by the window with his coffee. There was a morning breeze coming in, in spite of the lateness of the day.

He opened the pouch and began looking through the letters in it. There was another one from Kate—

He suddenly looked up.

I reckon she's sick again.

Sick.

Again.

Like Kate used to be. By God, *exactly* like Kate used to be.

Mrs. Russell had noticed it. She had wanted to lay the change in Maria Markham's well-being at *his* door. It wasn't overwork that had caused her to suddenly be so "puny."

Maria Markham was pregnant.

No, he thought immediately, not because he wasn't certain of the similarities between her behavior since he'd arrived and Kate's, but because he didn't want to consider who the man might be.

No, he thought again. *Surely not.*

Maria Markham wasn't that kind of woman.

And neither was Kate.

How could Mrs. Russell and the rest of the old biddies in this town have missed it?

Actually, he knew how. The same way he and his mother and father had missed recognizing Kate's condition for so long. It was the sheer improbability of it.

Maria—

Had someone charmed her into it?

Canfield?

He dismissed that possibility immediately, regardless of recent events.

Perhaps she had been forced. Hatcher—or some other occupation soldier.

He knew from reviewing the military records just after he arrived that there were few complaints—even minor ones—of any soldiers molesting the decent women of the town. Max had assumed that the women either didn't report it or Hatcher had purged the records—or never documented the complaint in the first place. The men here were a long way from home, and Rebel females were intriguing at the very least. Max had no reason whatsoever to believe that the men of the United States Army had suddenly become a pack of saints.

He remembered suddenly when he had carried Maria upstairs after her fainting episode at the literary society meeting. All the longing in her voice when she'd said her fiancé's name. Maria Markham was not a cold woman. Perhaps there was someone who reminded her of the martyred fiancé, and she had simply...succumbed.

It didn't really matter, of course. All that mattered was whether or not she was carrying a child. And if she was, then she was in one hell of a fix.

He gave a sharp exhalation of breath, and he realized that Perkins had returned.

"Sir?" Perkins said when Max glanced at him.

"Hot water," Max said. "I'm ready to shave."

He went through the motions, but his mind wasn't on his usual morning ritual at all. When he was through and wiping the last bit of soap from his face, he heard a noise behind him. He looked around to see Maria standing in the still-open doorway.

She didn't enter.

"I'm looking for Joe and Jake. Mrs. Russell said they came in here," she said, letting her gaze briefly meet his and slide away. She looked so pale and tired. Perhaps it was just fatigue. And the grief and worry about her father's illness, he thought. And all the while he knew better. It was so clear to him now.

"They were here," he said. "My information is that they are now somewhere partaking of 'baby coffee.'"

"I'm sorry they disturbed you." She dared to look into his eyes again, but the contact was fleeting at best.

"It wasn't a problem."

She was looking at him gravely—and she was...not leaving.

"I wanted to ask you about Mrs. Russell," he said, since she had given him an opening.

She continued to look at him, and he took that for a certain receptiveness on her part.

"You know about this matter between Mrs. Russell's daughter and De Graff?"

"Yes."

"Is it one-sided?"

"One-sided?"

"Yes. Is it all De Graff's doing with no encouragement on the Russell girl's part."

"I don't believe so."

"Is there anything I can do? Speak to Mrs. Russell, perhaps."

"No." She shook her head. "No," she said again. "It wouldn't help. Nothing will help. Even if Mrs. Russell could be persuaded to be more receptive to their courtship—which I assure you she can't—Major De Graff has ruined his chances. There would still be the matter of Nell—Eleanor Hansen. Everyone knows about what happened on the street. The major's behavior toward her indicated a…history between the two of them. It's public knowledge now. No one will forget it."

"I see," Max said. Then, "No, I don't see. How is it that there are both elements in this town?"

"Elements?"

"Yes, elements. Women who are stampeding to get their daughters married off to my officers and then women like Mrs. Russell."

"Necessity," Maria said simply. "There aren't a lot of men left here to marry, and times are hard. Some women seek the most prosperous and well-situated husbands for their daughters they can find—even if they are…former enemies."

"And some would rather see their daughters dead first."

"Yes," she said bluntly. "I have something I would like to say to you."

Max looked at her. "Very well."

"The boys are very taken with you. I ask you not to encourage it."

It wasn't what he was expecting, and it surprised him how insulted he felt. "Why?"

"Because they have lost their mother and they have a drunkard for a father. They are looking for attention wherever they can find it. It's better if they don't come to rely on you for it—or for anything. You have no reason to let them become attached to you—and every reason not to. Please don't encourage them. I don't want them to suffer any more losses in their lives.''

They stared at each other across the room.

''Do you understand?'' she asked after a moment.

''I understand,'' he said.

''Good,'' she said.

''But I think perhaps you are too late. I think they are already…attached.''

She had nothing to say to that, regardless of how much she clearly wanted to, and she abruptly left.

Max didn't see her for the rest of the day. He stayed at headquarters late, and when he returned, the house was very quiet. A different pair of women greeted him at the door and advised him that the children were asleep—as they should be—and that Miss Markham had gone to Suzanne Canfield's wake. Mr. Markham was resting.

Max wanted to ask about Phelan Canfield—what kind of state he was in—but he didn't. He asked about the funeral instead.

''It will be a house service, Colonel,'' one of the women said. ''At the Kinnards'.''

''When?''

''Tomorrow at two. There was no need to delay. There are no out-of-town relatives who needed time to arrive.''

''Is it by invitation?''

''Yes,'' one woman said.

''No,'' the other one said at the same time.

The two women looked at each other.

''I'm asking if I may attend,'' Max said bluntly.

"Well...I—Mrs. Kinnard has large rooms—but not so large as to be able to seat the same number of guests as the church could accommodate—" the first woman said.

"Could you make inquiries and let me know? I would like to pay my respects, but I don't wish to intrude or give insult."

He left them to twitter over his request. He had said that he wouldn't hide from whatever blame he bore in Suzanne Canfield's death, and he meant it. And, even if he were barred from attending her funeral, the town would surely know that he'd been civilized enough to ask to come.

There was no sign of Maria the next morning. He left for headquarters early, and shortly before eleven, a black-bordered invitation written in an elegant script was hand-delivered to him at headquarters. He worked until well after one, then went to the Markham house to change into his best uniform. Maria was not on the premises. Nor were the boys.

Did children attend funerals here? he wondered. He didn't know and didn't ask.

He did remain long enough to speak to Mr. Markham. The old man seemed more frail to him today. He still struggled to breathe—and he still probably would have smoked a cigar if given half the chance.

"I've delivered your instructions, Sir," Max said obscurely, because of the woman caretaker in the room.

Mr. Markham nodded his gratitude. "One...less... worry," he said.

Max took his leave and arrived at the Kinnard house just before two. The folding doors between the large front parlor and the dining room were open, and all the furniture had been removed save the piano. Rows of mismatched chairs had been placed from one end of the area to the other. Those assembled were expecting him. There was intense interest, but not surprise. He could feel it when he was escorted to his seat—next to Valentina Kinnard, who was enveloped in black silk and who wept beautifully.

He could see Maria on the front row with the boys on either side of her, their chairs pulled close so she could keep a hand on them. Even from that distance, he could tell that she wore the same drab black dress she'd had on when she'd come for him at the train station. The woman Max had seen weeping in the wagon the night Suzanne Canfield died sat next to Joe. Phelan Canfield was conspicuously absent.

Where is the son of a bitch? Max thought.

The funeral service began. The room was hot in spite of having all the windows raised. Whatever flowers were blooming now had been picked and brought in to fill a number of vases and urns. Here and there a wasp bobbed in the air over the gathering. A baby fretted. Someone sobbed.

And eyes bore into his back. He hadn't felt that sensation so acutely since the last time he'd had a Reb sharpshooter dog his every move.

Valentina Kinnard fanned herself vigorously next to him. He glanced at her.

"I think I shall faint," she whispered.

"I wouldn't if I were you," he said loudly enough for any number of people to hear. And he meant it.

The fanning abruptly stopped.

People were standing suddenly as Suzanne Canfield's casket was being brought in. Her pall bearers all wore Confederate uniforms—or what was left of them. Max still didn't see her husband.

Lieutenant Carscaddon's wife followed the procession, carrying a wreath of greenery and magnolia blossoms she placed carefully on the coffin. A reverend came and stood at the halfway mark in the room, then began the burial liturgy.

The room grew hotter still, and the service went on and on. Mrs. Kinnard played the piano for the hymns, and she was quite accomplished. Max shifted in his seat so that he could see Maria. Her back was ramrod-straight, but he thought she was crying—in the same quiet way she had when he told her the details of Suzanne Canfield's death. At one point, she took Jake onto her lap.

Finally, it was over. Max stood with the rest of the mourners as the casket was taken out. Maria gave no indication that she saw him as she joined the procession and walked past—but Jake did. He pulled out of her grasp and came running, wrapping both arms around Max's knees. There was nothing to do but pick him up.

"Come here, Jake," Max whispered. "I'll carry him," he said when Maria reached out for him.

She hesitated, her eyes looking directly into his.

Sad eyes.

The kind John Howe had written about.

He could see the question there as clearly as if she had spoken aloud.

Why? Why are you doing this?

And the truth was he didn't know. These people were nothing to him—less than nothing, given his prison experience. And yet, here he was. His presence wasn't a self-serving token designed to keep the peace, after all. He knew that. But he couldn't begin to say why it was so or when his attitude had changed.

Maria walked on, holding Joe by the hand, and Max stepped in behind her. When he reached the outside, he could see a company of soldiers from the garrison standing at attention at a respectful distance on the other side of the street. Perkins was there. And De Graff, and the regimental surgeon and a number of his other officers. Max hadn't ordered it, and whoever had perhaps understood these people better than he.

Max tried to give Jake back to Maria after she had climbed into the carriage that would take her to the cemetery. The boy only clung harder and began to cry.

"What do you want me to do?" Max asked her. He could feel the attention the scene was garnering. "Shall I take him on to the house? And Joe?"

She looked both relieved and bewildered by the suggestion. Her mouth trembled slightly, but she said nothing. It was clear to him that she had reached a point where she was too exhausted to decide.

"Come on Joe," Max said, holding out his hand.

Joe came to him easily—pausing long enough to give Maria a hug before he climbed into Max's other arm.

"I'll take them with me," he said.

Maria looked at him and gave him the barest of nods. Max stepped back from the carriage and watched it drive on.

After a moment he realized that Perkins was standing at his elbow.

"What?" he said.

"I thought you might like to know about the rest of the family, Sir," Perkins said.

Max took a quiet breath. He didn't know if he did or not.

"Where is he then?" he asked finally.

"Skedaddled, Sir. Last night. Lit out on the Western Railroad."

Chapter Eleven

"Where is my..." Joe said.

Max braced himself for the question.

"...Maria," Joe concluded, still looking out the window.

It was an easier question to answer than the one Max expected—but not much.

"She'll be here soon," Max said.

"Is she in the rain?"

"Don't worry. Maria will be all right."

The boy gave a quiet sigh. "No. Is my *mama* in the rain?"

Max hesitated. He had no idea what the child had been told or how much he understood about what had happened the night of the fire or today at Mrs. Kinnard's. Joe was looking at him now, and it struck Max that regardless of how much he looked like his father, he still had his mother's eyes.

"Your mama is in heaven, Joe," he said finally.

"Does it rain there?"

"I don't know. I've heard people say heaven is like a garden—with all kinds of flowers. So it must, I think."

"Mama likes flowers," he said. "She likes the rain."

He went back to looking out the window. "People going to church."

"What?" Max said, not understanding.

"See the rain? It's not rain. Mama said pretend it's something else. Pretend it's people going to church. Lots and lots of people. Is she coming back?" he asked.

"No, Joe."

"Is my papa coming back?"

"I don't know," Max said, because it was the truth. "I'm...not sure where he went."

"Mexico," Joe said. "Mexico is a long, long way."

"Who told you he went to Mexico, Joe?"

"Maria did. Is Mexico as far as heaven? Me and Jake can go to Mexico sometime, I bet. Maybe we can see Mama, too—when we go." He fingered the lace curtain, poking his small fingers into the holes that ultimately made the pattern of a rose.

"I'm not scared," Joe said after a moment, more to himself than to Max.

"Joe," Max said. "Come here."

The boy hesitated, then flung himself into Max's arms.

"You'll be all right, son," Max said, lifting him up off the floor and holding him. The boy hid his face in Max's shoulder. "I promise. You and your brother both. Don't worry."

Max looked around. Mrs. Russell stood in the doorway with Jake in hand.

"It's time for them to nap," she said, still using that confrontational tone of voice he had come to dislike intensely. He believed Maria's assessment of the situation. There was nothing he could say to this woman to smooth the way for Major De Graff.

"Go with Mrs. Russell," Max said. "Naps make you grow big and tall," he added when he sensed a budding mutiny. "You've got to grow into a big boy—so you can ride your own horse one of these days. I will see you and Jake later. Mrs. Russell, how is Mr. Markham?" he asked to irritate the woman as much as to find out about Markham's condition.

"He's stopped asking for cigars," she said tersely.

Joe reluctantly hopped down and trotted away with her. Max could hear him jumping up the stair steps—until Mrs. Russell made him stop.

He sat down in a chair near the window, his mind focused on Maria Markham and her situation. He kept seeing the way she had looked at him today, just before the carriage moved away. She had desperately needed his help—and, as John had said, she would rather die than ask for it. It was one thing to make a request for a doctor on her father's behalf and quite something else again when it was something she herself needed, no matter how small. He wanted to be with her now, damn it. He wanted her to rely on him, just a little. What could a man do with a woman like that?

And yet, he had made her laugh—once. The old Max—the one who had been the darling of all the eligible young ladies of Philadelphia—and some not so eligible—had reasserted itself the night of the thunderstorm, quite without his bidding, and had made a remark spontaneous enough and witty enough to catch her by surprise.

And what a pleasant experience her laughter had been.

He closed his eyes, still considering what could be done for her. He could hear people coming and going, most of them bringing food. He didn't know if the constant arrival of heavily laden plates and platters and bowls was a long-standing Southern funeral tradition or one born of their time of near starvation during the war.

He had only recently learned how hard times had been here then. There had even been a bread riot, staged by these strong-willed women on behalf of their hungry children, and, if he could believe Perkins, the women had essentially won.

In any event, it was as if, in Phelan Canfield's absence, Maria had been designated the primary mourner by default, and the gestures of condolence that would have been extended to him had been redirected to her.

Max wondered if Canfield had indeed gone to Mexico. If he had, then Maria's predicament was all the more dire. If her father died, she would be left to care for Canfield's children alone. And if she were pregnant and not married, the Kinnards and the Russells of this town wouldn't allow her to keep them. As far as he knew, there was no family to step in—or he hadn't seen anyone he could identify as such at the funeral.

Perhaps all the Canfields were accomplished at disappearing.

Skedaddled.

A soldier's term for running away under fire. Max supposed the word fit Canfield's situation as well as any, though he suspected that the man was likely a brave soldier. It was trying to endure what was left of his way of life and the strain of day-to-day living that had apparently driven him to drunkenness and ultimately sent him on the run.

Max suddenly got up and walked to the window and looked out at the rain in much the same way Joe had done. He, too, wanted to see Maria. He wanted to talk to her, to do something—anything—for her. Feed her. Hold her. Make her laugh again.

How right Perkins and John both had been about the allure of a woman who is certain she despises you.

He felt as if the house was closing in on him suddenly, and he was quite aware of the fact that he didn't have to stay here. He could remove himself to headquarters, or to a hotel or even to another residence. Mrs. Kinnard would likely be delighted to have him. But for the boys and Valentina's relentless determination, he might have actually sought an invitation.

Joe.

Jake.

When and how had he come to put the sons of an enemy above his own comfort? It didn't matter, he supposed. It only mattered that he had. He could still feel both sets of little arms around his neck and smell their little-boy smell, still see Joe standing at the window.

I'm not scared.

And he wouldn't be if Max could help it.

Carriages began to arrive out front, and people were coming into the entry hall—some of the funeral attendees, arriving hushed and drenched in spite of Mr. Markham's illness.

He had no wish to encounter any of them or to retreat to his room upstairs. He headed toward the rear of the house instead, where he found Perkins busily arranging the latest array of bowls.

"I want Major Strauss to see Mr. Markham again today," Max said.

"Yes, Sir. I believe he is planning to do that—come here as soon as he finishes up his work at the infirmary. Shouldn't take him long, Sir. Ain't too many of the boys sick or banged up for a change."

Max nodded and stepped outside. It was getting harder and harder to stay ahead of his sergeant major. The man was born to manage army officers, and manage them he did.

It was raining still. Max didn't mind it much. Four years of war had rendered the elements essentially meaningless to him—unless it was something extreme. In wartime, nothing was ever postponed because of inclement weather. Burnsides's infamous "mud march" was proof of that. In the prison, Max had lived outside for months, his only shelter a burrow in the red clay. And burrows were useless in the rain. It was only the thunderstorms that caught him when he was sleeping and sent him into the hell that was his past he minded.

He walked down the covered walkway to the summer kitchen. And he found Maria sitting on a stool by an open window in the far corner.

He didn't say anything, and neither did she. It occurred to him that he should withdraw and leave her to recuperate from the funeral and the worry about her father in private, but he didn't. He picked up the only other chair and set it in the doorway, dragging a piece of wood and his knife out of his pocket and sitting down with his back to her.

And just in time. Mrs. Russell appeared on the back steps.

"Are you available?" he asked Maria quietly.

"Have you seen Miss Markham?" the Russell woman asked before she could answer.

"Mrs. Russell, the regimental surgeon will be here to check on Mr. Markham soon," Max said instead of answering.

"I hardly think that is necessary," Mrs. Russell assured him. "Mr. Markham was awake just now and without complaint. He was able to drink some beef tea and take some bread. Now, have you or have you not seen Miss Markham?"

Max kept waiting for Maria to announce herself. "Sorry," he said when she didn't. "I can't help you."

He went back to whittling, paring the edges of the wood into what could almost be identified as a train engine.

"Thank you," Maria said after a time.

"You're welcome," he said without looking up or turning around.

"I just...couldn't—I needed..."

"The house is full of people," Max said. "Your father seems to be comfortable at the moment. There's no reason why you can't escape here for a while."

"It's hardly an escape," he thought she said.

It occurred to him that perhaps Canfield hadn't gone to Mexico, after all. Perhaps she was waiting for him.

"Where are the boys?" she asked after a moment.

"Mrs. Russell declared it time to nap. If they know what's good for them, I expect they are napping."

She didn't say anything else; she sighed.

"Miss Markham," he said. "What plans do you have for them?"

"Plans?"

"Joe says his father has gone to Mexico. Is that true?"

"I...so Phelan said."

"And he's left the children with you until further notice?"

"Yes."

"There is no other family who could take them? Joe mentioned a grandmother."

"No. She died this spring."

"It could be a long time, then. It could be a permanent arrangement."

"I suppose so. Yes."

"Then I suspect you have a very serious problem,"

he said, continuing to work the wood. "And I would like to ask what it is you intend to do."

"I intend to take care of them as best I can—"

"No, I'm asking about your condition, Miss Markham. What do you intend to do about that?"

He heard the stool scrape when she abruptly stood, and he turned to look at her, knowing that this was neither the time nor the place to ambush her with his suspicions—no, convictions—and that he was going to do it anyway.

"Please answer me, Miss Markham," he said.

She walked forward with every intention of getting past him and making her escape. He stood up to block the door.

"You have no right to speak to me in this way—"

"I know that. Nevertheless, I do speak to you. You may be insulted by my audacity, if you like, but it changes nothing. I believe you are…with child, Miss Markham. For the boys' sake, I would like to know how you will manage. Do you have the prospect of marriage? Will the child's father step forward or not?"

"Let me pass!"

"After I say to you what I wish to say. If he will not come forward—then what are your plans? Surely you recognize the difficulties here. Your father is very ill. You can reasonably expect to find yourself alone at some point. You father has arranged for the back rent he has been paid to go into a bank draft in your name—as protection from his creditors should he pass. I know this because that is why he asked to see me the other night.

"There will be some money for a time, but your father has debts, which I suspect will take whatever property he has—the roof over your head. There are the boys to think of. You yourself said that you didn't want them to have to endure any more losses. And you and I both know that, as the mother of a bastard child, you will not be allowed to keep them. You will be completely ostracized by Mrs. Kinnard and the others, and if there is no family to step in, who knows where they will—''

''I will not listen to this!''

''Do you plan to go somewhere with them and assume a new identity?'' he asked, ignoring her outburst. ''It might work. There must be 'war widows,' real and false, all over the South. Or will you follow their father to Mexico? Perhaps you think you can join your friend Nell in her endeavors in order to support yourself and them.''

Maria looked so pale, and she reached out to steady herself by gripping the edge of the table. He took a step toward her, but she backed away.

''I don't condemn you, Miss Markham. I am trying to help you.''

''Why! Why would you want to help me! Am I not indebted enough to you?''

''I have my reasons,'' he said honestly. ''Some of which I...can't explain.''

''You can't help me. No one can.''

''I think you're wrong about that. There is a solution.''

''And what would that be?'' she said sarcastically.

''Marriage.''

She gave a short laugh. ''Who would offer me marriage—even if I could deceive him? I have no dowry but an invalid father's debts and two children to care for.''

''I would,'' he said, and he didn't realize until he'd actually said it, that that was indeed the best solution for them all. ''I think we would be...compatible—intellectually, if not politically or temperamentally. And we would not have the distraction of an emotional attachment.

"I don't know how much longer the Occupation will continue—years, I expect. I have no plans to leave the military, and it would be very advantageous to me to have a Southern wife, particularly here. Your father apparently trusts me already to see to your well-being, so I don't believe he will object. And the boys are attached to me—as you have already noted.

"So. Please consider my offer. That's all I have to say. Except that it would be a good idea if you made your decision regarding this quickly—if we are to deceive the town and your father as to the real reason for the marriage."

She kept wiping furtively at her eyes with her fingers, as if she thought he wouldn't notice she was weeping if she did it quickly enough.

He stood back from the doorway to give her room to pass.

She took a deep breath and moved warily by him, clearly expecting him not to let her leave. When she had gone a few steps, she stopped. "It doesn't matter to you that I hate you and your kind?"

"What matters to me is that you don't hate me as much as you wish you did," he said.

She looked at him a long moment, then turned abruptly and ran into the house.

After a moment, Max sat down again and began to whittle, his mind firmly focused on the task. But he could only force his concentration on the wood for so long.

You and your kind.

John Howe had warned him of the dangers of becoming entangled with a Rebel woman. Clearly, it had been wasted advice.

Maria sat at her father's bedside, her heart still pounding.

I didn't deny it. Not once.

And she should have. It didn't matter that Max Woodard's suspicions were correct. She should have told him he was wrong. She should have said how offended she was.

Except that she hadn't been offended. She had been shocked. It was incredible to her that he could have even made a guess about her condition, much less be so certain of it that he would suggest marriage. At the very least she should have made more of an attempt to leave. She should have called for help—done anything—to escape the humiliation of having him tell her that he knew.

But she had simply been too exhausted to defend herself. She was still exhausted. She could hardly hold her head up, and she was only here now, playing the dutiful daughter at her father's bedside, because she was mortified that she would encounter Max Woodard in the hallway.

Her father was sleeping, and had been since shortly after the regimental surgeon had left. He didn't need her presence. Thanks to whatever concoction the army doctor had given him, he wasn't even aware that she was in the room. And the doctor had assigned not one, but two of his hospital orderlies to be on hand to assist with her father's care. She hadn't been able to find the will to protest that, either. She was slowly loosing control of everything in her life.

She closed her eyes for a moment. She could hear the rain on the roof, and her mind immediately went to Su-

zanne and her lonely grave in the church cemetery. She
had promised Suzanne she would always take care of
the boys. She would never forgive Phelan for leaving
the way he had. Never. Any more than she would forgive
Billy.

Max Woodard had been right about everything. About
her pregnancy. About her losing the boys. About how
very little time she had to make up her mind. He had
been right about the other thing, as well. She didn't hate
him as much as she wished she did.

Still, she couldn't believe that he had actually pro-
posed marriage, nor could she believe that what little
indignation she could summon now was directed, not at
his having offered, but at the way he'd done it, backing
her into a corner with his cold logic and his Yankee
arrogance the way he always did—and yet he had realized completely her need to evade Mrs. Russell for a
time.

She didn't understand the man, and she didn't understand herself. The reality was that however badly she'd
wanted to run away from him just now, she had just as
badly wanted to stay, even knowing that he couldn't be
serious and that there was no "emotional attachment."
She would be a bigger fool if she believed him sincere
than if she arbitrarily turned him down.

She covered her face with her hands for a moment as
she relived her humiliation. She had been so overwhelmed by everything else that she'd managed for days
not to dwell on the coming child and what she would
do.

My poor baby.

The encounter with Max Woodard had suddenly made
it all real to her. A child. *Her* child. A son or a daughter.
I don't know what to do!

Yes, she did. She would do what she should have done in the summer kitchen. She would tell Colonel Woodard that she would not marry him. If there was some money now, she would leave—and take the boys with her. There must be someplace she could go—

Her father stirred, and she gave a heavy sigh. Perhaps she *could* take the children with her, but she couldn't leave her father.

She was trapped. There was no one she could turn to for help.

No one.

"I can't think about this anymore," she whispered.

"Did you say something, Maria?" Mrs. Russell said behind her.

"Yes—no. I—I'm so…"

"Of course you are," Mrs. Russell said. "Come away now. You must rest. Someone will call you if your father needs you."

"I can't rest—"

"Look at yourself, Maria. You don't have a choice."

No choice, Maria thought. *Exactly.*

She let Mrs. Russell lead her from the bedside with no more resistance than she'd given Max Woodard's marriage proposal.

How could she say yes to that ridiculous offer?

And how could she say no.

Chapter Twelve

Maria slept much later than she'd expected. In fact, it was past noon when she awoke. Even so, she could have slept longer. She forced herself to sit on the side of the bed. All in all, she felt...better. Much better than yesterday.

She washed the sleep from her eyes and dressed quickly in her everyday dress and pinafore, braiding her hair into one long braid she let hang down her back. She was hungry, as well, but she took the time to look at herself in the mirror before she went downstairs.

She looked like Tragedy in a tableau—if she were being played by an unhappy, overage schoolgirl.

She went first to her father's room. One of the army orderlies informed her that her father was getting his bath and would be available to her shortly.

Maria hesitated then went quickly down the back stairs. All that food that had arrived yesterday, and she didn't see any of it. She did see Colonel Woodard, however. Surprisingly, he was in the backyard under the shade trees, sitting at the small folding table she'd seen in his room, working away.

There was no one in the kitchen or dining room. In

fact, she didn't hear anyone in the house at all. She took a deep breath. There was no time like the present. She would go right now and tell him what she had decided. She picked up her skirts and went outside, losing her nerve about halfway to where he was sitting and almost at the very moment he looked up and saw her.

He didn't say anything. He just looked at her expectantly. She forced herself to keep going, stopping when she reached the edge of the shade.

"Did you have a good sleep?" he asked.

"I—yes," she answered. If he wanted pleasantries, she would give him pleasantries. "Very well, thank you."

"The boys have gone on a wagon ride with Perkins. To get supplies."

"I see," she said.

She continued to stand.

"I wanted to—" she began.

"Would you mind sitting down?" he interrupted, putting aside the papers he was holding. "You're making me nervous."

"*I'm* making *you* nervous," she said.

"I'm afraid so," he answered. He looked up at her. "I don't throw out marriage proposals everywhere I go, Miss Markham. Actually, this is my first." He pushed a wooden crate near the camp table. "Sit," he said.

She didn't, and he moved it farther away from him and then gave her a pointed look. She sighed and sat down.

"I've seen your father—no, I didn't mention anything to him," he quickly added, apparently because of her look of alarm. "He seemed to be feeling better. I understand Mrs. Kinnard sent a telegram to John Howe's mother-in-law. And she sent back her recommended remedies for his condition—parsley tea—and I've forgotten what else—something to do with willow bark. Anyway, he seems a little perkier to me. Did you find that to be so?''

"I haven't seen him yet today."

"Ah. Well. I've also spoken to Nell Hansen. She came by very early—to the edge of the yard, that is. Hoping to catch a glimpse of you."

"How is she?"

"Very sad, I think. She says to tell you if you want Phelan Canfield shot, she will be more than happy to help you. I'm not sure she wasn't serious."

Maria had nothing to say about that. She glanced at Max. He was watching her closely, and it occurred to her that this might be what it would be like if they were married. They would meet at some point during the day, and he would share information with her. It was not an altogether unpleasant notion.

But this was clearly the point where she could say that she was declining his proposal. She didn't, however. She simply looked back at him, wondering again, *Why?*

"I've been thinking," he said.

But he didn't say what he had been thinking about. He reached over to a tin plate of peaches sitting on yet another wooden crate and selected one. Then he began to peel it with a knife apparently placed on the plate just for that purpose. He didn't ask her if she wanted any. He merely peeled it and removed the pit—and held half of it out to her.

She didn't take it.

"These came in on the train this morning," he said. "My mother sent them. I believe you'll like it."

She took the peach, and, eventually, she even took a bite. And another. And another. It was wonderful.

"The growing season is a little later in Pennsylvania," he said.

"Colonel—"

"Max," he corrected.

"Colonel—" she repeated.

"Before you continue, I would like to say something first. If you don't mind."

She stared at him, wondering now if he was about to withdraw his offer.

"Go ahead," she said. Her hands were juicy from the peach, and he gave her his handkerchief to wipe them on.

"I've been thinking that I haven't been entirely fair to you."

"In what way?" she said, sounding more wary than she intended.

"I've expected you to make your decision based entirely on the dire circumstances of your situation. And I think we should put all that aside for a bit. There are things you should know—about me—before you make up your mind."

He stopped long enough to eat his half of the peach, and she waited for him to continue, more than a little bewildered.

"It would help if you didn't frown so," he said.

She held up both hands. "What is it you want to say?"

"I should have given you some personal information. I should have said that I'm twenty-eight years old. I will be twenty-nine in December. I'm in good physical health—considering—and my mental health—well, you've seen the nightmares firsthand. My mother and father are both living. He's in shipping. I have one sister, who is younger than I. Her name is Kate. I'm very fond of them all—particularly her. Would you like to see their photographs?''

It was her polite upbringing and only her polite upbringing that made her say yes.

He reached for a small worn leather case hanging on the back of his chair and brought out two daguerreotypes—one of a man and woman—he sitting, she standing. His parents, Maria guessed, because he looked a little like each of them. The other one was of an incredibly beautiful young woman and two Yankee soldiers. She recognized them both. Max Woodard and John Howe.

''This is your sister?''

''Yes.''

''She's very beautiful,'' Maria said, because it would have been nearly impossible not to.

''Yes, she is. The remarkable thing about her is that she doesn't seem to know it.''

''You and John Howe have been friends a long time,'' she said, still relying on her early training for something to say.

''Long enough for the friendship to end. Twice,'' he said.

He didn't elaborate, and she didn't ask any questions. She handed him back the daguerreotypes.

''I'm reasonably well off financially,'' he continued. ''I didn't earn it, however. It came to me from my mother's father. I'm not sure how he got it. He was a bit of a rascal, so it's probably best that I don't know. I was in my last year at Harvard when the war broke out. I didn't sit for my final exams, and, much to my mother's dismay, I joined a cavalry unit. Rush's Lancers. I was young enough that I just couldn't resist the fine military figure they cut. John used to say we were nothing but nerve bred of ignorance and Philadelphia's best tailors.

"Ultimately, I ended up here—also twice. I'm not much of a church-goer, but that I would remedy, if need be. I drink occasionally and smoke a lot—cigars. I don't believe in beating horses, children, or women—even wives. I don't gamble—but I've had enough practice in my time to know how. I guess you could say, before the war, I led a man's life.

"You should also know that at some point, your father will be consulted. I will make whatever arrangements with him required to make sure he is easy about entrusting you to me."

"What does that mean? Money?"

"If need be. It should not be offensive to you. It's done all the time, I can assure—"

"Perhaps where you come from." She looked away. "You and I have every reason to hate each other."

"Yes," he said.

"Regardless of the fact that I personally had nothing to do with your imprisonment and I have no way of knowing whether you actually encountered my brothers at Gettysburg—we can't just establish some kind of blanket forgiveness for all that."

"No, we can't."

"I loved the man I was going to marry," she said bluntly.

"I know."

"How could you possibly know that?"

"I heard you say his name," he said simply, looking into her eyes.

She frowned, but she didn't say anything. The silence between them lengthened, and she looked down at her hands, the rough skin and the ragged nails. These were not the hands of a prospective fiancé for the son of a Yankee shipping magnate who was "reasonably well off."

"You…haven't asked me about the baby," she said finally. She had no intention of telling him anything, even if he had. It was a secret she would carry to her grave.

"I assumed that the father is not really a consideration here. Is he?"

"No," Maria said.

"If it's over and done, I have no need to know the details."

"I still don't understand why. Why would you ask me to marry you? If you need a Southern wife, this town is full of eager young women who will oblige."

"The bride fair."

"The what?"

"It's what Perkins calls it—this interest in marrying army officers."

Maria tried to be insulted, but the descriptive term hit far too close to home.

"So I'm to believe that it's because of our supposed intellectual compatibility and my usefulness as an occupation colonel's wife."

"Those are two reasons, yes."

"But not the only ones?"

"No."

"Am I to be advised of those?"

"No. Those are quite…personal, the details of which aren't mine to share."

"I don't understand."

"It's simple. Some things we won't discuss. Like the identity of the father of your child and my personal reasons for the marriage proposal. Neither matter in the overall scheme of things.''

''Colonel Woodard, I—''

''There is one last thing,'' he interrupted.

''What?''

''It wouldn't be a marriage of convenience,'' he said, and she could feel her cheeks flush as the question she'd barely dared to entertain was answered.

''It will be a true marriage in every way. We will take care of these two boys as best we can—and as long as need be. Neither of us has any way of knowing when Phelan Canfield will return or what he would do about them if he did. *Your* child will be made legitimate and my heir. Regardless of whatever rumors may surface, he or she will be raised as mine.

''This marriage will be an alliance for that purpose and to aid me in my military career. If you agree, I will ask for your word of honor that you will do your part to make this a success. I can't do it alone. I believe the union will be beneficial to us both—but neither of us should enter into it blaming the other for the political and personal circumstances that have ultimately brought us together.

''Now. You have much to consider, and I must leave shortly. I will be away for about three days on army business. When I return, I trust you will give me an answer. Do you think that is possible?''

''Very possible,'' she said, grateful for the reprieve in spite of her conviction that the answer would be no.

And she had no intention of changing her mind.

''Good,'' he said. ''Until then.''

He was gone longer than three days. Nine to be exact. Long enough for her to alter her decision—several times.

The house was very…empty without him somehow, in spite of having the boys very much in evidence. She still didn't know exactly where he had gone. ''Army business'' could mean anything and likely dealt with something which would not favor the people here.

Mrs. Russell and Mrs. Justice continued to spend part of each day helping with both the children and the chores. Maria was more grateful than she could ever have expressed. The three of them managed to set up some routine for Jake and Joe, and her father.

She actually thought her father was improving. He was drinking his parsley tea without complaint, which caused her to entertain the notion that he might somehow been enhancing its flavor with spirits of some kind. He certainly enjoyed having the company of the Yankee orderlies. She had even caught him playing cards.

He also enjoyed having the little boys in his room for a time every afternoon. As far as she could tell, Joe and Jake seemed to be doing all right. Neither of them mentioned Suzanne or Phelan except in their bedtime prayers. Max Woodard had been moved onto their prayer list, as well. They called him ''Con-el Mac'' and made sure he was blessed every night.

By the seventh day Max had been gone, Maria began to think that perhaps he wasn't coming back. Perhaps he'd been reassigned. Perhaps he'd had such a change of heart regarding his offer to her that he'd asked to be sent someplace else.

It which case, she had been suffering the agony of making and unmaking her decision for nothing. It surprised her somewhat that his being gone wasn't general knowledge. She knew that because Valentina Kinnard came to visit her father and bring him some damson preserves from the Kinnard cellar—she said. But all the while she listened intently to every footfall in the house like a cat listening for the tread of an unwary mouse.

The "mouse" didn't show in this case, and eventually Valentina was driven to ask about Colonel Woodard's whereabouts. Maria told her the truth.

She didn't know.

When Max returned on the ninth day, Maria was in the backyard scrubbing dirty linens, her sleeves rolled above her elbows and her hair coming undone from its braiding and falling into her face. She had been lifting piece after piece of scalding hot laundry out of the iron wash pot with a long stick and carrying it to a wooden tub and washboard to be scrubbed with lye soap.

Jake and Joe ran around and around her with their usual exuberance. She smiled from time to time at their antics in spite of the sorrow she felt at the loss of their mother. There was a fire under the big black pot where the sheets and pillowslips were boiling, and she kept a close eye on them to head off any interest in it. For once, they left it alone, she supposed because they now had all the experience with fires their young minds could handle.

The boys saw Max first, and she had to grab both of them to keep them from rushing his horse. She was surprised to see him and showed it, in spite of her wish not to. He looked...tired. And out of sorts. But he dismounted and endured both boys grabbing him around the knees. Maria went back to her scrubbing, all the while marveling at how glad she was to see him.

Not glad, she immediately decided. *Relieved.* Though why she would have been either, she was hard-pressed to say.

Max picked up Jake and gave Joe to his shadow, Perkins. They all went into the house—just as she expected.

She continued with the washing, letting her mind wander *almost* where it would. She considered the fine morning and the fact that there was breeze enough to dry the sheets quickly when she had them all rinsed and spread on the shrubbery. She considered the birds singing and the smell of the bread she had baking in the oven and the fact that the garden was doing well—but she would have to carry buckets and buckets of water to the plantings later, because of the lack of rain.

She didn't consider Max Woodard—at all—and she was so diligent at it that she didn't realize he was standing just beyond the wash pot. How long he'd been there, she had no idea, and once again she'd jumped because he'd caught her unawares, which was so disconcerting that she kept scrubbing long after that particular sheet needed it.

"How is your father?" he asked without prelude, as he was wont to do.

"I think perhaps he is better," she said, still scrubbing. She glanced at him. He was looking at her intently, and he was still unhappy.

"What's wrong?" she asked.

"Wrong? Nothing—as far as I know. No, that's not true. I had to lock De Graff up again. I arrived back in town just in time to see him go straight to the source of his misery. He was supposedly on duty—and he was drunk. He royally insulted Mrs. Russell on the square and with half the town watching. His language was so vile, it's a wonder the birds didn't fall out of the trees. Mrs. Russell already has her bad opinion of him—us—and he handed her all the verification she would ever require—wrapped up and tied with a bow. The man is an idiot."

Maria didn't say anything. She thought his assessment of the situation was quite accurate.

"This trip turned out to be more than I planned," he said after a moment. "I ended up having to go to Washington and then to Wilmington—by ship—which was…an experience. I'm not a good sailor—much to my father's dismay. He would have preferred not to have a son who is always too seasick to get out of his bunk every voyage he's ever taken. Shippers are supposed to produce better, I suppose. I did get to see him before he goes to London, though. He and my mother came down to Washington while I was there. They're waiting to hear—as am I."

She looked at him, not quite understanding what he meant. Surely he hadn't mentioned anything to them about this exceedingly tentative marriage proposal.

"That was a very broad hint, Maria," he said after a moment. "Have you made your decision?"

She ignored the question. "You told your mother and father about…me?"

"Yes."

"Why did you do that!"

"Why? Because they're my parents and I don't see them very often. Call me peculiar, but I thought the possible marriage of their only son would be of interest to them. I can make no excuses for telling them. When they asked what was new with me, it just fell out of my mouth. And as long as you're already upset about that, you might as well know, I've told my sister, as well. And she will likely tell John and Amanda Howe."

"But I haven't agreed!"

"I know that. They know that, too."

"You didn't tell them…everything, did you?"

"Only that I'd asked you. And that your father was

very ill—so if you said yes to me, we would likely marry in haste so that he can be witness to it.''

''That's all?''

''That's all. My word of honor—for whatever that might be worth to you.''

She vigorously rinsed the sheet.

''Maria,'' he said. ''Will you let go of the washing long enough to tell me if I'm a betrothed man?''

She stopped dunking the sheet and looked at him. It took a great deal of effort on her part to look into his eyes. The mere act of doing so altered her decision one more time.

''Yes,'' she said quietly.

''Yes what?'' he asked.

''Yes, I will let go of the washing. Yes, you are a betrothed man—if the offer still stands.''

He didn't say anything, and he was quiet so long that she reached again for the sheet. He caught her hand, not minding the wetness or the lye soap. He wasn't holding her fast. She could get loose if she wanted, but she made no attempt to pull free.

''Good,'' he said. ''And you give me your word that you will do all you can to make this marriage a success.''

''If I have yours in return,'' she said.

''Good,'' he said again. ''You do. Perkins!'' he suddenly yelled.

Perkins came out of the kitchen on the run, and Max let go of her wet hand to search his pockets. He finally brought out a slip of paper and a small stub of a pencil.

''Turn around,'' he said to the sergeant major, and he used the man's back to bear on while he scribbled something down.

''Have them send this telegram right away,'' he said.

"Yes, Sir!"

"I'll go see your father now," Max said to her. "Alone. I want this all to be done right. People will be watching, and I don't want to set a foot wrong anywhere in the process. I'll come get you when I'm done and we'll talk."

"'We?'" Maria asked, because there didn't seem to be much "we" to this, thus far.

"We," he assured her. "We'll have to decide what is to be done with—" he said as he walked away, giving her no chance to approve or disapprove the plan thus far.

"What?" Maria called after him, because she didn't hear all he said.

But he kept going, disappearing into the kitchen without a backward glance.

He stayed gone a long time. Maria tried to concentrate on the wash. She didn't dare let her mind engage in any second thoughts. It was done. Max Woodard knew her situation. He'd asked to marry her. She'd given her word. No emotional attachments to be found anywhere she looked.

And that was that.

She saw several soldiers arrive and go into the house through the front door. And Mrs. Russell.

Heaven help them if they cross her path, Maria thought.

She finally finished the washing, and she began carrying the water from the iron pot to the garden, bucket by bucket. She diligently used the last of the soapy water in the wooden tub to sprinkle down the bean plants to keep the beetles off. Her back hurt, and she was hungry. She hadn't felt sick in the morning for several days now, and it occurred to her that that heretofore regular event must have been what Max recognized as a symptom of her condition. If he'd arrived here to assume his post this week instead of when he did, he would never have guessed.

And she wouldn't be engaged to be married.

Engaged.

What have you done, Maria Rose?

The only thing she could do, given the circumstances. In spite of her brothers. In spite of Billy.

Oh, Billy. Look what I've come to.

She gave a quiet sigh. Her sudden prospect of marriage left her feeling no less abandoned than the day William Canfield left.

Max had been with her father a long time now. She stood at the edge of the garden, wondering if the news of her impending marriage would have time to reach Texas before it was a done deed.

No, she thought immediately. And it wouldn't matter if it did. The only Canfields in her life now would be Joe and Jake.

When the last of the soapy water was distributed, she turned the wooden tub over to drain and walked toward the house. Mrs. Russell came out of the back door to get the crock of butter that was kept down the well.

"Have you seen Colonel Woodard?" Maria asked her.

"I have—but that will soon be rectified."

"I…don't understand."

"Rejoice, Maria! Rejoice! The man is moving out."

"He's what?"

"He's leaving. Isn't it wonderful? You and your father shall have your home all to yourselves again."

Maria hurried into the house and headed for the back stairs. But she heard a commotion in the front of the house and went in that direction instead. Two soldiers were carrying Max's trunk down the stairs.

She stood back to let them pass, but she didn't ask about Max's whereabouts. She waited for a moment, then went to the kitchen. She found him there, and Mrs. Russell stomping up the back stairs in a huff.

"What a very short engagement," Maria said, more than a little dismayed.

"What?" Max asked.

"What have you said to my father? Why is he throwing you out of the house?"

"He isn't—"

"I saw them carrying out the trunk. Mrs. Russell said you were leaving."

"So I am—but for the sake of appearances. Mr. Markham pointed out—and quite rightly—that I shouldn't be living here under the same roof with you now. There may be at least six people here at all times, but there is no logic to gossip, and I defer to his judgment. Our meeting went quite well, actually. He gives his blessing and expects to see you after his nap. May I ask what kind of wedding you have in mind?"

She looked at him blankly.

"Church or here, so your father can attend," he said.

"Here."

"Attendants?"

"None," she said, thinking of Suzanne. And Nell. Nell would probably be an appropriate bridesmaid for this kind of marriage.

"When will it be?"

"I don't know. I leave that to you."

"All right, I will work for the earliest possible date. What's wrong?" he asked suddenly.

"Nothing."

"You aren't going to faint or anything—?"

"No. I'm quite fine."

He had come closer, and she looked up at him.

"I am quite fine," she said again. She wasn't feeling faint; she was feeling overwhelmed. This was actually happening. She had said yes to Max Woodard, and he was going forward with the plans as if she'd meant it.

She did mean it. She had no choice but to mean it.

No choice.

Chapter Thirteen

Ceily Carscaddon ambushed Maria in the summer kitchen. There was no other word for her sudden appearance outside the doorway mere seconds after Mrs. Russell had gone through it with the rice and broth Maria had made for her father's noon meal.

The kitchen was stifling hot, and Maria all but trampled Ceily trying to get outside and onto the walkway in the hope of finding some small breeze before she was completely overcome.

"Maria!" Ceily whispered urgently, grabbing her hand and pulling her aside, as if she hadn't really expected to find her here and was more than a little worried that she might suddenly take off. "I'm sworn to secrecy, but I just had to come. Dear, *dear* Maria."

Still perplexed, Maria smiled, because Ceily had that kind of effect on people. They had never been close friends, but she had always liked Ceily very much.

"James says I'm not to mention it to a living soul—but I can mention it to you, of course."

"Ceily, what are you talking about?"

"You, silly—and Colonel Woodard. I mean, who

would have thought it? Does Valentina know? No, of course not. It's a secret—''

"Ceily—''

"I know, I know. *No one* is supposed to know about it—but I just had to come, you see? I had to know if I could help—with the wedding or the reception. Or the wedding night," she added, whispering again. "You don't have a mother or any female relative to tell you the things you should know about that, and I *am* a married woman, after all. So tell me—what can I do?"

"Nothing," Maria said, thankful she'd had a little over a week to get used to being engaged so that Ceily's offer regarding the wedding night hadn't completely bowled her over.

"Oh, of course. Suzanne would have explained to you all about being married and sleeping with a man. But I can do something, can't I? Anything at all. All you have to do is say."

"Thank you. I will say—as soon as I need something done. How did you find out about the…" Maria tried, but she just couldn't make herself say the word.

But Ceily didn't require completed questions. "James, of course," she said, whispering again.

"Well, how did he find out?" Maria asked in a normal voice.

"I don't know. The colonel must have mentioned it to his officers, I guess. So when is it?"

"I'm…not sure. Colonel Woodard is making the arrangements—according to his…availability."

"Yes, of course. The United States Army comes first in all things, doesn't it? If there is one thing I've learned in my marriage to James, I've learned that."

Ceily suddenly hugged her. "You clever girl!" she cried. "I still can't believe this! Even if the colonel was living in the same house. Tell me. Tell me *right now*. What did you do to the man to send him on the path to the altar?''

''I—nothing,'' Maria said truthfully.

''Well, whatever you did, Valentina Kinnard is going to hate you for it. I think Acacia was already seeing herself being invited to visit the colonel's parents in Philadelphia.''

''Germantown,'' Maria said absently, because Suzanne had told her that was where Max Woodard was actually from.

''Maybe Valentina would like to be a bridesmaid,'' Ceily said mischievously, putting her hand immediately to her mouth to hide her laugh.

There's no time for bridesmaids, Maria almost said, stopping herself when she realized how it would sound. She looked around at the arrival of a carriage. It stopped in the shade in front of the house, and Perkins jumped down and came trotting across the yard.

''The colonel's compliments, Miss Markham. I'm to tell you that—''

He glanced over his shoulder. The two women in the carriage had disembarked and were coming right behind him. He immediately speeded up his message.

''The colonel's mother and sister just arrived. He wants them to stay here, miss.''

''He what!'' Maria said. The women were nearly in earshot.

''Mother and sister,'' Perkins whispered. ''He wants them to stay here—excuse me now, miss. Colonel's expecting me,'' he added, wisely running for his life.

Maria stood there, speechless.

''Oh, my,'' Ceily whispered beside her. ''Look at those *hats*. Look at those *dresses*.''

The older woman was wearing a very pale mauve dress—almost the color of ashes—with a brilliant turquoise-and-mauve hat and trimmings. The color alone was an indicator of her financial security, that she could travel in a dress of that light color and that kind of fabric and not worry about getting it ruined or dirty. The younger woman had on a shimmering deep green dress that reminded Maria of a cool pond in summertime. Both women were absolutely stunning.

Oh, my, indeed.

"Miss Markham?" the younger woman said, looking expectantly at Ceily.

Of course, they would make that mistake, Maria thought. How could they not? Ceily was well dressed and was worthy of an "Oh, my" in her own right. Maria, on the other hand, looked—and felt—like the scullery maid.

"No, Kate," the older woman said. "I believe this is Maria—may I call you that, my dear?" she asked, extending her hand in Maria's direction.

Maria took it, and the woman squeezed her fingers warmly. "Yes, of course," she said. "I—this is Mrs. Carscaddon."

"Mrs. Lieutenant James Carscaddon," Ceily said with a pride that made the older woman smile.

"I'm very pleased to meet you both," Mrs. Woodard said. "I realize we've caught you quite by surprise, Maria. Max said your father was ill. How is he, my dear?"

"He's better of late," Maria said.

"Now, we have no wish to burden you unduly. I'm sure we can go to one of the hotels."

"No—no, that won't be necessary. There's the room Col— Max had when he was billeted here. I believe you will find it more comfortable than the hotel—at least quieter.''

"You're sure we're not intruding?''

"Very sure,'' Maria said, hoping the lie was convincing. She gave Ceily a desperate look. *Now* she needed help. "Please. All of you. Come inside.''

"And where are the little boys Max told me about?'' Mrs. Woodard asked.

Maria looked at her in surprise. "They're napping. They'll be awake soon.''

"Wonderful,'' Kate said. "I am so looking forward to meeting them.''

Maria looked around at another arrival—Mrs. Russell. She had forgotten all about Mrs. Russell.

But she had no choice but to blunder on and pray earnestly that Mrs. Russell wouldn't spit in anyone's eye.

"Mrs. Russell,'' Maria said. "This is Colonel Woodard's mother and sister. Mrs. Woodard, Miss Kate Woodard—Mrs. Russell.''

Mrs. Russell gave them the barest of nods. "I will be going now, Maria,'' she said, immediately ignoring them. "I see you have no need of my company.''

"Mrs. Russell—'' Maria began, then broke off. There was nothing she could say to placate the woman, and there was no point in trying. "Thank you for your help,'' she said to the woman's retreating back.

"Is she the Mrs. Russell who is Major De Graff's nemesis?'' Kate whispered.

"I—yes,'' Maria said, completely taken aback. Max Woodard may not have told his family the specifics about her—but he'd clearly told them everything else.

"It's very sad, isn't it,'' Kate said. "Life is too short

to waste on hating people. She should take a lesson from you and Max.''

Maria said nothing to that.

''I take it she doesn't know about the coming marriage,'' Kate added.

''No. No one does really—except Ceily—Mrs. Carscaddon.''

She led the way for the women to go inside.

''You must be tired,'' she said to Mrs. Woodard and Kate. ''I'll show you to the room. You can rest for a bit. I was about to make some lemonade for my father. I'll bring you some, as well.''

''Maria, you mustn't feel you have to wait upon us,'' Mrs. Woodard insisted, but that was precisely the way Maria felt. She took her leave as graciously as she could and stopped to check on the boys. The pallet where they should have been sleeping was empty.

She hurried down the hallway to her father's room. He was awake and playing cards with his current orderly.

''Father, have you seen the boys?''

''No, can't say that…I have. Have you…misplaced them?''

''Yes,'' she said. ''And I have to find them before they get into something.'' She hurried out of the room, then stuck her head back inside. ''Colonel Woodard's mother and sister have arrived,'' she said. ''Here,'' she added.

''Good,'' her father said, clearly not recognizing it for the calamity it was. ''Bruno here…will make me…presentable. Then I shall…meet them both. Right… Bruno?''

''Yes, Sir, Mr. Markham,'' Bruno said.

Maria didn't wait to hear any more of the plan. She

hurried down the back stairs, still looking for little boys along the way. Ceily was waiting in the kitchen.

"What can I do?" she said, taking off her hat and gloves.

"I can't find the boys," Maria said. "And I've promised Mrs. Woodard some lemonade—"

"I'll make it," Ceily said.

"Thank you, Ceily," Maria said in relief. "The lemons and the sugar are in the locked pantry. The key is hanging on the peg there. I'm going outside to see if I can find them."

She crossed the backyard, looking behind the summer kitchen, in the garden and in the stable.

No children.

Then she took a deep breath and approached the soldiers camped at the edge of the property.

"I'm looking for the boys," she said. "Have you seen them?"

"Yes, miss, I did. They were heading that way, toward downtown. I would have stopped them if I'd had any idea they'd jumped the fence."

"Thank you," Maria said, and started down the street at a half run, calling as she went.

She came to the Kinnard house, and she still didn't see them.

"That way, Miss Maria," the Kinnard's longtime butler called to her from their upstairs portico.

Maria waved her thanks and kept going—and she kept calling. She caught a glimpse of them as she crossed the main road that led in and out of town.

"Joe! Jake!" she yelled. Both boys broke into a run, Jake's little short legs pumping hard to keep up with his brother.

She ran through a backyard to head them off. She had

a good idea where they were going now—to military headquarters.

Her petticoat got caught in a hedge of wild blackberries at the edge of a vacant lot, and she had to stop to try to get the last decent undergarment she owned free without tearing it. In the end, she just had to jerk it loose, cringing as she did so at the sound of the rip.

She had lost sight of the boys now, but when she took a shortcut through an ally behind the hotel and came out across from the military headquarters, she saw both children disappearing up the stairs to the second floor where Max's office was located.

The street was at least knee-deep in mud and horse droppings, and she ran down to the end of the block to cross on the tall granite stepping stones.

By the time she reached the headquarters, several people had gathered to wait for an audience with the colonel. The private on duty at the foot of the stairs wouldn't let her or anyone else pass.

"No, miss," he insisted. "I can't let you go up there without seeing if the colonel says you can first."

"I've come for the boys—I'm sure you saw them come in," Maria said, trying to get past.

"Miss, you are making trouble for yourself and me. Now go over yonder and sit down!"

"Sir, there's this woman downstairs."

"What woman?" Max said without looking up.

"Don't know, Sir. But if you don't let her come up here, I think I'm going to have to shoot her."

"I don't have the time to see anyone, Briggs."

"Yes, Sir. I said that to her, Sir. More than once. She just ain't listening."

"Did she say what it was about?"

"I reckon she's looking for somebody, Sir."

Perkins suddenly stuck his head in the door. "Sir, Miss Markham's downstairs."

"Miss Markham. Briggs, you didn't say it was Miss Markham."

"Sir, she didn't tell me her name. She didn't tell me nothing but to get out of her way—"

"She's mad, Colonel," Perkins interrupted.

"Well, get her up here, damn it—did you get the boys cleaned up?"

"Some of it, Sir. Them young'uns must have waded through every manure pile between here and home—except Jake. He did a belly flop. It's going to take some major scrubbing to get them fit for decent folks again. Briggs, don't just stand there. Go get the lady!" Perkins barked.

"Yes, Sergeant Major!"

In no time at all, Max could hear Maria coming up the steps. He stood to greet her, and the minute she stepped into the doorway, he knew that Perkins had been correct in his assessment. She was, without a doubt, angry.

"Where are the boys?" she said, her carefully quiet voice belying her riled state.

"Perkins, where exactly are they?" Max asked his sergeant major, but he was looking at Maria. Her hair was coming undone and the color was high in her cheeks. She was out of breath and disheveled, and, he suddenly realized, quite…lovely.

"They're still getting washed up—at the pump, Sir. It's the manure, Sir," Perkins added unnecessarily.

Maria looked at the man in a way that didn't invite further elaboration.

"I want them, please," she said. "And I want them now."

"I take it they are in some kind of trouble," Max said, still trying to keep it light.

"They aren't the only one," she answered.

"Maria, is this about my mother and sister—"

"This is about the boys running off from the house and coming here when they were supposed to be taking a nap—and about you not even wondering for one instant how it is they came to be here or why they weren't accompanied *or* if anyone would be worried."

She stepped forward then, and with no warning whatsoever, smacked him on the arm. Hard. "*This* is about your mother and sister," she said. "Perkins, I want those boys!" she said as she strode out.

Max stood staring after her, fighting down his amusement and finally losing. Desperately in need of marrying or not, she had actually *hit* him. He chuckled to himself and rubbed the place on his arm where her small and he had once thought delicate fist had connected, then walked to the window, watching for her to come out of the building. He supposed that a good swat on the arm of an exasperating male came easily to a girl who had grown up with two brothers. Kate had certainly been known to resort to such a response on more than one occasion.

His amusement abruptly faded. Thanks to the war, Maria had no brothers now—and Kate didn't have much of one.

"Sir," Private Briggs said behind him.

"Now what is it?"

"Another woman, Sir."

"Well, who?" Max said, thinking perhaps Mrs. Russell would like to come hit him, as well.

"Me," Nell Hansen said in the doorway.

"Nell, I *told* you—"

"I know, Briggsie," she said mischievously. "But I just couldn't wait down there. If I'd stayed much longer, a couple of those old biddies would have gotten out the tar and feathers. Colonel Woodard will give me five minutes, won't you, Colonel?" she said, turning her considerable charms on Max, as well.

"It's all right, Briggs—but this is the limit for the day."

"Yes, Sir!" Briggs said, clumping back downstairs to take up his busy post.

"Is it true?" Nell asked as soon as Briggs had gone.

"Is what true?"

"Are you marrying our Maria?"

Max looked at her and didn't answer. Neither did he inquire as to where she had gotten her information.

"Are you?" she persisted. "Tell me."

"I am," Max said after moment.

"Are you fit to marry her? Because if you're not, for God's sake, don't do it. I've watched one friend suffer the miseries of Holy Matrimony, and I don't want to go through watching another one. You and Phelan both—"

"I'm not like Phelan Canfield," he interrupted.

"No? How do you know? Maybe you're worse. You were both in prisons during the war. He took to drink to keep from thinking about it—and you. I don't know what *you* do to get by. I keep thinking about when Suzanne and Maria and I were little girls, you know? The three of us, we used to plan our weddings all the time. We'd dress up in these old lace curtains our mamas gave us. Maria—Maria wanted a candlelight wedding ceremony with flowers and cut-glass candelabras all around the room. And afterward her new husband would waltz her around the floor. Just her and him—with everybody else looking on—and a fiddler playing a beautiful and sad three-quarter-time waltz. She's the only one of us left to—''

Nell abruptly stopped, and Max thought for a moment she was going to cry, but she recovered quickly. ''I just don't want you to hurt her, all right?''

''It's not my intention to do so,'' Max said.

''Good.'' She was looking at him intently. ''You're not a bit like Billy,'' she said after a moment.

''If that's all, I'm very busy this afternoon,'' Max said. He was *not* interested in hearing a point-by-point comparison to the dead fiancé.

''No, it's not all,'' she said bluntly. ''I came to ask you about my mother.''

''Your mother,'' Max said, drawing a blank.

''She was staying with Suzanne when she died in the fire. That's what my mother does for her living—she looks after sick people. She won't take any money from me, and it's hard for her to go live with any of our family—because of what I am. I was wondering if maybe you could hire her to help out with Mr. Markham—since you're going to be the son-in-law and you've got the coin.''

''He has two male attendants from the army hospital already.''

''Then hire her to help Maria with the boys. She loves those two little hell-raisers. It would help her a lot if she had them to take her mind off what happened to Suzanne. Hire her to do that—or let her cook or whatever else Maria needs. What I'm asking is that you give her something to do. So she won't be blaming herself because she didn't die when Suzanne did—and it isn't like Maria doesn't need the help. Maria's all worn out trying to keep her daddy alive and looking after Suzanne's children. You should have seen her before the war, Woodard. She doesn't look much like she used to then. She was so pretty. It was no wonder Billy and Phelan both wanted to marry her—''

''Anything else?'' Max interrupted.

''Yes. Don't tell either one of them I said anything about this. My mother won't work for you if she thinks I had a hand in it. Will you help me out here, or not?''

''I'll...consider it.''

She looked at him in surprise—as if his consideration was much more than she ever expected.

''All right then,'' she said, smiling. ''Good. You know what, Woodard? Maria might be better off married to you after all.''

Max sat down at his desk after Nell had gone. He had papers to read and sign, reports to be made and sent to Washington, but he didn't do any of it. He just sat—until he realized Perkins had come to stand in his usual spot.

''Perkins,'' Max said.

''Yes, Sir!''

''I want you to find me some cut-crystal candleholders.''

Chapter Fourteen

Maria stood on a low stool in the middle of her bedchamber. The woman, who had arrived on the doorstep with the rest of Mrs. Woodard's baggage, circled her intently with her mouth full of straight pins. The ivory satin gown Maria reluctantly wore, which had also accompanied Mrs. Woodard on her trip south, was still unfinished. The side seams of the bodice had only been loosely basted, and there was a whole basket full of satin roses of varied shades of white and ivory and ecru yet to be sewn onto the skirt and train. The woman pulled and pinned and gave small sighs, which Maria could only interpret as barely restrained responses to the utterly hopeless. She had asked the woman her name at one point, only to have the question dismissed with a wave of her hand. Clearly, the woman had no need for pleasantries when she sewed.

Until this moment, Maria hadn't given a thought to what she would be married in. She certainly hadn't considered anything so elegant as this. It was far too beautiful for her kind of bride, and she had tried every way she could to refuse it.

''Please don't say no, my dear,'' Mrs. Woodard said.

"I know you have your Southern pride—Mrs. Howe, John's wife—explained that to me very specifically. She also explained that for Max's sake, you might be willing to suffer this small gesture of mine—and I most sincerely ask you to do so. I expect any number of his officers may be attending the ceremony. Will you do this for him—and for me?"

Maria had capitulated—in what she saw as likely a whole series of capitulations before this thing was done. A bunch of strange soldiers baked and cooked in the summer kitchen. Ceily and Mrs. Woodard and Kate were on the back porch—still in their finery—trying to scrub the smell off Joe and Jake. To say that she barely recognized her life anymore would be beyond understatement.

There was also the matter of hitting the groom. Maria had been so angry with him for not telling her his mother and sister were arriving. To let them just *appear* with no warning like that, when she looked so awful, so totally unpresentable. And then having the boys run off to see him without permission had only added fuel to her already justified ire. It had simply been the last straw. She'd been angry with Max Woodard before, but this time she'd resorted to violence.

"Turn, turn, turn!" the woman said around the pins in her mouth. "Stop!"

Not for one minute had Maria expected his family to come here for the wedding, much less bearing a dress, a coronet, tulle veil *and* a more than disconcerted seamstress. And even if it had occurred to her, she would never have expected to be received with such open acceptance from the women in Max Woodard's family. She was completely unnerved by the fact that Mrs.

Woodard and Kate seemed to know everything about her.

Almost everything.

She couldn't for the life of her imagine Max sitting in a parlor somewhere, reciting information about this Miss Markham he suddenly planned to marry. But he must have. They knew about her father's illness, about Suzanne and the boys, and, Maria suspected, Phelan's disappearance. If Mrs. Woodard was the least bit scandalized at the haste associated with the marriage, it certainly didn't show. Mrs. Woodard had spent a long while with Maria's father after she arrived, and he now thought she was the most gracious woman he'd ever met in his life, Yankee or not. And she was—which only added to Maria's dismay. How could the woman possibly be at ease with her son's plan to marry an embittered Rebel like Maria Rose Markham?

Maria looked around at a soft knock on the door. Ceily Carscaddon peeped in.

"I've been invited to dinner here tomorrow night," she said.

"Is there going to be a dinner?" Maria asked.

"So I'm told," Ceily assured her. "We've got the boys all shined and polished again—and what a job *that* was. James has come to fetch me, so I'm going home—he's invited tomorrow, too, of course. Acacia Kinnard and Valentina are downstairs. And Mrs. Russell and Mrs. Justice. My guess is Mrs. Russell told Acacia the colonel's mother was here—and she didn't believe a word of it and had to come see for herself. I expect poor Mrs. Justice simply got caught in the stampede. And I *know* the Kinnards will have extracted dinner invitations of their own by the time the dust clears."

"We won't have enough chairs," Maria said.

"Maria, Maria, haven't you noticed? The Yankee army has only to command, 'Let there be seating,' and there will be chairs aplenty. I'm thinking this is going to be a rather formal affair. Do you have a suitable dress?"

"Of course I don't have a suitable dress. I haven't had a suitable dress since before the war."

"That's what I thought. So I'm going to lend you one of mine. I think the rose silk will fit you and look wonderful with your color. I'm going to take a Yankee soldier with me now and send it back with him. So 'bye—and you're going to make a lovely bride," she added appreciatively.

Ceily closed the door, only to open it again with one last bulletin before she disappeared.

"The groom is here, by the way. He said something about speaking with your father."

The groom.

Maria did *not* want to encounter the groom.

"James says he's in a bit of a huff. I couldn't tell by looking at him, but James could. See you tomorrow!"

"Ceily, thank you!" Maria called after her, not knowing if Ceily heard her or not.

She sighed and gave herself up to twirling on the stool again. If Max was in a bad mood, she didn't have to think very hard to conclude why. She would have to see him, of course—huff or not. She was marrying the man—as far as she knew. In light of the smack she had given him, he could have gone to see her father in order to withdraw his offer of matrimony.

She heard the door to her father's room open and close, then heavy footsteps down the back stairs.

Good, she thought. If Max was going downstairs, he would surely be cornered by Valentina Kinnard. And that should keep him busy for a time—until Maria could shore up enough nerve to face him. She had no intention of apologizing—and oh, how her late mother would frown at that. Whatever the provocation, true ladies did *not* go around hitting.

The seamstress put in the last pin and urged Maria off the stool and out of the wedding gown, completely ignoring whatever modesty Maria might have wanted to uphold. Maria put on her everyday dress quickly in a feeble effort to hide her ragged underpinnings, but the woman was totally absorbed in her alterations and paid Maria no attention whatsoever.

Maria looked in both directions before she stepped out into the hallway. It was empty, but she had no idea how long it would stay that way. She decided to go down the main stairs—but when she reached the top step, she heard Mrs. Woodard calling her. She immediately turned and hurried to the back stairs, just in case Mrs. Woodard had Max with her. As she descended, she heard someone calling him, as well, and she realized too late that he was trying to make his own escape and coming up the stairs in the opposite direction.

He didn't say anything, and neither did she. He stopped on a step below her; it put him directly into the shaft of sunlight from the porthole window that kept the stairs from being so dark.

She stared down at him, wondering how it was that she had never really noticed much about him before, and why now, at this moment, she was seeing everything. The color of his hair—brown and several shades lighter than hers. The stubble on his chin and the slight cleft. His straight brows. His finely shaped mouth…

He took a step upward. And then another.

They were at eye level.

Had she noticed the piercing blueness of his eyes before? Perhaps not. Perhaps she didn't dare register such things, because he would become a man and not merely an enemy.

His eyes were so sad—that, she had noticed. He was looking at her so gravely.

Such pain.

What happened to you? she thought. *What terrible thing did you see—or do?*

Maria had no sense that he reached for her, nor she for him, but she was in his arms somehow. He held her tightly, both of them caught in whatever this moment was. Their foreheads touched; their breaths mingled. And suddenly his mouth was on hers. She gave a soft moan, completely overwhelmed by the feel and the taste of him. It was as if she suddenly couldn't get close enough, couldn't touch him enough, kiss him enough. She had never felt such need, such hunger.

She held on to him, her fingers digging into the back of his tunic.

Some part of her registered the hated uniform—but her only reality was *him* and not the dominance he represented. Nothing else mattered. She didn't care who she was or where she was or that people still called both of them from below.

"Maria!"

"Colonel Woodard!"

He broke away just long enough to look into her eyes—he was as incredulous at what was happening as she was—and then his mouth found hers again.

"Maria!" someone said sharply at the bottom of the stairs—Mrs. Russell.

He released her abruptly. "Go!" he whispered, sending her on down the steps, reaching out to caress her cheek as she slipped from his grasp. She could still feel the brush of his fingers against her mouth as she stepped reeling into the kitchen.

"What's wrong with you?" Mrs. Russell demanded, catching her arm. "Are you about to faint again? Sit down."

"No," Maria assured her. "I'm fine."

It wasn't faintness she felt. It was white-hot carnal desire, the kind that surely must be a sin. She didn't want to sit. She wanted to look at herself in the mottled washstand mirror by the back door. Surely, surely what she had felt on the stairs, what she still felt, must show. Had Ceily experienced this with James? Or Suzanne with Phelan? The only thing she knew with certainty was that she had never felt like this with Billy, even the night they parted.

"There you are, Maria!" Max's mother said, coming in from the central hall. "We have two handsome young gentlemen who are anxious to see you."

Kate was already bringing the boys in, both of them with clean, shiny faces and still wet hair and both of them wrapped in flannel.

"Well, who is this?" Maria said, kneeling down to see them.

"It's me, Joe," Joe said, grinning. "And this is Jake."

"*My* Joe and Jake? It can't be!" Maria cried, hugging them both in spite of her pretended lack of recognition. "Mmm—sweet, *clean* boys."

"Joe was stinky," Jake said, grinning his lopsided grin.

"Was not," Joe said. "*You* fell in the manure—not me."

"Come on, come on," Maria said. "Let's go get your

clothes on so you can have some supper—tell Mrs. Woodard and Kate thank you very much for making you presentable again.''

''Thank you very much,'' Joe said dutifully.

''Wood and Cake!'' Jake said, breaking into a giggle and a run.

Maria intended to take the boys up the back stairs, but dashing down the wide hallway with their flannel wraps flying behind them was infinitely more exciting. She ran after them, and she didn't catch up until they were halfway up the stairs—and naked. She snatched up the discarded flannel as she went, but they weren't about to stop long enough to be wrapped again. There was nothing to do but shoo them along ahead of her toward the small dressing room that had been turned in to a nursery of sorts and hope that the seamstress didn't decide to emerge from her sewing. Maria already had the distinct feeling that the woman thought she'd been dragged to the most godless place on the face of this earth. Little naked boys running about would surely erase all doubt.

''This way, this way,'' Maria whispered in an effort to steer the boys from a distance.

For once, they actually went in the direction Maria intended. Her father's door stood ajar, and she could see Max in the room, his gaze holding hers as she passed.

Max stood quietly, waiting for Mr. Markham to wake enough to notice that he had company. He didn't mind the wait. The truth of the matter was that he was very glad to have a moment to recover from his encounter with Maria on the stairs—if he could. Even the glimpse of her at the door just now was enough to stir his desire again.

Maria.

What an unexpected development *that* was. Would she ever and always surprise him?

Apparently so, he decided.

"Maxwell," the old man said, opening his eyes. "Welcome to the…house of…all manner of…bedlam, tumult and…turmoil. And that's only on the…ground floor. Sit down…my boy. It's safer in…here, is it not…Bruno?"

"Yes, sir," the orderly assured him.

"Have you seen…Maria?" the old man asked.

"Briefly," Max said.

"I hear…my daughter was having a…fitting of some sort in…her bedchamber. Or perhaps it was a…fit…she was having. Your lovely mother…had the presence…of mind…to bring a half-constructed…wedding gown… with her *and* the seamstress to do…the sewing. It took some doing…to get Maria Rose to agree…to accept it, but accept it…she has."

"Is all this too much of a bother for you, sir?" Max asked him.

"Me? No, indeed. I live for adventure…and I get precious little of it…these days. I understand…in spite of…all the excitement going on…there may actually…be some dinner in the offing…at some point…this evening. And right now…Bruno and I…are biding our time, ever hopeful—"

Mr. Markham closed his eyes and struggled to catch his breath. Max stood to take his leave. The old man was not nearly so improved as he might have first seemed. "I'll leave you to that, then, sir. Perhaps I can hurry them along in the kitchen."

But Mr. Markham motioned him closer, and Max bent down to hear what he had to say.

"Your regimental surgeon…is a…blunt man. And

my…own doctor agrees with his…opinion. The wedding…must be…soon, Maxwell. If I am…to see it. Make that…seamstress…sew fast. Do you…understand?''

"I understand," Max said. And he did. He had seen the look of death too many times in the prison not to.

"Don't worry Maria…about it. Just…make haste. Will you do…that?''

"I will," Max said.

The old man nodded and closed his eyes.

Max stepped from the room into the hallway. Valentina Kinnard stood hovering outside the door.

"I am so ashamed," she whispered, leaning close.

Max looked at her, expecting her to elaborate. She didn't.

"I don't understand," he said.

"What *must* you think of us here? It's no wonder you've moved out of this house—what with Maria Markham throwing herself at you like that."

"I don't know what you mean."

"How very gallant of you, Colonel, to try to protect her reputation. But I saw what she did just now on the stairs. I saw everything—''

"Not quite everything, Miss Kinnard." She had clearly missed his enjoyment of it. "As long as you're guarding the upper hallway and back stairs, would you happen to have seen where Maria went just now?" he asked.

"Oh, it's safe, Colonel Woodard. Truly. She's well occupied in the nursery—dressing the boys and giving them their supper. You don't have to worry about any more of those…those—*incidents* with her. Honestly, she's becoming just like that friend of hers, Nell. But my mother will speak to her, and you won't be troubled again, I can assure—''

"Excuse me, Miss Kinnard," he interrupted, moving by her. He wasn't quite sure which room was the nursery, but he could hear Maria singing. As he came closer, he recognized that same song again, Trooper Hazeltine's song.

Bushes and Briars.

She had a lovely voice—soft and soothing. He couldn't hear anything from the boys at all.

He quietly opened the door and went inside, in spite of Valentina's gasp. Maria was kneeling by the cot where both Joe and Jake lay quietly on the verge of sleep. Maria looked surprised to see him, but she didn't stop singing. The room was hot and stuffy. He removed the bowls that had held the children's cornbread and milk supper from a nearby chair and sat down. Then, he took the fan from her hand and began fanning the boys for her. She suffered his participation without comment, but her cheeks grew pink. She was quite undone by what had happened on the stairs, he suddenly realized. She was embarrassed, while he, on the other hand, couldn't be more complimented.

Jake opened his eyes long enough to grin and then closed them again. Joe appeared to be already asleep. Both of them were worn out by their adventure—or the consequences of it. Max wondered idly if his mother had ever scrubbed a little boy clean before. He had certainly gotten dirty as a child—but he'd always had a nanny to make him right again. He couldn't help but think of Kate and how very much of her own lost boy she must see in these two.

Maria stopped singing. Neither child stirred. She

glanced at him. She couldn't get out unless he moved, and he wasn't moving. He stopped fanning.

"Your father has asked me not to worry you, but I think you should know," he said quietly, more because he thought Valentina might have an ear to the keyhole than to keep from waking the boys.

Maria looked at him with alarm. Jake stirred suddenly, and she reached out to pat his back. Max took up fanning again.

"He asks that the wedding take place quickly," he continued after a moment, his voice still low.

Maria seemed poised to ask a question, but then she clearly understood the implication of what he was saying and looked away from him. He could see her take a quiet breath, the rise and fall of her breasts.

"I see," she said. "What was to have been an excuse has become an actual reason."

"I intend to oblige him. Is that all right with you?" he asked.

She didn't say anything.

"I would appreciate it if you would say what's on your mind."

She gave a soft laugh and shook her head. "Very well. I'm feeling trapped. Completely, utterly trapped. But you wouldn't understand that."

"Wouldn't I?" he asked. "I have had some… experience with that sensation. Enough to know there is only one thing to be done."

"And what is that?"

"You have to realize your options. And once you've done that, you either pick one and damn the consequences or you simply endure."

She was looking at him now, directly into his eyes in that unsettling way she had.

"There is one other thing," he said.

"What is it?"

"Valentina saw what happened—on the stairs."

"Oh, no!" Maria said.

"It doesn't matter. The marriage will cancel out anything Valentina decides to tell."

"Are you certain you want to have a marriage? I have no explanation for what Valentina saw. I was..." She blushed and looked away.

"I am certain," he said without hesitation. "It's only in that song you were singing that a man is put off by a woman's so-called boldness. The rest of us are flattered beyond words."

She gave him a perplexed look, but she didn't say anything more.

"We'll just have to move everything forward, which needs doing anyway, for your father's sake. Just be prepared to get a lecture on proper behavior from Mrs. Kinnard."

"I shall certainly look forward to that," she said with just enough of what he was beginning to realize was her characteristic drollness to make him want to smile. He also wanted to touch her again. And taste her. His mind filled with the memory of their "incident" on the stairs. At that moment she had needed him, in precisely the way *he* needed her.

He abruptly stood and walked to the door, then turned to say one more thing. "I warn you now that getting everything done quickly probably won't meet local standards—so try not to hit me again, all right?"

Chapter Fifteen

"Carscaddon is about to faint."

"Is she?" Max glanced at his sister, but he didn't stop rocking Jake, who hovered on the edge of sleep.

Kate came into the room and sat down on the footstool nearby. "Not *she*. *He*. Being the only representative of the occupation army *and* the entire Yankee population at a blatantly Confederate dinner table is clearly not his cup of tea."

"He'll survive," Max said, and Kate smiled. She reached out to touch Jake's small hand.

"How is this one—he's not sick, is he?"

"No. It was just a nightmare."

"About the fire?"

"Yes, I think so."

"Why didn't you tell Maria you were the one who got them out of that burning house? She didn't know—until I told her."

"It never came up," he said.

"Max—"

"What?" he said pointedly.

"What is going on?"

"I don't know what you mean."

"I mean, my darling brother, you omitted one little detail about this so-called mutually beneficial marriage of yours—"

"I told you the situation as I see it."

"And you left out the part that you are totally smitten."

"I am not 'smitten.'"

"Well, of course you are. You look at Maria the exact same way John Howe looks at Amanda."

"And how is that?"

"*Smitten,*" Kate insisted. "And believe me, I am an authority."

"I told you I respected Maria and admired her."

"You didn't say you'd die for her, go into a burning house for her."

"I went for the boys."

"Whom she dearly loves."

He took a quiet breath so as not to disturb Jake.

"Have you seen Harry lately?" he asked, because he suddenly felt that Kate wanted to talk about her son.

"Not lately," she said. She tried to smile, but didn't quite make it. "He's off somewhere with the senior Howes. They really don't like for me to know much about his comings and goings. They don't trust me to maintain my discretion, I suppose." She gave a small shrug.

"About Maria," she said, renewing her inquest.

"Shouldn't you go back to the table and protect poor old Carscaddon?" Max said pointedly.

"He'll survive," she said, throwing his words back at him. "Max, I don't think you realize how changed you are."

"For the better, I hope."

"Yes," she said. "And no."

"Kate—"

"You're more at peace than I've seen you since the war ended—but you've walled yourself off from your feelings, Maxwell. I know you had to—so you could survive what happened to you in the war and in the prison—and so you could get past John's leaving you in that horrible place. I just think you should be aware of it, that's all. So you don't mess up a real chance for happiness with a woman you truly care about."

"Kate, it's all right. *I'm* all right."

She looked at him, then at Jake. "Yes," she said after a moment. "That child loves you, you know. And his brother does, as well. It was clear when he woke up afraid just now, no one would do but you."

"Well, neither of them seem to notice the uniform."

"But the thing is, Max, there's more to this situation than you and Maria wanting to take care of these boys and her making you more acceptable to the Rebel populace—"

"Kate, enough. Will you please return to the table now and save Carscaddon? I'll be down shortly."

"Aren't you going to enlighten me at all?"

"About what?"

"About where Mother has gone for starters—that's why I came up here—to find her. And why are all those unescorted women downstairs? Why are we having this clearly important dinner tonight instead of tomorrow night as planned, and why does Perkins have his 'sack and burn' face on?"

"Mother and the Methodist minister are in with Mr. Markham. The man—and his doctors—feel that he doesn't have much time. He wants me to get the marriage done before he dies. Unfortunately, I need Mrs.

Russell and Mrs. Kinnard and Mrs. Justice to keep the haste required as respectable as possible.''

''Then why are Valentina and her mother ready to pounce on Maria? When you took Jake back upstairs, and it looked as if she might go with you, I thought they both were going to leap out of their chairs and restrain her bodily.''

''They aren't privy to the wedding plans.''

''You mean Mrs. Kinnard has hopes for Valentina and doesn't know you're already taken.''

''Correct.''

''So when are you going to enlighten *them?*''

''Any minute now,'' he said. There was a sudden commotion outside in the hall. It continued down the main stairs.

''What on earth is that?'' Kate asked.

''That would likely be Perkins and Mother dragging the minister downstairs so he can announce the impending marriage.''

''He's not willing to do that?''

''I doubt it. I'm asking him to go against the way things are done here. But I have every confidence Mother will bring him around gently, however. And if she can't, there's always Perkins. If the minister is lucky, he might even get some cake and coffee out of it.''

Kate looked at him, then threw up her hands and laughed. ''Leave it to my brother to make the already exciting absolutely sensational.''

''I do my best,'' he said, smiling.

''And have as long as I can remember. So when will the nuptials be?''

''Wednesday.''

''Wednesday!''

''Shh-hh. Don't wake the boy.''

"Max, that is two days away. You can't have a wedding by Wednesday."

"Indeed, I can. You yourself saw Perkins's 'sack and burn' face. And if all goes according to plan, the minister is going to ask those women downstairs to help me."

"Let me see if I understand this. You expect Mrs. Kinnard to help you marry Maria—when she's got plans for you and her own daughter."

"That's right," he said.

"And that hateful Mrs. Russell—whose idea of a happy occasion would be to wear a red dress to your funeral."

"That's right," he said again.

"And you think they'll do it because it comes from the minister and not you."

"Exactly."

"You are insane."

"Be that as it may," he said, refusing to be daunted by mere logic.

Kate leaned back and smiled again. "Well. Wednesday. I think—"

She stopped because Maria appeared in the doorway.

"I think I will go give poor old Carscaddon some moral support, after all," Kate abruptly decided, taking her leave. She gave Maria a brief hug and whispered something in her ear on her way out the door.

Max put Jake in his bed beside his brother, delaying a moment to see if the rocking took. The boy slept on.

Maria waited for him in the hallway.

"Are you ready to see the elephant?" he asked when he joined her.

"What?"

"See the elephant," he said. "Until a soldier has gone into battle, he hasn't 'seen the elephant.'"

"I don't know if I am or not," she said, looking up at him.

"Are you all right?"

"I'm not going to faint, if that's what you mean." She shook her head. "How can you be so…?"

"So what?" he asked when she didn't go on.

"So calm about all this."

"I can assure you that, at the moment, I have no kinship with calmness whatsoever."

"I still don't know why you're doing this."

"I've told you why."

He stared into her eyes as long as she would let him, then took out his pocket watch. It was well past nine. He didn't have much time to get the announcement made, suffer the immediate repercussions, and still uphold the existing ten o'clock curfew—which he was determined to do.

"Last chance," he said.

"It's too late for last chances," she said. "I have given you my word. If the elephant is ready, so am I."

He offered her his arm, and surprisingly she took it, until they reached the head of the stairs. He followed her down the steps, thinking all the while about what had happened on the other set of stairs.

The minister was standing at the head of the table by Mr. Markham's empty chair when they entered the dining room. Neither Max nor Maria took their seats. Instead, they stood together just inside the doorway. It was clear to Max that only his family—and somehow the Carscaddons—had any idea of what was about to transpire.

"Sir," Max said, giving the minister his cue.

"Yes. Yes, indeed," the man said. "Now that you are both here, I will begin. I've come here tonight—at Mr.

Markham's invitation and with his permission—to make a very special announcement. As you all know, my dear friend is very ill. He has made a last request of me—and Colonel Woodard—and Maria—which may at first seem unusual, but is not at all—given the circumstances. I trust you will, in Christian charity, extend to the three of us all the help we may need to accomplish Mr. Markham's wish.

"I would, therefore, without further delay, like to announce the coming marriage of Colonel Maxwell Prieson Woodard to Miss Maria Rose Markham. The ceremony will be held…here?" He looked pointedly at Max.

"Wednesday evening," Max said, causing Maria to give him approximately the same startled look his sister had.

The minister, on the other hand, didn't seem to be the least bit intimidated by the time frame. "Wednesday evening," the man repeated. "As you can see this is very imminent. Mrs. Kinnard and Mrs. Russell—Mr. Markham has asked that you handle the guest list. The colonel will advise you as to who among the military officers *must* be invited, and Maria will give you her particular preferences. Then, we are to fill in with invitations to other local persons, as available space dictates. You ladies will know best who should be included—"

"That won't do," Mrs. Justice said from her position well below the salt, startling everyone with her daring, including herself.

"Mrs. Justice?" the minister said.

She looked panicked for a moment, then pulled herself together.

"Well," she said. "This is an important occasion." She cleared her throat. Several times. "Only a few people can be accommodated here in the house—and given the situation, that is as it should be. But there must be a way to include more people. I was thinking if it was done in three…tiers—''

"Tiers?" Mrs. Kinnard interrupted. "Mrs. Justice, what *are* you talking about?"

"I'm sure Mrs. Justice is about to tell us," the minister said. "Go on, Mrs. Justice."

"Well…the notion came to me the minute I heard the word 'marriage.' Just like that," she said, snapping her fingers. "If the wedding was held in the upstairs hallway—it's very wide, you see—then Bud—I mean, Mr. Markham—could be a part of it without having to venture very far—or at all. The persons who stand with Maria and the colonel would be the *first* tier. And then there can be those who are *in* the house, but stay downstairs during the ceremony. That would be the *second* tier. Then, there should also be guests who participate in a reception only—a special reception somewhere, you see—maybe in the yard if the weather is fine—for those who can't witness the actual ceremony *or* be inside the house. So no one will feel slighted. That's what I think…" she concluded, her boldness abruptly leaving her.

"What an excellent idea," Max's mother said. "We certainly don't want hard feelings because of the lack of an invitation. Don't you agree, Mrs. Kinnard?"

Mrs. Kinnard sat stonily next to Valentina, who looked ready to bolt from the table.

"I'm sure I don't—"

"Mrs. Kinnard," Max interrupted. "Before I forget it, I need your husband to come to my office to see me as soon as he returns from his business trip. At his convenience, of course."

The woman looked at him. Max could feel her weighing the import of his remark and once again trying to decide whether or not to offend him. He watched her as she re-evaluated her objectives. If she couldn't advance her daughter, then she would advance her husband.

"I...don't see any reason why there can't be three sets of invitations," she said after a moment. "Valentina has a beautiful hand. She will help write those of first importance. We shall need the list right away—and the vellum cards, as well as someone who will personally deliver them and wait for the response—we simply cannot allow any leeway in waiting for RSVPs if the wedding is to be Wednesday evening. They will have to answer immediately or be passed by."

Valentina took a deep breath, and then another, as if she might make good her previous fainting threat. But she didn't say anything.

"The reception must be in keeping with your position, Colonel," Mrs. Kinnard continued, clearly recovered and feeling her power now. "It will take much effort—more than I or Mrs. Russell can supply ourselves."

"I will see to it that you and Mrs. Russell have all the help you need. My sergeant major will be your liaison. You have only to tell him your needs and he will see to it."

Max thought at first that Mrs. Russell was going to balk, but, apparently, having a Yankee soldier at her beck and call had its appeal.

"Is it all settled then?" the minister asked. "I see we are fast approaching curfew."

There was a murmuring of assent.

"Then I expect you will all want to meet about this again tomorrow. For now, we must bid each other good night."

Max glanced at Maria. She looked so...determined—

the way she had at the train station that first day. She was the obedient daughter, and her father had spoken.

He shook the minister's hand and accepted Carscaddon's flustered congratulations. Then he moved into his mother's embrace, followed by Kate's, realizing as he did so that Perkins waited in the hall and that he did indeed have on his "sack and burn" face. But it was Perkins's pacing back and forth that got Max's attention.

"I have to see about this," he said to Maria.

"What is it?" Max asked as soon as he and Perkins had walked out of earshot.

"I got them glass candle-holding things," Perkins said. "About a dozen. And I got a fiddler what can play a decent waltz, and a bunch of the boys lined up what know how to make a brush arbor in a hurry—if you're wanting to hold any of this here wedding outside and the weather turns iffy."

"And?" Max said, because none of these announcements were enough to make Perkins agitated.

"The son of a bitch who set the fire what killed Mrs. Canfield—I think we got him treed, Sir."

"Who? Where?" Max asked, lowering his voice.

"Name's Jimmy Julian, Sir. His uncle's got a farm six or seven miles out of town. I had some of the boys keeping a watch on the place because I heard here and there he might have had something to do with all this incendiary activity around town. Sure enough, him and his men have showed up there."

"What men?"

"He runs with a bunch that claim to be Union veterans. I'm thinking most of them sat out the war safe as you please up in the mountains—just like he did. Anyways, Sir, seems he thinks we need help keeping these ex-Rebs in line—especially in the western counties—so he'd got himself a little 'army' organized. He comes back here every now and then to show off for his kinfolk. I reckon he found out about that thing on the street between De Graff and Phelan Canfield, Sir, and he thought he'd show Canfield what was what.''

''How many of them do you think there are?''

''About a dozen, Sir. There's a lot more of them altogether—but he didn't bring the rest of them with him this time.''

''Has he got any kind of authority or is he just doing this out of the goodness of his heart?''

''No authority that I know of, Sir—but he sure as hell acts like he thinks some kind of free hand from the governor is on the way.''

''Then I expect we better get him before that happens,'' Max said, turning and heading back to the dining room. ''Carscaddon!''

''Sir!'' the lieutenant barked.

''You're in charge of the wedding!''

''Me, Sir?''

''Yes, damn it, you! Unless you think Mrs. Carscaddon can handle a company of soldiers well enough to get it done.''

''I expect she can, Sir,'' Carscaddon said, glancing appreciatively at his wife.

''Perkins is going with me. You'll have to take over as liaison for Mrs. Kinnard and Mrs. Russell. Whatever they want—you do. Understand?''

''Yes, Sir!''

''Where's Maria?''

''Here,'' she said from the dining room. She had a basket of leftover biscuits in her hands.

''I have to go,'' he said. ''I'll be back in time for the wedding.''

She nodded, putting the basket down on the table, then picking it up again.

"Maria," he said.

She looked up at him. The look held. And that was all he wanted.

Chapter Sixteen

I can't believe it.

Maria stood transfixed, staring at herself in the full-length mirror. The hastily finished dress fit perfectly. And her hair...Kate had performed some kind of miracle with her hair. How long had it been since she'd looked anything like this? Years.

Years.

"I remember you," she whispered.

"Did you say something, Maria?" Kate asked.

"No," Maria said. She took a deep breath and reached for the velvet case that held the garnet earrings, but she kept fumbling with the catch.

"I'll do it," Kate said, taking it from her hands and opening it. "Ah. These must be the ones Hatcher stole from you."

Maria looked at her.

"What?" Kate asked.

"I-it just surprises me that you know about them."

"Max said they were a parting gift from your brothers and that both of them were killed at Gettysburg."

Maria looked away, still trying to reconcile herself to

this openness Max Woodard had with his people. About the small things, in any event.

"It will please him very much that you're wearing them," Kate said.

"I doubt that."

"Well, of course, it will. It's really a very kind gesture on your part. If you wear them today, on your wedding day, as your brothers intended, then it will mean that you accept Max and all that he must represent to you. You see?"

Maria did see. But she didn't say so.

"Come sit down," Kate said, leading her to a small table and placing a cushion on it, then spreading out a muslin sheet over all of it so that she could lift her skirts and sit and not muss the roses on the train.

Maria took another deep breath and asked the question that had preyed upon her mind all day.

"Do you think—" Maria stopped.

"What?" Kate asked.

"Do you think he'll make it to the wedding?"

"Of course he will."

"We don't even know where he is."

"Max will be here, Maria. He may be late. He may even arrive a little grumpy and rough around the edges— but he'll be here."

With Kate's help, Maria sat down. And she tried to feel reassured. All these people, in the house and out- side—and Maria Rose Markham all dressed up and no- where to go. What an incredible humiliation it would be if Max Woodard didn't show up for the ceremony— almost as humiliating as the real reason for it. Her preg- nancy didn't show, and she supposed that she could be grateful for that. Valentina Kinnard had come into the room twice on various and sundry errands, and the closer it came to the appointed hour and Max hadn't arrived, the more elated she grew.

Someone tapped lightly on the door, and Maria braced herself, expecting the increasingly happy Valentina again.

"I'll bet that's news of him now," Kate said. "Yes?" she called.

Mrs. Justice opened the door. "Maria, Warrie Hansen is here. She wants to see you. Acacia doesn't much want her up here, but I thought you should say if she can or not."

"Of course, she can," Maria said.

"That's what I thought," Mrs. Justice said. "I'll go get her."

Warrie arrived shortly. She looked…better than when Maria had last seen her.

"I've been trying to see you for two days," Warrie said, hurrying into the room to take both of Maria's hands. "Lordy, what a sight you are. Your mama—well, she'd cry her eyes out, wouldn't she? She was like that, so tender-hearted about things."

"What did you want to see me about?"

"Your Yankee colonel," Warrie said. "He's done hired me—to help take care of them young'uns. I'm telling you, Maria, I tried not to like him, but he sent word for me to come and do this—and I feel like the sun's come out after a rainy day. But I got enough sense to know I need to ask you, too. Is it all right that I come here and work? I believe I can help you, darling. You know I love you—and those boys. Might be, I'm a kind of a wedding present," she said, laughing softly.

"I think maybe you are," Maria said. "Thank you, Warrie. I need you."

"Well, that's music to my ears. Now. Those boys are

busting at the seams to get in here and see you. Can I bring them in if I hold on to them so they don't topple you?''

''Yes,'' Maria said, laughing.

''Well, good! Brace yourself, my dear,'' Warrie said as she hurried out again.

Nell's mother as a wedding present, Maria thought. What an unusual idea.

She suddenly smiled. She couldn't think of anything she needed more than having someone around who was so firmly entrenched in her memories of ''better times.''

''The earrings, Maria?'' Kate said.

''Oh, yes.'' Maria took them from the case and put them on.

She would never forget her brothers or her love for them. But it was getting harder and harder to recall their faces. Whatever would they think of all this?

Warrie brought the children in. They were both giggling in the hall, but at the sight of Maria, they became what could only be described as dumbfounded.

''It's me,'' she said, smiling, and immediately they both would have rushed forward if Warrie hadn't kept them in hand. She brought them close enough for Maria to touch them if she leaned forward, but not close enough for them to trample the hem of her dress.

''Jake thought you *died*,'' Joe said. ''Like Mama.''

''No, I'm here, Jake,'' Maria said, whispering just to him, because she knew he preferred whispering when he was worried. ''Do you like my pretty dress?''

Jake nodded, his finger in his mouth.

''Let Warrie hold you up so I can give you a kiss.''

''I'll do it,'' Kate said, and she lifted the boy and held him so that Maria could kiss his forehead and cheek.

''Me! Me!'' Joe cried, jumping up and down, and

Kate handed over his brother to Warrie and picked him up, as well.

Maria kissed him gently, a kiss he promptly returned with a big grin.

"Now. You and Jake go with Warrie—and I'll see you in a little while. And do you know what I think? I think there will be cake later," Maria said mischievously. Whether Max Woodard showed up for the ceremony or not, she thought she could safely promise them that.

When they had gone, Maria took as deep a breath as she could manage and repositioned herself on the cushion. She was so tightly laced that there was no chance of her slouching. She smoothed the front of her skirt, picked at a satin rose or two. Sighed. Waited.

"He'll be here," Kate said. "I'm going to go downstairs and see how things are progressing. Do you need anything? Something to drink?"

"No, thank you. Nothing."

"All right then. I'll be right back."

But she barely made it outside the door before she returned. "Maria, your father wants to see you."

"Is he all right?" Maria asked, trying to get to her feet and not step on anything she shouldn't.

"I think so. I believe he just wants to see you up close."

Kate helped Maria get down the hall, carrying the train of the dress carefully as they moved along. The upstairs was all ready, transformed into a bower of ferns and white ribbons. Someone had crafted the marriage bell; it, too, was wrapped in white ribbons. Two hassocks had been appropriated from somewhere for her and Max to kneel upon during the ceremony. No one had thought the preparations could possibly be completed in two days—no one except the groom.

Where is he?

The door to her father's room stood ajar. As Mrs. Justice had predicted, he would be able to witness the entire ceremony from his bed. Maria smiled slightly to herself. Mrs. Justice had known her father since they were children, and she wondered idly when it was that everyone—except Mrs. Justice—had stopped calling him ''Bud.''

Kate followed her inside the room and took a few moments to carefully arrange the train, then gave her father a little wave and discreetly left. Her father smiled and managed a weak wave in return. The effort it took made it necessary for him to rest before he could speak.

Maria waited quietly. The room smelled of camphor and lavender. The window was open and a fly buzzed around the sill. The shadows were growing long. The sun would go down soon. She could hear the voices of the people gathering on the lawn outside for a wedding that might not even occur.

''Daughter...'' her father said finally. ''You are a...vision...to behold. Is she...not...Bruno?''

''Colonel Woodard is a very lucky man, Sir,'' Bruno said.

''I wish...your mother...were here,'' her father said. ''And the...boys. My...fine...boys. What a day...they would have...made this. Wouldn't...they have...made it a grand...celebration?''

''Yes, Father.''

''You're wearing...the earrings.''

''Yes.''

''Beautiful. As you...are. Are you...happy... today... Maria Rose?''

She didn't answer him immediately, and he reached out and took her hand. His fingers were so cold to the touch, cold in a way she never remembered before.

"Maxwell...is a...good man," he said after a moment. "I think—" He stopped abruptly and closed his eyes.

"Father?" Maria said, growing alarmed.

He suddenly gave a deep, rumbling cough that went on and on. Bruno stepped forward immediately to lift him up and wipe the spittle from his mouth.

"I think...you already...know him...better," her father said when he'd recovered.

"Better?"

"Than...you ever did...Billy."

Maria looked away from her father's quiet gaze, suddenly overwhelmed with sadness at how little he understood of the situation. She didn't know Max Woodard at all.

"Hurry...away now...before the groom...comes and...sees you. We don't want...any bad luck...this day."

"Father—"

"Go," he said, shooing her feebly with his hand.

She caught it and pressed it to her cheek for a moment and then placed it gently on the bed.

Bruno opened the door, and Kate came in immediately to help maneuver the train. Maria gave her father one last look as she went out, but his eyes were closed.

"Are you all right?" Kate asked as they walked back to the sanctuary of Maria's room.

"Yes—no."

"All will be well."

Maria looked at her, trying hard not to give in to the urge to cry.

"It will," Kate insisted.

Maria nodded, but the truth was that she didn't know Kate Woodard—any more than she knew her brother—and she couldn't find any comfort at all in her well-meaning words.

When Kate had Maria situated on her perch again, she handed her a handkerchief and quietly left the room.

Maria gave a wavering sigh, but she didn't weep. And for once she was glad that the grandfather clock was gone. At least, she didn't have to hear it chime every fifteen minutes of the wait. Whether Max came to marry her or didn't, the anxiety was the same.

Whose duty would it be to call the wedding off if Max didn't show? she suddenly wondered.

The minister, she decided. He announced it; he could unannounce it.

The door opened just a crack, and Mrs. Woodard peered in.

"Maria?" she said tentatively. "I think we should talk."

And Maria's heart fell. The wedding was off—and Mrs. Woodard had come to tell her the bad—good?—news.

"Maria," Mrs. Woodard began again.

"Please," Maria said. "It will be better to just say it, I think."

"Yes," Mrs. Woodard agreed. She took a deep breath. "About the wedding…night. You have no mother to ask and I thought—if you have questions—questions that I can perhaps answer for you—about what happens…"

Maria could feel herself blush.

"Oh, dear," Mrs. Woodard concluded. "Perhaps I've been indelicate."

"No," Maria hastened to say. "Ceily has already...made the offer to...advise me."

"Ah. Well. That's all right, then. I'll just go and leave you to your thoughts. And, dear Maria, may I say you look lovely?"

"Yes," Maria answered, smiling slightly. "As often as you like."

"Darling girl," Mrs. Woodard said, giving her a careful hug before she left Maria alone again. "You have made my son care about his life again—and for that I shall always be grateful."

After Max's mother had gone, Maria alternated trying to decide what the woman had meant and trying to listen to whatever was going on outside. The room grew hot and stuffy. She felt sticky and half smothered. After a time, she reached the point where she just wanted it all to be over—one way or the other.

There was a rapid, staccato knock on the door suddenly, and she jumped. The door opened before she could say anything.

"He's here, he's here, he's here!" Ceily whispered frantically as she lunged into the room. "The minister's waiting. Mrs. Woodard is waiting. The Kinnards and Mrs. Justice are waiting. James and his kind are waiting—so let's go. Are you ready? Where's Kate?"

"I don't know," Maria said, flooded with relief and ready to bolt all at the same time.

"Where's the bouquet?"

"Over there," Maria said pointing.

He's here, she thought, dazed. *He's really here.*

She tried to stand up. Her legs wouldn't quite cooperate.

"Wait, wait, wait," Ceily insisted. "Let me fix the veil, then we'll get the bouquet. Do you know what

Colonel Woodard asked me? He asked me if he had time to shave. I said, 'For heaven's sake, *no,* you don't have time to *shave!*' The very idea! Of course, James had a fit—he says you can't say things like that to a colonel—they do as they please. I told him *he* can't say things like that. *I'm* not on the troop roster. Anyway, the colonel's very handsome if un-barbered self is waiting right outside—and he is most presentable in a dress uniform, even if it is the wrong army—wait till you see. Are you ready now? Can you stand up?''

"Yes—and yes," Maria said, managing to get to her feet.

"You look so beautiful, Maria. He's going to be so surprised!"

Maria couldn't help but laugh at the left-handed compliment.

"No—I meant...well, you know what I meant!" Ceily said, dissolving into laughter with her.

"Now, we can't stand here giggling," Ceily said. "It's just not done. Come on. If Kate's not here, I'll get the train. No, I'll get the door—*then* I'll get the train."

Somehow Maria made it out into the hallway intact. Max stood near the head of the stairs, and his startled look made her see the truth in Ceily's observation. She couldn't say with any great certainty that *she* was beautiful—but she could definitely say that *he* was surprised.

But no more surprised than she. In need of a shave or not, he was indeed splendid in his dress uniform. And he was tired. Whatever he'd been doing in the two days he'd been gone, it hadn't involved rest or sleep.

Someone started playing the piano downstairs, and Max came forward to meet her. "Miss Markham," he said with great formality, offering her his arm. She took it, holding on for dear life, while Ceily fussed with the train.

When Ceily—and a harried Kate—had taken their places, Maria dared to look at him. He was smiling—almost.

"It's a very good thing I made it in time," he said.

"Is it?"

"Do you see my staff over there?"

She glanced in the direction he indicated with a slight movement of his head. A significant number of Yankee officers stood along the row of potted ferns, all of them looking in her direction.

"They were going to duel each other for the right to step into my shoes if I didn't get back here."

He was deliberately teasing her, and she knew it—perhaps to negate any distress he might have caused her by his late arrival, perhaps because he liked to unsettle her and had since the day they met. Even so, she smiled.

"There's something you should know," she said quietly as the minister motioned for them to come forward.

"What?"

"The 'obey' part of this ceremony? I'm probably not going to mean it."

Chapter Seventeen

"I require and charge you both, as ye will answer at the dreadful day of judgement when the secrets of all hearts shall be disclosed, that if either of you know any impediment why ye may not be lawfully joined in Matrimony, you do now confess it..."

An unborn baby with an unnamed father, Maria thought.

Was that an impediment?

No emotional attachment.

Was that just cause?

She pushed both questions aside and forced herself to concentrate on the minister, answering when she was suppose to answer, receiving the heavy gold ring Max had provided, until finally it was done.

"I pronounce that ye be man and wife together..."

Man and wife together.

Aside from wanting to give as good as she got, she had meant what she said about not "obeying." But at the same time, it surprised her how much she did mean the rest of it. She intended—if not to love, then to respect and honor—in sickness and in health. Max had stated plainly that he did not want a marriage in name only—and she would oblige him in that, as well. It came as a great surprise to her how much she wanted the marriage to succeed, and she would do her part to make that happen.

"God bless, preserve and keep you, Maxwell and Maria," the minister said. "Maxwell, you may kiss your bride."

The kiss Max gave her was brief and chaste, a gentle brushing of his lips against hers. Yet, it was a reminder of what had happened earlier and a promise of what was to come—and they both knew it.

Max immediately led Maria to speak to her father.

"Just…right," her father whispered to her. "A ceremony…long enough…to take, but not to…torture. I rejoice…that I have…lived to witness…this day. See that…Bruno…gets something…good to eat from the… bridal table…will you, daughter?"

"Yes, Father," she said, kissing his cheek.

"And me…too…while you're…at it."

"It's already taken care of. All the things you shouldn't have will be on the way shortly—except cigars."

Her father laughed softly and feebly patted her cheek.

"Take her…to your…guests…Maxwell. So…I can get…fed."

"I'll do that, Sir," Max said.

He led Maria away to his mother and Kate—both of whom cried, as did Mrs. Justice. Acacia Kinnard, on the other hand, was quite in control. And, with much effort on her part, so was Valentina. Mrs. Russell had been invited to witness the ceremony, but she was conspicuously absent.

The faces of the Yankee officers passed by in a blur,

all of their well wishes to the colonel and his lady seeming surprisingly heartfelt.

Maria glanced at Max from time to time, but she couldn't read his expression. If he was happy—or even content—about the situation or if he had regrets, she couldn't begin to tell.

Perkins appeared at the head of the stairs and disappeared again as soon as he'd caught Max's eye. Kate immediately stepped forward to help Maria find the wrist loop on the train so she could walk with at least some ease now that they were no longer concerned about crushed roses.

The downstairs was jammed with people. Clearly, the invitation committee had outdone itself.

As she and Max came into view, a round of applause began among the guests in the foyer and spread through the house. Still holding on to Max's arm, Maria spoke to the people she'd known all her life, one by one: the mayor and city council, friends of her father and her mother—some of whom she hadn't encountered in ages—schoolteachers, people from church, the doctor and his wife. She accepted all their well-wishes as graciously as she could, trying not to blush at the heavy-handed references to a hopefully quick arrival of little Woodard-Markham babies and marveling that her new husband seemed to take the remarks all in stride. She marveled, too, that, as with the Yankee officers, the well-wishes seemed genuine.

"One more tier," Max said in an allusion to Mrs. Justice's ingenious plan. He led the way through the dining room and out the side door into the yard.

Maria had known that Ceily's husband had kept a number of soldiers busy decorating, but she had no idea to what degree. As she and Max led the guests outside, she hardly recognized the grounds. The soldiers had built a low wooden platform and placed long tables with starched, white-linen tablecloths and numerous chairs all around the edge of it. Maria could see a number of cut-crystal candelabras like the ones she had once thought, in her young girl's naiveté, she would require to celebrate her first appearance with her new husband.

Billy. It was supposed to have been Billy.

The candle flames flickered in the early twilight, but stayed lit. There were more white ribbons and greenery placed all around—and there was a huge wedding cake and piles and piles of food: thinly sliced bread and butter, cracker bonbons, sweets of all kinds, tarts, meat pies, nuts, pickles and punch. Lanterns hung from the trees to light the celebration, and nearly as many soldiers as it must have taken to put all this together, now diligently waved fans and branches to keep any insects away.

"Ladies and gentlemen," James Carscaddon announced loudly. "I give you Colonel and Mrs. Woodard."

Once again there was a round of applause. People stepped forward to offer their congratulations—many of whom Maria knew. Perkins approached and snapped to attention.

"Now, Sir?"

"Now, Perkins," Max said.

The sergeant major immediately trotted to the side of the platform and picked up a fiddle. And, incredibly, he began to play—a poignant, three-quarter time waltz. The beautifully haunting music swirled around them, and Max held out his hand.

"Will you dance with me, Mrs. Woodard?" he said.

Maria hesitated, then took it, letting him lead her out onto the middle of the platform. It had been a very long time since she had waltzed—she wasn't even certain she remembered how. But Max Woodard was a gifted partner, and he danced her easily around the floor. The music rose, and everything became a blur—the faces of the people looking on, the candlelight and decorations—everything but him. She felt as if she were in a dream, with no sense of how she had gotten to this point or where she was going from here. Max's sad eyes looked into hers, but he said nothing. There might have been no one in the world but the two of them—and Perkins.

Someone had told him, she suddenly realized. About the crystal candelabras. About the waltz.

The song ended, and the regimental band promptly took over with another more lively tune. Max gave her a bow and handed her over to Lieutenant Carscaddon, the first in a series of young officers determined to dance with the bride and tread mercilessly upon her toes. Max turned away to partner his mother, and then Kate.

When he finally rescued Maria from his staff, they made the rounds again, speaking with every guest, encouraging them all to partake of the food and celebration. Outsider or not, arbitrarily reviled or not, Max Woodard was completely at ease in the situation. But then he had always seemed in command, Maria thought—except for the night of the thunderstorm.

At one point she looked up at her father's window, surprised to find him sitting there, propped up by pillows and Bruno—and Joe and Jake. The boys waved vigorously, and, with Bruno's help, her father held up a plate to show her he was well-supplied with every forbidden food available. Maria blew him a kiss, and Max gave him a solemn bow.

"Thank you," Maria said as they began to dance again.

"For what?" he asked.

"For all this—and for getting it done in time for my father to see it."

"It...meets your expectations?"

"It is beyond my expectations. I thank you, too, for my wedding gift."

"And what gift would that be?"

"Warrie Hansen. She says she thinks that she is my wedding present."

"Well, I didn't have time for much else," he said, and another of his officers respectfully cut in and whisked her away.

The mayor made his obligatory speech and toast, giving Maria a brief respite from soldiers with two left feet. She and Max cut the cake—with a cavalry sword—and then there was more dancing.

Once, when Maria was waltzing with the regimental surgeon, she thought she saw Nell standing among the trees on the other side of the street. Nell and a man— Phelan? She couldn't tell for certain in the twilight.

She tried to get a better look but there were too many people in the way.

It couldn't be Phelan, she decided. He was long gone, and even if he were here, he would never hang back and hide in the underbrush, particularly on the occasion of her marriage to a Yankee colonel. He'd be right here, happy for an opportunity to save Southern womanhood from yet another Yankee soldier's clutches.

And just how different was she from Nell? Maria thought suddenly. She was no less mercenary in her dealings with Max Woodard than Nell was with her soldier clientele—only Maria's reward was a tenuous respectability and legitimacy for her child rather than hard cash.

Poor Phelan would never understand that neither she nor Nell needed saving.

Maria glanced up at her father's window again. He and the boys were no longer in view. She supposed that between Warrie and Bruno, all three of them had been put to bed for the evening.

The regimental surgeon said something she didn't hear over the music.

"I beg your pardon?" she said.

"I said my name is Strauss. Major Edwin Strauss. It occurred to me that I have been here to see Mr. Markham many times, and while you have always thanked me kindly after every visit, we have never been introduced."

"How do you do, Major?" Maria said politely, and he laughed. He also abruptly stopped dancing. "I believe the colonel has some concern about the celebration," he said, taking her firmly by the arm.

Maria looked around her until she spotted Max, deep in conversation with Perkins and looking toward the woods where Nell had been.

"Colonel Woodard has us all on the alert for any trouble," Major Strauss said. "I believe I will let you sit out the rest of this dance, Mrs. Woodard—inside the house."

"But I—"

"Inside," he said again. "The colonel has said your safety is the prime concern."

He escorted her firmly toward the house whether she wanted to go or not. She thought he would leave her inside the door, but he didn't. He took her all the way upstairs to her bedchamber.

"I would like to check on my father," she said when he opened the door.

"I will do that. If he's awake, I'll come and tell you. For now, wait here, Mrs. Woodard. I mean it."

And to show her that he did, he summoned another soldier to keep vigil outside the door.

"Am I allowed to know nothing?" Maria asked. "Please," she said when he was about to dismiss her concern.

"There is a vigilante group about. They have taken up the business of keeping *your* people in line. I believe your husband has made an enemy of them. That's all I can tell you. Now stay inside. For both our sakes. I can assure you, if any harm comes to you, your husband will have my hide. If you must light the lamp—stay away from the window."

He waited until she had stepped back, then firmly closed the door.

Maria waited a few minutes, then opened it again.

"I'm sorry, ma'am," the soldier posted outside said. "I can't let you pass—except to go to your father if he needs you—or to the little boys. And they're all asleep."

"I want to know what's happening," Maria said.

"Nothing yet, ma'am. But the colonel—he don't take chances."

Except when it came to marrying, Maria thought.

She closed the door again and went to peer out the window. She could see her bridal bouquet lying on the table next to the wedding cake where she'd put it aside. Everyone seemed to be leaving. She couldn't locate Max or Perkins—or any of the officers.

She sighed heavily and stepped back from the window, hesitating for a moment, then closing the draperies and lighting one candle. She realized as she did so that the room had been made ready for the wedding night. Whatever clutter she had left had all been neatly put away. The bed now had a crocheted wedding ring counterpane on it, and it had been turned down, and someone had sprinkled the crisp, white sheets with rose petals.

Who had done this? she wondered with some dismay. Was she expected to lie down with Max Woodard on rose petals?

More roses had been placed in vases around the room—the same lilac-pink Hermosa roses that had made up her bridal bouquet, the ones that could have only come from Acacia Kinnard's side yard.

A nightdress made of a fine sheer lawn lay spread out at the foot of the bed. Not hers—any more than the wedding dress was hers, or the one-piece chemise and drawers, the corset, the stockings and the petticoats she had on under it. They were all part of an unexpected trousseau that kept magically appearing, piece by piece, whenever she needed yet another undergarment of some kind. Because of her "Southern pride," she had to be handled delicately.

Cornered.

Trapped.

Eventually, she sat down on the same low table where she had had to perch before the ceremony. Without help, she couldn't get out of the wedding dress; she could only sit here and wait—and take off the veil and coronet at least.

At one point she heard Kate and Mrs. Woodard—apparently being shepherded to their room, as well. She considered opening the door again, then let it go. Encountering the two Woodard woman in a room so obviously made ready for the intimacies of a wedding night was far too daunting.

An errant breeze billowed the curtains and blew the candle out. She continued to sit in the dark. There was nothing else to do—except challenge the soldier outside the door to see how far he would go to carry out his orders. She looked down at her hands. She could just make out the gold ring on her left hand.

This is ridiculous, she thought, intending to stand up again and open the door. But she heard voices suddenly.

Max.

"Where's my wife?"

"In here, Sir."

"Is she mad?"

"I...couldn't say, Sir."

"That's what I thought," Max answered.

He didn't knock. He just came in without a by-your-leave—and she could have been standing in her birthday suit for all he knew.

"Why are you sitting in the dark?" he asked.

"I'm making the regimental surgeon happy," she answered. "What's happening?" She got up from her perch too quickly and stepped on her dresstail. He had to grab her to keep her from stumbling.

"Everything is fine," he said, letting her go.

"Don't do that," she said.

"Don't do what?"

"Answer *your* questions instead of mine. I didn't ask you if everything was all right. I asked you what was happening."

He moved to light the candle, then stood looking at her in a way that was nothing if not disconcerting.

"So you did," he said. "Will you sit down?"

"No."

"Then do you mind if I do?"

She made an impatient gesture with her hand for him to sit. He did so—on the bed—after he picked up the nightdress and looked at it with far too much interest, in her opinion, and set it aside.

"I thought I saw Nell," she said.

"You did. She came to warn me."

"About what?"

"About a man named Jimmy Julian," he answered, unbuttoning his tunic—as if they had been together like this for years.

"The vigilante."

"Yes," he said, clearly surprised that she had that much information. "Nell thought he was going to try something here this evening—against me. He was looking to kill two birds with one stone, as it were."

"I don't know what that means."

"It means that getting me out of the way—or least an attack upon my person—could be blamed on ex-Confederates. And that would give him—and his so-called army—a free rein to do as they please, even more so than they already do. I believe he's the one who set the fire that killed Suzanne Canfield. Somehow he's gotten the notion that he has the authority to punish the Rebels at will. It rather surprised him to discover that I took exception to that. He managed to get away, but he's not very happy with me—are you going to sit down or not?" he suddenly asked.

"I need help," Maria said.

"Help," he repeated, as if it were a foreign word which had no meaning to him whatsoever.

"I can't sit down in this dress and I can't reach the buttons."

"Do you want me to get Kate or—"

"No!" she said with a certain amount of alarm. "I...think you should unbutton them." She realized immediately that it was far less mortifying to have him perform the rightful honors than to have his mother or his sister come in and see all those rose petals.

"Ah," he said. She thought he was going to smile, but he didn't. He rubbed the side of his nose with his forefinger instead. "Well, then, do you want me to come over there or are you coming over here?"

Maria gave a small sigh and gathered up as much of the skirt as she could and dragged herself and the dress closer and presented her back to him.

"If you would just turn around again first," he said.

"The buttons are in the back," she whispered.

"I know where they are—why are you whispering?"

"Because I feel as if everyone in this house is listening," she said.

"Well, I expect they are."

"And that doesn't bother you, I suppose."

"Not particularly—people take an inordinate amount of interest in the first night a newly wedded couple spends together. Will you turn around this way again?"

"Why?"

"Because," he said. "Turn around. Please."

She turned and faced him—eventually. He sat calmly on the side of the bed and looked at her. She was absolutely determined not to let his inspection get the best of her.

"You look very beautiful, Maria," he said finally, and that was the last thing she expected to hear.

"So do you," she answered. "We have both benefited considerably from a more elegant style of dress. I suppose it's good that we are able to appreciate it."

"Are you always this difficult to compliment?"

"It all depends on where the compliment originates."

"Harder to accept if it comes from a damn Yankee, I guess."

"Something like that."

He took off his uniform tunic and draped it on the bed post.

"Suzanne told me something once—about you. She said you would never believe what I said—only what I did."

"Why would she tell you something like that?"

"I asked her why. She said it was because of her illness. It made it possible for her to get away with having opinions about things. I think she rather enjoyed the freedom." He motioned with his hand that she was to turn around again.

She did so, but she was too far away. He put both hands on her waist and backed her up so that he could reach her. His hands were warm and strong—the way she remembered the night of the thunderstorm. She had to close her eyes against the surge of feeling the memory evoked.

"Did she tell you about the crystal candelabras and the waltz, as well?" she asked.

"No. Nell told me about that."

Maria sighed.

Nell.

She had very informative friends, it seemed.

"Nell said it was something you always wanted. I didn't intend to offend you," he said.

"I wasn't offended," she said truthfully. And she hadn't been. It wasn't offense that she had felt at seeing what he had arranged for her, but an incredible sadness.

There were a lot of buttons on the dress, and it was taking him a long time. At one point, she thought his fingers trembled.

"Now what?" he said when he had finally undone the last one.

She considered this carefully. She had made what was essentially a business agreement with him, and she was not a shy virgin bride. Or she wasn't a virgin, at any rate. It would be hypocritical for her to behave as if she were.

"The corset laces?" he suggested when she had no answers forthcoming.

She realized immediately that he was not a man bewildered by the logistics of undoing a woman's underclothing. The laces were tied in front, and his hands slid around her waist beneath the dress to pull her corset cover up so he could reach them. Then he deftly untied and loosened them.

Who else had he done this for? she wondered. He had a definite expertise—but he was not entirely blasé about it. She was certain now that she could feel his hands trembling.

"I can do the rest," she said over her shoulder.

"Would you...allow me?" he asked. "Now that we've set a precedent," he added. The question was a token one at best, and she knew it. She couldn't see his face, but she had the distinct impression that he was somehow...amused.

She turned around to face him again and, after a moment, she let go of the bodice she'd been holding so tightly. The high-necked dress slid off her shoulders slightly, but no farther.

He stood to help her get her arms out of the sleeves and to lift the dress over her head, gathering up the rose-bedecked skirt as best he could. One of her hairpins still got caught and fell to the floor.

He took the dress and spread it out carefully over her grandmother's upholstered rocking chair, then picked up the hairpin before he came back and sat down on the edge of the bed again.

She stood very still while he searched for whatever kept her hoop slip in place, his hands sliding around her waist front to back.

More buttons.

He undid those without making her turn around, and she studied his face as he did so. He was looking at her, but he was still concentrating on mastering what he couldn't see.

With his help, the hoop slip collapsed in concentric circles at her feet. He unloosened the ties on her under petticoat so that it fell, as well, and held her hand so she could step out of them.

"Shoes," he said, and she dutifully stepped out of her white satin slippers.

She would have bent to pick up the petticoats and put them away, but he wouldn't let her. He merely pushed them aside with his foot.

Once again he put his hands on her waist and brought her closer. And he looked into her eyes for a moment before he proceeded. For what, she didn't know. Not permission. She understood that much, regardless of the polite request he'd made earlier. Did he expect revulsion on her part? Panic?

She was…uneasy, but she was not panic-stricken.

Yet.

"I have thought about this for a long time," he said, reaching up and taking a dangling pin from her hair and placing it into the palm of her hand. Then another. And another and another—until her hair tumbled down around her shoulders. His fingers searched carefully through the tresses for more pins. She didn't say anything, but she wanted to. Surely he didn't mean *this?* And if he did, then when had it first come to mind?

"Have I shocked you?" he asked easily.

"No more so than usual," she answered, and he smiled. How very different he looked on those rare occasions. Younger. More vulnerable.

He was still smiling when he reached for the corset cover and began undoing yet another row of tiny buttons. He slipped it off her. She stood there in her stockinged feet, glad that there was no more light in the room than one candle. He let his fingers move lightly over her shoulders and downward, stopping just short of the swell of her breasts.

She closed her eyes and felt him undo the top hook on the front of the corset. Then the next one. He was in no more of a hurry than he had been in his search for hairpins. There was nothing between the backs of his fingers and her bare skin but the thin material of her chemise.

He undid the last hook on the busk and gave the corset a toss, not particularly noting where it landed. She stood there in the one-piece chemise and drawers that was supposed to be the very latest style. Perhaps it was. He seemed fascinated by it.

He reached out and rested his hands on her waist again. "Are you afraid of me?" he asked after a moment, staring into her eyes.

"No," she said, grateful that her voice didn't give her away, because she was afraid now. Afraid of the pounding of her heart and the weakness of her knees and the growing warmth in her belly.

"I always thought you were."

"At first," she qualified. "When I thought you would be like Hatcher."

"Am I not...like him?"

"No," she said again.

He was waiting for something. She could feel it.

For what? she thought.

He kept looking at her, and she stared back, unabashed now, her shyness giving way to curiosity—and anticipation. She was acutely aware of him again, in the way she had been that day on the back stairs. And, if she were truthful, the way she had been since that first day at the train station. Impulsively, she reached up to touch the stubble of his beard. When she did so, his eyes closed, and he gave a soft exhalation of breath.

She immediately leaned into him and his arms slid around her. His mouth almost...*almost*...touched hers. She could feel his warm breath as he gently nuzzled her cheek.

He was holding back, and he trembled with the effort it took for him to do so. Why was he holding back—when he wanted this, when they *both* wanted this?

But when he kissed her—finally—she knew why. The first touch of his mouth on hers took her breath away.

I love the way he tastes, she thought. *I love the way he smells. I love the way he feels.*

She had to cling to him to keep from falling. The hairpins spilled from her hand. He lifted her up off the floor and placed her gently amid the rose petals. She could smell their heady scent, and she lay with her knees bent, watching while he took off his shirt and undervest.

He undressed quickly and came to her naked, letting her see all of him, letting her witness his desire. She was not a virgin, she thought again, and yet she was. The other time, the only time, had been all fumbling and desperation. It was not the same as what she knew— *knew*—she would experience with this man.

He lay down beside her and brought her to him, holding her close as he stroked the length of her body. She took a deep, wavering breath, and his arms tightened around her. He was lean and strong. She pressed her face into his shoulder. His skin smelled of soap and the out-of-doors.

He's not Billy, she thought. And incredibly she didn't want him to be. That part of her life was over and done.

He was impatient now, too impatient to be bothered with removing the chemise and drawers. There was no need. The inside seam, thigh to thigh, was open. She felt his fingers seeking her bare skin above her stockings and then moving higher. The first touch made her jump, but he didn't stop. His mouth found hers, and he kissed her deeply, caressing her between her legs until her body rose to meet his hand. And then he was kneeling between her thighs, lifting her hips, pushing himself inside. Her head arched back, not in pain, but in acute sensation.

At his first thrust, she gave a soft moan, her fingers digging into his back. He thrust deeper, and her need for him intensified. She could identify a pinpoint of pleasure deep inside her, and suddenly she had to bring it to the surface. Her body began to meet his with the same ardor, the same need and hunger, the urgency growing until the pleasure soared and soared and finally burst in them both.

He lay heavily on top of her for a moment, then moved away from her, heaving himself onto his back, his breathing still ragged—as hers was. He didn't say anything, and she lay there, feeling the abandonment, not knowing what to say or do.

Had she done this all wrong—offended him with her wantonness?

After a moment he reached down and took her hand,

his fingers sliding between hers, a gesture so needed and so comforting that it made her want to weep. She held on to his hand until his fingers suddenly relaxed, and she realized that he was fast asleep.

"What are you thinking about?"

The question surprised him, because he had been lying in the dark wondering the same about her. There was a faint rumble of thunder in the distance, and a strong breeze that heralded a storm billowed the curtains outward.

"The truth," she said before he could answer.

He took a deep breath and stretched, wondering, too, how long he had been asleep.

The truth.

"I was thinking about Gettysburg," he said. "About your brothers. And your fiancé. I was thinking about how little I remember of the battle—it's all run together now. What I remember most are...the little girls."

"Little girls?" she said, turning her head to look at him.

"Schoolgirls—standing on the streets...singing us into town. Singing—because they didn't know what hell on earth really is or that they—and we—were about to fall headlong into it."

He was looking at her, but he couldn't make out her features in the darkness. "Did I...hurt you?"

"No," she said, and her answer came quickly enough that he believed her. She sat up on the side of the bed, and he moved so that he could rest his hand on her shoulder, because he suddenly had the feeling that she was about to flee. At his touch, she came to him. He held her tightly in his arms, immediately feeling the return of desire.

"How did we ever get here—you and I?" he said against her ear.

"I don't know—I don't know—"

His mouth found hers, and he kissed her deeply, fumbling to get her out of the clothes he had been too aroused to worry about earlier. He wanted nothing between them this time. Skin to skin, perhaps heart to heart.

The storm was closer now. Thunder rumbled overhead. He could hear the rain begin to fall. But, for once, the storm without had no meaning for him. There was only the storm within.

Chapter Eighteen

Smitten.

Max turned the word over in his mind, trying to decide exactly what it meant in his particular case.

Outwardly, except for the addition of the Hansen woman and the two boys to the household, nothing appeared to have significantly changed since the marriage. Mr. Markham's health neither improved nor deteriorated, and Max followed the same daily routine as when he first arrived. Because he needed a quiet place to work, he reclaimed the front bedchamber as soon as his mother and Kate left to return home and ultimately to join his father in London. He went to military headquarters in the morning—except when he had his staff meetings in the dining room—and he came back home again as soon as his duties permitted. During the daytime and in the presence of others, it was as if he and Maria had arrived at some kind of unspoken, mutual agreement to give the appearance that their relationship was as formal and restrained as it had been before the marriage.

But at night—ah, God, at night.

From the very first, he had intended his alliance with Maria to be a straightforward business arrangement, one which allowed him certain sexual privileges. But the passion they shared when they were finally alone was beyond his wildest expectations. Sometimes she came to him when he was working late on some impossible bureaucratic tangle. He would look up from his papers and find her standing there in her nightdress and bare feet, with no shame whatsoever as to why she had come. Knowing that she desired him in that way was an incredible compliment to him. He basked in it, and he simply couldn't get enough of her.

Smitten.

If that was his condition, then there was more to it than just the lovemaking. He liked being in Maria's company—he had *always* liked being in her company, even when he was doing his best to "inconvenience" her. He liked living with her and the boys. He even liked spending time with her father.

Maria was proving to be a great help to him regarding the occupation, explaining the intricate relationships of the people in this town. Who got along and who didn't. Who owed favors to whom, and who carried lifelong grudges—and why. She explained the fine points of the pecking order that he himself would have missed, and his knowing these things did much to put the occupation on a more even keel.

His very life was on a more even keel—because of her. He found that he wanted to take care of her, feed her, clothe her, take her any place she wanted to go. He wanted to keep her safe and well and happy.

And he wanted not to think about the father of her child.

She was always on his mind—like now—when he should be working or at least giving the appearance that he was.

He realized that Perkins had come to stand in the doorway, but he didn't immediately acknowledge his presence. Instead he abruptly decided that he'd had enough of the army and its doings for one afternoon.

"I'm going home for a while," Max said. He opened a drawer in his desk to retrieve the cloth sack that held the two trains he'd finally finished whittling for Joe and Jake.

"Yes, Sir," Perkins said in such a way that Max looked up at him.

"What are you grinning at?"

"Nothing, Sir. It's a fine day for going home. Yes, Sir, I'd say it was a *very* fine day."

"You mind your own damn business, all right?"

"Yes, Sir!" Perkins assured him.

Max didn't smile until he'd reached the street. He really wasn't planning on going home in the middle of the day for *that* reason—but it certainly wouldn't hurt to be alert to the possibility. All he had to do was find Maria then outwit Warrie Hansen, two small boys, Bruno, and Mr. Markham—and anyone else in town who might be wandering through the household.

He'd faced worse odds in his time.

He rode down Main Street and on to Innes Street, spurring his horse into a cantor and appreciating the fine afternoon. Several people nodded as he passed, people who, before the wedding, would have turned away.

His mount was in high spirits, and Max gave him his head, arriving at the Markham house at a gallop, scattering dust and chickens all the way.

He expected to find Maria in the summer kitchen this time of day, but it was empty. He could hear Warrie and the boys somewhere in the house. Sack in hand, he went back inside and hurried up the back stairs. He looked in

on Mr. Markham and found him—and Bruno—napping
in the cross breeze from the open windows.

He continued down the wide hallway straight to Maria's bedchamber. She wasn't there. He stared at the bed
for a moment, wondering idly if he would ever look at
rose petals in the same way again. Then he moved to
the window. He saw Maria standing at the far edge of
the yard. She was talking to a man.

No. He realized immediately. Not "a man." Phelan
Canfield.

In the weeks since the wedding, Max had all but forgotten about him. He stood for a moment, watching, then
abruptly turned and went downstairs. There would be no
more trying to eavesdrop on Canfield's conversations
with Maria. He would confront the man and find out
firsthand what he was doing here.

Warrie and the boys were in the kitchen now. He went
immediately to the window, but he couldn't see Maria
from this vantage point. Both boys grabbed him around
his legs, nearly toppling him.

"Whoa!" he said, reaching down to touch them both.
"Now what are you two up to?"

"We went to Mrs. Kinnard's house," Joe said. "She's
got cake."

"I'll bet she does," Max said. "Did she give you
any?"

"No," Joe said morosely. "We were too wild."

"I see. Well, sometimes it works out that way. You
get too wild, you don't get cake." He disengaged himself from the boys' grasp, intending to go outside.

"Colonel," Mrs. Hansen said, putting herself between
him and the back door. "Would you stay awhile? The
boys have missed you today."

Max looked at her. She was lying.

"Please, Sir," she said, her voice gone urgent now. "For them?"

"Mrs. Hansen, I don't—"

"Please. Maria will be here in a minute," she said pointedly, and what he was supposed to take from that, he wasn't quite sure. Except that she didn't want him going out to where Maria was.

"Here I am," Maria said suddenly from the doorway. "Are you looking for me?" she asked. She appeared rushed, flustered, but she was smiling as if she were glad to see him. There was that, then. In spite of whatever Phelan Canfield was up to, she was glad to see him.

Or was she?

She began to move busily around the kitchen, but she was distracted in a way that reminded him of the night they'd announced their engagement. She kept picking up things and then didn't seem to know what she intended to do with them.

"Will you eat with us, Maxwell?" she asked after a moment.

"No—I have to get back. I just came to bring the boys something."

"What is it!" Joe cried, and both of them had him around the knees again. He handed the sack with the trains to Warrie.

"Mrs. Hansen will have to say if you've been too bad to have it. Can you do that, Mrs. Hansen?"

"Lordy, Colonel Woodard, these are not bad boys— they're just *boys,* that's all. Acacia Kinnard just don't know a thing about how they are. Come along, Joe— Jake. Let's us go up and find us a nap."

The boys groaned in unison, and Max smiled.

"Of course, we will be looking into this sack first,"

Warrie told them and was nearly rushed off her feet for it.

Max stood watching until they disappeared up the back stairs.

"So what have you been doing today?" he asked Maria, watching her closely, waiting for her to tell him about Canfield.

"Well...making watermelon syrup," she said, busy again doing things that didn't need doing.

"I don't think I know what that is."

"You would if you'd gone without sugar for years," she said. She made an attempt to smile and didn't quite make it this time.

"Maria—"

"Colonel Woodard!" someone called from outside.

Max walked to the kitchen doorway.

"Patrol's back, Sir!" one of his men called. "They got Julian!"

Julian.

Yet another plague Max had tried to keep from intruding upon his post-wedding bliss. He still had men out looking for the son of a bitch.

"Keep him under lock and key," Max said. "I'll be there shortly."

"He's raising hell, Sir."

"Let him," Max said. "Bring my mount around before you leave."

He looked at Maria. He couldn't tell if she was paying attention to the exchange.

"I have to go," Max said. "I'm not sure when I'll be back."

She nodded absently, then looked at him. "They say you aren't going to do anything—about Julian."

"Who says?"

"People."

"You mean the people who intercept the military telegrams? Those people?" *Or Phelan Canfield.*

Maria ignored the question. "Are you going to let Julian go?"

"Yes," he said, because he didn't want to lie to her. Julian had friends in high places, and Max had gotten the word early that morning that the man was to be allowed to move about the state unmolested by the military.

"Then why even bother locking him up—if it's all just for show?"

"I can't hang the bastard—but I can worry him, and I will."

"Suzanne is dead because of him."

"Yes," he said again.

Maria looked at him a long moment, then turned away.

"Maria, are you all right?" he asked, giving her one last chance to tell him about Canfield.

She gave a small sigh. "Just a bit of a headache," she said. "That's all."

He waited a moment longer, but she didn't say anything more. She didn't even tell him goodbye.

He left the house, looking for some sign of Canfield as he did so. He saw Mrs. Russell driving her buggy along the street. And if she intended to stop, it was clear that she wasn't going to do it until after he had gone.

He rode back to headquarters with but one thought on his mind.

Why didn't Maria tell him Canfield was here?

Surely they had reached a place in their relationship where she could do that. Surely she didn't consider him an outsider in this matter, at least. The boys were important to him, and he to them. He had a right to know what had brought Canfield back here. Whatever it was it didn't seem to be his children. The boys didn't know their father was skulking about—but Warrie Hansen did and she'd clearly wanted to keep it from them.

There were no answers Max could reach logically, no matter how much he worried the facts as he knew them. He would have to ask Maria—and he intended to do so as soon as he got home.

He put off dealing with Julian—too long if Perkins's fidgeting was any indication. By not letting the man go, Max was flying in the face of an official decree from the duly elected governor of this state—and it made his sergeant major more than a little nervous.

Or perhaps it was the mood Max had been in since he'd returned.

Perkins disappeared from the outer hall, only to reappear again almost immediately.

"Sir, Mrs. Russell is asking to see you," he said.

"De Graff's Mrs. Russell?"

"That's the one, Sir. She's riled up about something—won't tell me a thing. Just that's she's got to see you—and right now."

"All right. Send her up here," Max said. There was no point in making any more of an enemy of the woman than she already was.

He put some papers away, and when he looked up again she was standing at the doorway with clearly no intention of coming any farther.

"Your wife is ill," she said without prelude.

"What?"

"I think you heard me, Colonel. I suggest you go home."

With that she turned and left, going down the stairs as noiselessly as she'd come up them.

"Mrs. Russell!" he called after her, but she didn't stop.

Max stood, annoyed by the woman's sense of the dramatic.

"You want me to find the surgeon, Sir?" Perkins said in the doorway, eavesdropping as always.

"No," Max said. He had no idea what was wrong—if anything. "Yes," he amended immediately, because his annoyance had become cold fear. "Tell him what Mrs. Russell said and send him to the house."

"Yes, Sir!"

But Major Strauss was already at the Markham house when Max arrived. Warrie Hansen waited on the front porch, both boys clinging to her skirts.

"What's wrong, Mrs. Hansen?"

"Lordy, Colonel Woodard, I don't know. Maria was talking to Mrs. Russell and she just keeled over. I thought it was another of them faints like she's been having, but she was burning up with fever and she didn't seem to know where she was. Mr. Markham's orderly—that Bruno—he carried her upstairs. He said he didn't like the looks of her one bit, and he went for your doctor—"

"Major Strauss," Max said.

"That's the one. He's been up there awhile. He said you was to wait here until he come down again."

Max had no intention of waiting—until he saw the boys' faces. He immediately knelt down and held out his arms for both of them to come to him.

"Maria wouldn't get up," Joe said, his mouth quivering, and Jake began to cry loudly.

"I know," Max said, holding them both. He wanted

to say something comforting, but they already knew the harsh realities of life. He didn't dare tell them everything would be all right.

"Here's the doctor," Mrs. Hansen said. "I'll keep the boys out here."

Max went inside immediately. "Strauss—what's wrong?"

"Typhoid fever," the major said bluntly.

"And?"

"And you know as well as I do that time will tell. With good care, we can be hopeful. Fortunately, there are no added stresses."

"Stresses?"

"Like a recent illness. Or pregnancy. All her energies can go into recovering."

"And if she is pregnant?"

"An early pregnancy would probably not—"

"If it's not that early," Max interrupted, looking Strauss directly in the eyes.

"Then the situation is more dire," the man said after a moment. "You can go up to see her now, but don't expect her to know you."

Max nodded, and Strauss waited until he was halfway up the stairs.

"Colonel Woodard," the man said. "She will likely lose the child."

Max continued up the stairs. He could see Bruno standing in the doorway to Mr. Markham's room, and he wondered if Strauss had spoken to Maria's father.

Maria.

She had been put to bed, in the same bed he'd been more than happy to share with her since they'd married. He was surprised to find Mrs. Russell in the room. And Mrs. Justice.

He didn't speak to either of them. He pulled up the chair that must have been provided for Strauss and his examination and sat down, taking Maria's hand in his.

"Maria," he whispered, his face close to hers. Her eyelids fluttered, but she didn't open them. He sat there a long time. Looking at her, trying to find a way around his fear. If she died...

"Maria," he said out loud, reaching to stroke her face. She was burning with fever. She moved her head restlessly on the pillow, but that was all.

"Mrs. Russell, where can I find a woman to act as nurse—"

"There will be no need, Colonel," she said, and at first Max thought she meant because the situation was so hopeless.

"Mrs. Justice and I will be here to see after her—so that Mrs. Hansen can take care of the boys and the household. Some of the other ladies from the church will help, as well. We want no strangers taking care of our Maria."

Her none too subtle message wasn't lost on him.

Strangers.

Like himself.

"Whatever you need..." he began, but he couldn't quite finish, because he was overwhelmed suddenly by the ache in his throat. He gave a sharp breath and struggled for control.

"The doctor left a list of things," Mrs. Justice said.

"Give it to Sergeant Major Perkins," Max said after a moment. "I expect he is downstairs by now."

She quietly left the room. Mrs. Russell hesitated, then followed.

"Maria," he whispered urgently as soon as the door

closed. "Stay with me. Can you hear me? Stay with me!"

But she didn't hear him, nor did he really think that she would. He had witnessed the stages of this disease many times when he was in the prison. He knew what to expect. Fever. Delirium. Terrible pain.

He couldn't bear to just stand by and let Maria suffer like that.

"Give her something to ease her, damn it!" he said to Strauss at one point.

"Enough to take the pain away is enough to kill her, Colonel," Strauss said.

By evening Maria's condition had grown worse. Max kept a vigil at her bedside—in spite of Mrs. Russell's disapproval. He didn't care about the Russell woman. He only cared about his wife.

Wife.

It had taken only a little time for her to become that to him, and he couldn't bear the thought that it might all end.

He delegated his military duties to his staff and did what he could. He lost all track of time. He sponged her to help keep her cool; spoon fed her water and broth and the chocolate concoction Strauss recommended; did battle with Mrs. Russell to keep her from cutting off all Maria's beautiful hair. People came and went—women who wouldn't leave Maria to the care of a stranger.

At one point she opened her eyes.

"Maria," Max said, leaning closer to her because he thought she wanted to speak. She seemed to try hard to say something to him, then closed her eyes again.

Max slept fitfully—at the bedside and for short intervals across the hall. From time to time he went to see Mr. Markham, not to offer the old man comfort so much

as to seek it for himself. The boys and Mrs. Hansen had
been sent away to Mrs. Kinnard's house—an indicator
of the high regard even the Kinnard woman had for Maria, he supposed, if she would try to help by taking in
the boys he thought of now as his own.

They *were* his. In his heart. In his soul. Just as Maria
was.

On the eighth day of the illness Maria lost the baby.
It made no improvement in her condition as Strauss
hoped. She was so agitated that he increased the laudanum, after all, and he offered no encouragement. Even
if he had, Max would not have believed him. There was
nothing to do but wait.

Max sat dozing in a chair by the bed when he heard
a commotion at the front door. He left Maria and went
halfway down the main stairs to find Nell Hansen going
head-to-head with the church women who refused to let
her into the house.

"They won't let me see her, Woodard!" Nell called
when she saw him. "Please! I want to see her!"

"Let her pass," Max said, ignoring an array of incredulous and affronted looks inspired only partly because he was allowing a woman of ill repute to enter by
the front door. The primary reason was his having signed
Jimmy Julian's release. He'd had no choice. None of
these women knew that, and he absolutely refused to be
put into the position of justifying his actions to them.

Nell followed him as far as the room then slipped past
him to go in first. She sat on the side of the bed and
held Maria's hand, weeping openly. The scene suddenly
became too painful for him to watch. He knew too much
about "The Three Musketeers" now and the long-
standing regard they had for each other. He went down
the back stairs into the kitchen. Perkins was there, and

he immediately brought a cup of coffee and put it into Max's hand.

"Anything you want done, Sir?" Perkins asked.

"No. Yes. I want you to bring the boys by."

"Yes, Sir."

Max realized that Nell was standing at the bottom of the back stairs. She kept wiping at her eyes with her fingers.

"Thank you," she said. "Don't give up, Woodard. She'll stay if she can. Honest to God, she will."

He nodded and looked away.

"How much trouble are you in?" she asked

"Trouble?"

"You kept Jimmy Julian locked up when you weren't supposed to. Are they going to do anything to you for it?"

"I don't know."

"Well, people here will know you tried," she said, and he gave a short, humorless laugh.

"Maria will know you tried," she said pointedly.

Maria.

He left Nell Hansen standing and went back upstairs. As he sat down in the chair by Maria's bed, he realized that she was awake and trying to say something.

"Maria, what is it?" he said, leaning forward and taking her hand. Her voice was weak, but he understood her perfectly.

"I should...never have...married you."

Chapter Nineteen

"She has lost her child. She needs time to grieve."

Max heard Strauss, but he gave no indication that he did. The remark was neither welcome nor accurate. It wasn't only grief that Maria suffered. It was also regret. For her, the only reason for their marriage no longer existed.

"She's growing stronger every day," Strauss said.

Max still made no comment.

"Colonel, about the pregnancy—"

"I don't want to discuss that."

"There can be other children," the major said anyway. "And you needn't be concerned that the women who were in the room at the time of the miscarriage are privy to the details of…a private matter."

"Is there anything else?" Max said.

"No…except—"

"If there is nothing else, you are dismissed, Major."

Max waited until the man had gone, then got up wearily from his desk and walked to the window. The evening was hot and muggy, but he could hear the rumble of thunder in the distance. The streets were deserted.

And there were no pressing military duties to keep him from going home.

Home.

His home was where *she* was, and he couldn't tell her so. Such an admission was the last thing she would want to hear from him.

The house was dark when Max got there but for the lamps kept lighted in the foyer and in Mr. Markham's room. Still, he didn't expect to find the old man awake. Mr. Markham's illness had left him afraid of the dark. And Maria's had made her retreat into it.

He saw to his mount, and then smoked a cigar before he went inside, looking up at Maria's window from time to time. It was dark. It was always dark.

He thought he heard someone in the front yard, and he walked in that direction, expecting a messenger with yet another aggravation concerning the occupation of the conquered South. But he didn't see anyone or hear anything else, so he went in by the front door, walking along the hallway toward the parlor. He had gone halfway down the hall when he heard the rasping click of metal behind him. The hair stood up on the back of his neck. He stopped dead, instinctively reaching for the cavalry side arm he no longer wore.

"Old habits die hard, don't they?" someone said behind him. "Don't turn around."

"What do you want?" Max asked.

"Where is Maria?" the man said.

Max turned his head slightly, trying to see him. "My wife is not here."

"I don't have time to play games with you, Yankee! Where is she!"

"The war is over. Whatever grudge you still harbor, it is against me. She has no part in it."

"I will ask you one more time. Where is she!"

There was a slight creak on the stairs, and Max turned to see Maria on the landing.

"Maria! Stay there!" he said, taking a step forward.

"Don't!" the man said, leveling his revolver at Max's chest.

"Maria," Max said in warning. She had said she wouldn't mean the "obey" part of her marriage vows, and clearly she meant it.

"Why are you here?" she said to the man, and Max realized suddenly that she knew him. She came slowly down the steps, one by one, holding on to the banister with both hands until she reached the bottom.

"I came for you," he said, his eyes on Max. "Whatever hold *he* has over you, I can put an end to it right now—"

"No!" she cried as he took careful aim, and she stepped forward and put herself between Max and the gunman.

"Maria, get out of the way!" Max said, intending to move her bodily, if he could get to her.

"Stand still, Yankee!" the man cried, and Max stopped. "Maria, move aside—what are you doing?"

"I don't want you to hurt him. I'll do whatever you want, but don't hurt him."

"Whatever I want? Maria, what's wrong with you! I'm here now—"

"He is my husband," she said, swaying slightly from the physical effort it had taken her to get this far. "I gave him my word."

"Not willingly," the man said, taking a step to the side. Maria moved with him.

"Yes. Willingly. What terrible thing do you think he

could do to me to make me marry him if I didn't want to?''

"There had to be something. I know you, Maria. Rob and Samuel would—''

"Rob and Samuel are dead! And I'm going on with my life—if you'll let me. I'm taking care of Phelan's children so he can follow you. The three of us are fine here.''

"What about your word to me?''

"You broke the bond between us, not I.''

"You love me, Maria!''

"Yes, and what did that ever mean to you?''

"I'm here! I have come back for you!''

"You have come back too late.''

There was another creak on the stairs—oblivious, happy-go-lucky Bruno, on some errand for Mr. Markham.

At the sound, the man swung the revolver in the orderly's direction, and Max lunged forward to get Maria behind him. The sudden movement caused the man to fire blindly at Max instead. The bullet struck him in the side, knocking him off his feet. Maria screamed, and he tried to get up, making it to one knee before he fell over onto his back. The pain was excruciating. He could feel a hot warmth spreading under his shirt.

All that time, he thought incredulously. *All those battles—and I'm shot in a damned downstairs hallway. Maria—*

He tried to say her name out loud and couldn't. She had her arms around him, trying to lift him up. He could feel her hands searching for the wound.

"Maria! Come on!'' the man said.

"Get out of here!'' she cried. "Someone will have heard the shot—''

"Leave him, damn it! You're coming with me!"

"Don't you understand, Billy!" Maria cried. "He's a good man! He is my husband! I love him! How much more will you take from me before you're satisfied! Max," she whispered against his ear. "I'm so sorry—"

Max heard her, and he tried to ask the question.

Billy—how can that be Billy?

There was a great roaring in his ears. He could only let the blackness pull him down.

When the roaring stopped, voices began to swirl around him.

"Move aside, ma'am. Turn him loose, so I can see how bad it is."

"Don't let him die, Bruno! Please!"

"Here comes Major Strauss. He's bleeding bad, Sir—"

"Goddamn it, just look at this—is this some of Julian's doings?"

"Don' think so, Sir. It was a different son of a bitch altogether."

"Hand me a probe—not that one! Damn—it's still in there. Get him on the dining-room table—and find me some more lamps and some mirrors so I can see. Are you hurt, Mrs. Woodard?"

"No."

"Then stay out of the way. If I need you, I'll call you."

"Damn your sorry hide, Maxwell, I can't begin to tell you what horizontal bliss you interrupted—"

"Bullet's out, Sir. Can you hear me, Sir? Major Strauss has got the hole plugged. It didn't hit nothing you need. You're going to be all right."

"Will...you look at...this—Bruno? My whole house—has become...an—infirmary."

"Maria!"

"Maria—"

"She's not here, Sir. Major Strauss made her go lay down for a while."

Max opened his eyes, not realizing he'd spoken aloud. "Today—"

His mouth was so dry. He had to swallow and lick his lips. The orderly was there immediately with water. "Today is Sunday. Again," he said as soon as he'd had a few swallows.

"Yes, Sir. Sunday again. You're absolutely right, Sir."

Max looked around the room. He knew where he was every time he woke up now—the Markham-Woodard infirmary. He was definitely improving. He'd been out of bed and sitting in a chair several times. And he was making short walks to the chamber pot.

But he hadn't talked to Maria. She came in to see him often, visits that were too brief and too strained to get anything settled between them. But today was the day. He couldn't stand it any longer.

"Is my wife all right?" he asked.

"Yes, Sir. Major Strauss was kind of worried about her using up all her strength. The fever ain't come back, though, and that's good. Sir, Perkins sent word a while ago that they caught the son of a bitch who shot you."

"Where is he?"

"They're bringing him here, Sir. So you can identify him."

Max closed his eyes and took a quiet breath. It hurt—but not terribly. He could hear a commotion downstairs, voices and footsteps in the outer hall.

"You ready, Sir?" the orderly asked, and Max nodded.

In a moment Perkins shoved a shackled Billy Canfield

into the room ahead of him. In broad daylight, Canfield looked a great deal like his brother Phelan, in the same way Jake looked like Joe. They stared at each other, but Max made no effort to speak, giving the man time to arrange his hostility to the best advantage.

Max looked at Perkins. "I want to talk to him. Alone. Wait outside."

"Sir, that's not such a good idea."

"You, too," Max said to the orderly, ignoring the protest. "Now."

Perkins hesitated, then complied, but he wasn't above giving one of his eloquently disapproving looks on his way out.

"You are one more witless bastard," Max said as soon as the door closed. Canfield flashed him a look.

"But I'm grateful for it," Max continued, thinking Canfield's stupidity in breaking his engagement to Maria. "So grateful, I've decided to let you go."

The man laughed. "Is that a fact? What am I supposed to do? Kiss your boot?"

"You and your brother are very much cut from the same cloth," Max said. "I seem to keep having the same conversation with both of you. In answer to what seems to be a standard Canfield inquiry—no."

"What then? What do you want?"

"I want you to understand. I'm not doing this for you. I'm doing it for Maria and me. She and I have too many things to get past as it is. We don't need any more sorrows or regrets added to the pile."

"Just like that. You're going to let me go."

"I am."

"How do you know I won't kill you next time?"

"I don't. I'll just have to live looking over my shoulder, won't I? You wouldn't mind that, I'm sure. Now let my sergeant major in.''

Canfield stood for a moment, then hobbled toward the door. ''Did Maria ask you to do this?''

''No,'' Max said. ''She didn't.''

Canfield stared at him; Max could feel him trying to decide if he believed him. And he realized suddenly that the man wanted Maria to have made a plea on his behalf.

''That night—I would have had to shoot you at some point. I knew you weren't going to let me take her.''

Max didn't say anything, because it was the truth.

''How did you manage it? How did you make her forget who she is?''

Max made no reply to that, either, and Canfield gave a short, bitter laugh and shook his head. ''All right— you win—this time. Because *she* wants it. You be good to her,'' he said before he opened the door. ''Or I will come back and kill you, you Yankee son of a bitch.''

''This is not the man,'' Max said as Perkins pushed his way into the room. ''Let him go.''

''But, Sir—Bruno has already identified—''

''Bruno was not on the business end of the revolver. I was. It's not him. Let him go.''

''Yes, Sir,'' Perkins said, shoving Canfield back outside. ''If you're sure about this, Sir.''

Max lay back and closed his eyes. He was only sure of one thing. He wanted his wife back. After a moment he made an effort to move, to sit up on the side of the bed.

''Whoa, Sir!'' the orderly said. ''Where are you going—if you don't mind my asking?''

''Across the hall—''

''Sir, you ain't up to that.''

''Then you can carry me.''

"Well, Sir, I can do that rightly enough, but Major Strauss—"

"Major Strauss is a major," Max said, upright now. His head was spinning, but it soon stopped.

"I see your point, Sir."

"If I'm going to die—it's going to be in that bed, not this one, understand?"

"Ah…yes, Sir. Let me get Bruno, Sir. He could carry both of us if he had to."

But Max didn't require carrying after all, only a considerable amount of propping up. Maria wasn't lying down when he and his entourage entered the room. She was standing by the window, staring down into the yard. And how beautiful she looked to him, in spite of her illness. And how unhappy.

Maria.

"Go on about your business," Max said to Bruno and the orderly.

"Sir—" Bruno began.

"I assure you, Bruno, Major Strauss will know that you were only following my orders."

"Begging your pardon, Sir, but who's going to tell him that if you can't?"

"Mrs. Woodard will," Max said. "She'll even try to do so ahead of the firing squad—won't you?" he asked her.

"I…yes," Maria decided.

"See? Now get out of here."

Max sat on the side of the bed after they'd gone, head bowed, working hard not to fall on his face now that he'd made it this far.

"I saw Perkins in the yard just now," Maria said quietly.

Max didn't say anything.

"Have you let Billy go?"

"Yes," he said. When he looked up, Maria was standing close to him, tears streaming down her face.

"Don't," he said. "Don't cry." He was so tired suddenly, and he took her hand and lay back on the bed. Incredibly, she came to him, stretching out beside him, her arms going around him cautiously at first and then clinging to him hard. He held her tightly—she felt so good!

Stay with me, Maria!

"I didn't keep my word to you," she said after a moment. "I didn't do my part to make the marriage work." She moved so that she could see his face.

"You wanted to go with him."

"No! How could you think that?" she asked, but she didn't wait for an answer. She pressed her face into his shoulder. He could feel her trembling. The windows were open. He could hear the boys playing on the lawn below. Trains. They were playing with the trains.

"Tell me how it is with you—and him," he said. "Because I don't know, Maria. I don't know what you want."

She didn't say anything for a long time. He thought she wasn't going to tell him anything, but then she wiped her eyes and took a deep breath.

"Billy...was reported dead at Gettysburg. I thought he *was* dead. But he was in a prison—Elmira—until the end of the war. And then, afterward, who knows where? Texas. Mexico—with men like himself who wouldn't admit the South had been defeated. He came to see me not long before you arrived here. He was so...changed. He wasn't the man I once knew. His mother had died. He had no family but Phelan. He intended to make his new life elsewhere—but then he decided I deserved to hear that face-to-face. Or so he said. I think it was just an…afterthought. I think he really came here to recruit Phelan to come join him and the army they were trying to raise in Mexico.

"I couldn't believe he was really here—really alive. I still…loved the man he once was, so I tried to…persuade…him to stay—the only way I knew how." She sighed heavily. "He left anyway, and he never looked back."

"But he knew about the baby. He came back for you."

"No. I never told him. There was no place for a baby in his life—or me. He would have been even less of a father than Phelan was." She sighed again and wiped at her eyes. "I didn't want to live like Suzanne," she said simply.

"And then Billy heard about the marriage. He sent Phelan. He wanted Phelan to bring me and the boys to Mexico. I told Phelan I wouldn't go. I told him I was happy in the marriage, that his boys were happy now, as well. I thought—hoped—he believed me, but I was afraid."

"Afraid of what?"

"Of the man Billy had become. Without the war, he had no direction, no purpose. I thought he might come here—not out of love for me, but because he needed another justification for his 'cause.' He was going to use my marriage to you. But then I lost the baby, and there was no reason for the marriage anymore—"

"I am sorry about the child, Maria," he said quietly, and she gave him such a stricken look that he reached up to touch her cheek. "I know you have regrets now—"

"What I regret is that I nearly got you killed. I should have told you."

"I saw Phelan here, Maria."

"You saw him?"

"I waited for you to tell me. You didn't."

Tears rolled down her cheeks. "What you must think of me—"

"It hurt my pride that you didn't trust me enough to say—I can't deny that. But my knowing the details wouldn't have changed anything."

"It might have."

"No. Billy Canfield would have still come for you. And I can't blame him for that."

She sighed and rested her head against his shoulder again.

"You told him you loved me," Max said quietly.

"Yes," she said. "I told him."

"Why?"

"Because it's true."

"Is it?" he asked, lifting her chin so that he could look into her eyes.

"Yes."

"And if I say I love you, as well. If I say I love you with all my heart and I want us to start again—then what?"

"Then…I suppose…the part about 'no emotional attachment' goes right out the window," she answered.

The response was so unexpected and so typically her that he laughed out loud and tightened his arms around her.

Maria.

"How did we ever get here—you and I?" he whispered, echoing the question he'd asked once before.

"It doesn't matter," she said. "It's where we go now that counts."

"I love you, Maria. I love you—"

He kissed her, and then again, and he held her close to him, the love he felt for her so strong it was akin to physical pain. And he realized that what she said was true. It was the future that mattered, not the past.

He and Maria and the boys would start again. None of them were untouched by the war, but they would still go forward, loving each other, picking up the pieces of their shattered lives and their shattered country as they went. The bond between them had been forged by all that had come before, and whatever happened in the future, they would face—together.

Epilogue

July 4, 1869

The ceremony and the speeches were over. Maria hadn't been able to brave the intense summer heat to attend, but now, in the cool of the early evening, she rode with Max in the buggy to the prison.

Max had wanted her to see all the bunting decorating the town—in spite of her recent politics—and she wondered if he realized that the route he had chosen, past the depot, mirrored that same ride they had taken the first day he arrived. He had been an arrogant stranger to her then, the very personification of the enemy.

Today, people on the streets nodded to them as they rode past, some of the same people who had been shocked to see Maria Markham in a buggy with the new military commander all those months ago. She tried not to smile at the well-chaperoned officers out promenading with young local girls on their arms, wondering if they realized that they were knee-deep in the "bride fair."

Max was very quiet, and understandably so. When they had crossed the railroad bridge, and he stopped the buggy, she got down with him, taking his arm to walk the grounds. How different the place was now. All the brambles and debris had been cleared away, replaced by grass and flowering shrubs and neatly graveled paths.

And rows of white headstones—all of them "Unknown."

But they weren't unknown to the man beside her. He had been imprisoned with many of them, and he had ultimately survived. And today the town was filled with former soldiers who, at his invitation, had come to pay their last respects to those who had forever remained behind.

Maria stood in this quiet place, acutely aware of the still terrible past.

So many lives lost.

The old infantryman who had taught Max to whittle was here.

"Rest in peace," she whispered.

She thought suddenly of Billy and Phelan, who desperately wanted to keep the war going. And of Rob and Samuel, hoping that wherever they lay, someone cared enough to make their graves a place of honor as these were.

The baby kicked her ribs suddenly, and she caught her breath.

"Are you all right?" Max asked, placing his hand over hers.

"Your son or daughter, the acrobat—that's all," she said.

He looked into her eyes for a long moment, then smiled. He would always carry the sadness of this place with him. She knew that. But he smiled much more easily these days.

And she liked to think that Maria Rose Markham Woodard had some hand in it.

*   *   *   *   *

Author Note

I was eleven years old the first time I visited the National Cemetery located on the site of the Confederate Prison in Salisbury, N.C. The rows of unmarked graves had a profound effect on me, so much so, that this is my second work of fiction dealing with soldiers who were imprisoned there.

There are no ''real'' people in this book, only those created in my imagination, but, if you would like more historical information about the prison itself, you can find it online at:

http://www.salisbury.nc.us/prison/csprison1.htm

CHERYL REAVIS

is an award-winning short story and romance author who also writes under the name of Cinda Richards. She describes herself as a "late bloomer" who played in her first piano recital at the tender age of thirty. "We had to line up by height—I was the third smallest kid," she says. "After that, there was no stopping me. I immediately gave myself permission to attempt my *other* heart's desire—to write." Her Silhouette Special Edition novel *A Crime of the Heart* reached millions of readers in *Good Housekeeping* magazine. Her books *The Prisoner*, a Harlequin Historical novel, and *A Crime of the Heart* and *Patrick Gallagher's Widow*, both Silhouette Special Edition titles, are all Romance Writers of America's RITA Award winners. *One of Our Own* received the Career Achievement Award for Best Innovative Series Romance from *Romantic Times*. A former public health nurse, Cheryl makes her home in North Carolina with her husband. She loves hearing from readers, and invites them to contact her at creavis@salisbury.net.

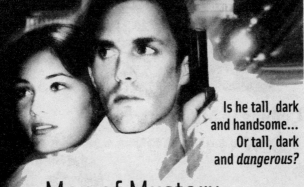

TRUEBLOOD, TEXAS

Coming in May 2002...

RODEO DADDY
by
B.J. Daniels

Lost:

Her first and only love.
Chelsea Jensen discovers
ten years later that her father
had been to blame for
Jack Shane's disappearance
from her family's ranch.

Found:

A canceled check. Now Chelsea
knows why Jack left her. Had he ever loved her, or had she
been too young and too blind to see the truth?

**Chelsea is determined to track Jack down and find out.
And what a surprise she gets when she finds him!**

Finders Keepers: bringing families together

HARLEQUIN®
Makes any time special®

Visit us at www.eHarlequin.com

TBTCNM9

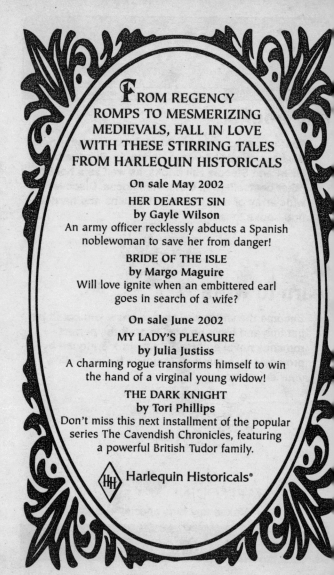

FROM REGENCY ROMPS TO MESMERIZING MEDIEVALS, FALL IN LOVE WITH THESE STIRRING TALES FROM HARLEQUIN HISTORICALS

On sale May 2002

HER DEAREST SIN
by Gayle Wilson
An army officer recklessly abducts a Spanish
noblewoman to save her from danger!

BRIDE OF THE ISLE
by Margo Maguire
Will love ignite when an embittered earl
goes in search of a wife?

On sale June 2002

MY LADY'S PLEASURE
by Julia Justiss
A charming rogue transforms himself to win
the hand of a virginal young widow!

THE DARK KNIGHT
by Tori Phillips
Don't miss this next installment of the popular
series The Cavendish Chronicles, featuring
a powerful British Tudor family.

Harlequin Historicals®